Here Was A Man

A Tree of Life Book

Published by arrangement with the author's Estate.

Copyright © Clive Lofts 2022

First published in Great Britain by Hodder & Stoughton, 1984. Published in the USA by Doubleday, 1986.

Cover illustration: Kate Garrett

Typed for Tree of Life Publishing by James Charles

A CIP catalogue record for this book is available from the British Library.

ISBN: 978-1-905806-99-7

Tree of Life Publishing
United Kingdom

Here Was A Man

Norah Lofts

PART ONE

Chapter 1

Budleigh Point in the County of Devon
23 June 1568

We've only one virginity to lose,
And where we lose it, there our hearts will be.

Old Harkess paused in his dragging of the boat to the water's edge and listened. There were no sounds except the sighing of the summer sea and the swish of the wind through the rough grass of the cliff's top and he was not listening to those. He sighed, for he was an old man and lazy, and a little help with the bunching and the rowing was very welcome on these warm nights. He spat on his hands and took a fresh hold on the boat. Twice after that he paused and the third time heard what he had been waiting for, the quick step, the hurried breathing, and presently the voice calling breathlessly, 'Harky, Wait for me, Harky.'

Urgent as was the call, it was not loud and the old man smiled in the darkness; a cautious one, Wally, for all his eagerness. He called back quietly, 'Ahoy lad.' Out of the shadows a figure came stumbling, threw itself silently upon the boat and, with the old man's apparent help, dragged it onto the water. As they clambered in the boy said, with reproach in his voice, 'I believe you were going without me.'

5

'I didn't want to. I like a bit of company, as you know. But 'twas getting latish and the nights are short now. I thought they'd keep you up in the house.'

'They tried. Father locked me in but thank God I'm still thin enough for the window and light enough for the wistaria.'

'You won't allust be. What'll you do then?'

'I'll be gone by then. I'm to go to Oxford this autumn.'

'I shall miss you, Wally.'

'Not as much as I shall miss you, Harky. Any boy who'll lend you a hand is the same to you. You're Odysseus to me.'

'What's that?'

'A bald sailor who was always talking.'

'Nice thing to call me.'

'High praise really. Where're you making for?'

'Straight out from the Point. 'Tis a French ship with a cargo of best Bordeaux. 'S' a pity your father's so set against the night wine, Wally. Many's the cheap drink he might have.'

'Oh father.' The boy's voice was a shrug. 'He's got trouble enough without running foul of the Excise men. Devon men are always wrong, they upset Mary by being Protestant and now Elizabeth is now against the privateering.'

'Only when it's near home, lad. If your father and his friends were busy in the Indies, she'd call them the brightest jewels in the crown.'

The word "Indies" struck like a gong in the boy's mind.

'Here, I row, Harky. You take a rest. She'd be heavier coming back.'

Nothing loath, the old man drew in his oars and sat back.

'Why's your father so set against the sea for you, Wally? He's a seaman himself?'

'That's just why there's nothing in it, he says. I'm to study for the law or the church and then look for preferment. Kate Ashley's a cousin of father's and she has a queen's ear and will speak for me.'

'Well, no doubt that'd be a steady safe thing to be. But you'd be wasted as a clerk, lad.'

'Maybe. Still, learning can do you no harm. Anyway, I can't

6

be a sailor like Humphrey, I'm always sick at sea. Nights like this are all very well. And oh, but I've a mind to see the Indies and all that vast country beyond them.'

'Ah, it's fair enough, some of it, and rich too. But you ain't so welcome there as you was in my young days. Thick with Spaniards and the Indians so savage with the treatment they've had that they're waiting behind every tree to put a poisoned arrow through your guts.'

'They'll all be wiped out soon, though. Remember what you were telling me the other night.'

'About the thousands that were driven into the silver mines and never came out again? Yes, I dare say you're right. Still anybody that sets foot in that continent from now on'll have to fight every step, I'm thinking.'

They both fell silent, the old man thinking of the far countries that had held no romance for him, that had been places where one was hungry or thirsty or in danger, and the boy thinking of the far countries, too, but as places that drew him as inexplicably as a magnet draws a needle. He knew that Harkess would mock at his thoughts, could he know them. Harky said that four thousand slaves were driven into a silver mine but he didn't see them in his mind's eye. He couldn't see, in that driving, the gesture of the conqueror. He didn't see the silver delved for by dark slaves from the dark earth, pouring its silver stream into the treasure galleons that sailed with it, stately into Cadiz. He didn't want Harky to think like that. Enough for him to supply the fact and to leave an image unsullied by his thoughts. And in Harkess's simplicity and realism may have lain the secret of the enormous influence of his casual words upon young Raleigh's life.

Presently the dark bulk of a ship loomed up; Harkess took up his oars again and they drew alongside carefully. The wine in its roped casks was stowed neatly in the bottom of the boat; money changed hands, a few sentences were spoken in the smugglers' peculiar tongue that was neither French nor English, and Raleigh and Harkess began pulling for the shore. They spoke little, for the laden boat demanded all their care and strength; once Harkess spoke but only to say, 'Second cave, Wally.'

Within about a hundred yards of the shore Raleigh halted his oars and turned his head, listening. Harkess stopped rowing and said quietly, 'What is it?'

'Somebody's at the cave if I'm not mistaken. Can you hear anything?'

'Hearing's not what it was. But there... there was a light. God's breath, it's that Trebor, he's been on the watch for weeks. We can't land, Wally. We must pull round the Point and hope to get it all under cover at Mother Shale's before morning. If we don't you'll have the pleasure of the sight of me in the stocks. As for you, your father'd...'

'Flay me,' said Raleigh.

Already there was a hint of coming light in the sky to the east and they bent their backs, working the oars like slaves in the galleys. To get round the Point was always a hard task; currents met there and at intervals a swirl of frothy water betrayed the presence of hidden rocks. By the time they were round they could see each other, they had both discarded all clothes but their breeches and the sweat was running off them in streams. Once round, however, they were out of sight of whoever had been watching the cave and stood a reasonable chance of retaining both their cargo and their liberty. Mother Shale's stood in the dip of the cliff, sheltered from view of all sides except that facing the sea. It was a long, low, rambling building which could be ale house, farm, smugglers' rendezvous or brothel according to who came inquiring. There were always barrels in her cellar but seldom the same barrels two nights running—and the same might be said of the horses in her stable.

She herself was a villainous old woman. She bore on her back the marks of a whipping that she received through the streets of Exeter for being a wanton, long ago. The whipping had put her definitely on the side of the law breakers and many a smuggler, rogue and wench in trouble had had cause to bless those stripes.

She came to the window in response to a shower of pebbles

sped from Raleigh's hand. Ten words from Harkess informed her of the night's doings and brought her stumbling to the door. In a quarter of an hour the wine was in her cellar and the boat a foot below the sand in the cove beside the house. Meanwhile someone within doors had stirred up the ashes of the fire that seldom died completely and soon Harkess and Raleigh, shivering in the cold morning air, were crouched beside it, wooden platter of fat bacon on their knees and horn cups of strong ale in their hands. The boy, who had been awake all night and subjected to unusual strain for some hours, could barely stay awake long enough to finish his breakfast. He roused himself long enough to say to Harkess, 'I must be getting back', but he never heard Harkess reply, 'You can't go in that state. And anyhow you can't get home before they miss you.' His head had fallen forward and he was asleep.

When he woke he became cautious first of the scent of the new hay and then of the red glow with which he was surrounded. Then he saw the girl who waked him looking at him. She had red smiling lips and she was laughing at him. He sat up quickly and began to pick the hay from his hair and clothes, blushing slightly at the indignity of being caught so by a laughing girl. She laughed again and, catching up a handful of loose hay, tossed it over him, and said, 'Sleepy head. You've been asleep all day. Harkess is having his supper.'

Raleigh scrambled to his feet, shaking the hay from his head, brushing it from his clothes. But the girl was in a teasing mind and fast he cleaned himself she tossed more on him. At last, more to gain time than from any desire to play with her, he gathered a great armful and dropped it on her from his superior position on top of the heap. With a little squeal she threw herself on him, the hay flew widely for several minutes. The red rays of the sunset danced with dust; and at last, spent and breathless, they dropped down beside one another on the tousled mound and looked at each other, panting. He saw then that she was both older than himself and very pretty. Her hair that was black where it hugged her head had a web of reddish light over it where the loose strands stood up in the sun. Her skin was honey and her

NORAH LOFTS

parted lips showed little white teeth and a pink, pointed tongue.
In her sharp nose and chin lay the threat that in a few years she
would be unmistakably old Mother Shale's granddaughter but
for the time being she was lovely. She pouted her lips to blow
away a wisp of her hair that had fallen over her nose and then
she leaned back, back until she was lying on the hay with her
arms curved around her head. The rolled-up sleeves of her cotton
frock revealed the little blue veins that ran, slanting, from wrist
to elbow, and the whole pose drew attention to the base of her
neck where the untanned skin was startlingly white and to the
budding breasts that thrust their nipples against the thin material.
Something unknown caught the boy by the throat. 'You're
lovely', he breathed. She laughed again and threw out one
arm to catch his head and draw it down to her face. He kissed
her, clumsily and shyly at first, as he kissed his mother when
occasion demanded. But in this, as in all things, he was fated to
be a quick learner and an expert when learned. And to the girl
it was no new road. It was very easy.
Harkess's voice rang through the barn, 'What are you at
Wally? I can't wait any longer. You can finish your sleeping
at home.'
Shaking, the boy rose to his feet. The girl whispered, 'Don't
say I'm here. Come again.'
'I will', he whispered, and slipped off the mound of hay and
came, with a well-stimulated yawn, out of the shadowy barn to
where Harkess stood in the last glow of sunset.
'Never see such a boy for sleeping', grumbled the old man.
'Come on now, put your best foot forward and I'll come home
with you and tell your father that the fault was none of yours.'
'You needn't trouble, Harky. I can deal with my father.'
There was something in the tone that made Harkess look
at him sharply. True he had said 'Harky' in the old, boyish,
friendly way but there was something arrogant in the voice and
in the rest of the speech that made Harkess suddenly cautious
that this was the Squire's son and that he was only a foremast
hand turned smuggler. Still, his kind old heart made him persist,
'Are you sure? I'd hate for you to get into trouble through me.'

10

Raleigh said, absently, 'That'll be all right,' and they walked on in silence.

This then, thought the boy, was to be a man, with a man's pleasures and privileges. He had known about it, of course, and rather recoiled from it but he had never guessed. How sweet she was, soft and yielding and wise! Better not to dwell on her wisdom perhaps, it emphasised his own ignorance. But oh what paths, what prospects of pleasures had been opened tonight! With the Indies forgotten, he bade Harkess a careless good night and went to face his father. He was a man now, he was not going to be flogged on this or any or any other night. The very idea of an irreverent hand being laid upon him made him burn with shame where yesterday there would have been fear only. And so deep was his new assurance, so soundly rooted in natural laws, that his father, after one glance at his flushed and defiant face, put all thought of corporal punishment behind him for ever.

Chapter 2

The Netherlands
17 November 1572

It was a November evening. Three men sat huddled over a brazier in a leaky tent waiting for a fourth. They might have been waiting for him to complete the number for a card game, for the cards lay in a pile on an upturned box which held also a bottle of wine, three parts empty, and some horn cups. But there was an expression of anxiety among their faces and a certain tension in the way that they sat upon their stools that belied the peaceful supposition. Humphrey Gilbert was boring fresh holes in a belt that had stretched from constant soaking. The nail that he used squeaked in the wet leather and every now and then he paused with it uplifted in his hand and listened; then, assured the sound was not the one that he awaited, he would shake his large head, lower the nail and resume his squeaking. Philip Sydney would hold his pen still and look towards the door of the tent and wait. Then, as Gilbert shook his head, Sidney would look towards him, catch his eye with an expression of sympathy and go on with his writing. The third man seemed less seemed less concerned. He tilted his tool upon one leg and swivelled round upon it; he hummed softly behind his closed lips; he eyed the bottle and grimaced as he realised how little was left in it; and at every pause of Gilbert's, he let out an impatient sigh.

Presently Sidney laid down his pen, closed the little vessel that contained his ink and folded his paper.

'It's useless,' he said in his quiet voice, 'the boy has been and gone twelve hours or more. Something must have happened.'

'I don't trust the country people,' said Gilbert miserably. 'If it comes to blows they're as likely as not to turn against their allies, to curry favour with the Spaniards. It's my fault, I should have never have let him go. He's but a lad when all's said.'

'Well,' said Gasgoigne, righting his stool with a thud, 'if aught has happened to him it's an end he would have chosen for himself. And I for one would as soon have a Spanish bullet or, for that matter, a Dutch pike through my spleen as hang about here up to my eyes in mud for the rest of my days as we look like doing.'

'We weren't taking to you,' Sydney spoke quietly still but there was a wealth of dislike in his voice, 'You may have little to live for. Walter is young far too young to...'

'Don't talk of it,' said Gilbert. He stood up and tossed the unfinished belt into the corner of tent where the light of the swinging smoking lantern did not fall. 'He's barely twenty; it's his first campaign.'

Gasgoigne, determinedly pessimistic, murmured as though to himself, 'Those whom the Gods love ...'

'Quit it!' snapped Sydney. 'A foolish old saying that means anyway that if the gods love you you're young at eighty. Be of good cheer, Humphrey. The horses may be bogged. And Walter is canny. Besides, you can't stand between him and danger for ever, you know.'

Gilbert sat down again. The soft leather of his breeches, stiffened by the rain, cracked as he moved. Gasgoigne flung a fresh handful of charcoal on the brazier and resumed his humming. A fresh spatter of rain hissed on the wet canvas overhead. For some moments there was silence in the tent except for the crackle of the charcoal and the monotonous repetition of Gasgoigne's ditty. Then that stopped too. The singer gave another impatient sigh and picked up his cards.

'For the love of God let's do something. Otherwise I shall go crazy and drink what's left of our last bottle. And I don't want to do that, it'll make a splendid welcome for Walter. There's faith for you Philip, "the evidence of things unseen," as the clerics say.'

'Don't mock,' said Sydney. 'And I don't want to play now.'

13

'Come on man. I've not lost all hope of playing my nag against yours and winning. We shan't do any good by sitting here like mutes at a funeral.'

'Oh very well. My Peg against your Pan. Going to risk your spavined steed, Humphrey?'

Gilbert shook his head. Gasgoigne began to shuffle the cards that were amongst the most treasured possessions. Each card was a slice of ivory, so thin as to be almost translucent, and the Kings and Queens were painted as carefully as miniatures. The Queen of Hearts was especially beautiful; she had the red hair, thin lips and exquisite hands of Elizabeth Tudor. The others were all dark, all nonentities. Gasgoigne had never been in the Queens presence but when he did achieve his ambition and stand before her he was going to tell her that through many years, on many strange journeys, he had carried her portrait with him. He had just turned over his cards and seen with pleasure that the red-haired Queen had fallen to him when Gilbert jumped up again, overturning his stool as he made for the tent opening. Sydney laid down his cards and asked, 'Where are you going?'

'To Leicester. I must do something. I'll get him to let me take ten men and go out to look for the boy'

'I'll come with you,' said Sydney. He handed his cards back to Gasgoigne who rose too, taking out a calf-skin case as he did so and slipping his cards inside it before he said, 'And I.'

The three stepped out into the street of the canvas town. On either side of the muddy track the tents stood in order. From some came the sound of voices and laughter but most were dark and silent, filled with sleeping men.

They plunged through the mud and turned left at the end of the road. The new road, even muddier than the first, gave upon an open square where the great tent that was Leicester's headquarters stood. As they drew nearer, they could hear the noise of men's voices, and a "plop" of horses' hooves in the mire. Lanterns bobbed about, carried by men in a hurry. 'It's they,' exclaimed Sydney, and seizing Gilbert's arm he began to run, unmindful of the mud that his flying heels sent into the face of Gasgoigne who was close behind. Gasgoigne cursed and fell back a pace or two. There was no hurry, he thought. If this were Walter the good news would keep and if it were ill tidings on him, why hasten towards it?

Just within the circle of lantern light the two runners stopped and the more leisurely Gasgoigne came up to them. He put a hand on Sydney's shoulder and leaned upon him while he stood on his toes to see over the ring of men who were crowded round talking. After one glance he lowered himself and turned excitedly to Gilbert. He ignored the look of impatient dislike that Sydney had levelled at him when he saw whose weight he had been bearing. He knew Sydney disliked him and would have quarrelled with him often and gladly enough if it had not been that Walter was their mutual friend.

'Look at the horses, Humphrey, Spanish bits and bridles, Before God, the boy's brought in some captives!'

'Has he come in himself? That's what I want to know.' Gilbert shook off Gasgoigne's hand and began to elbow his way through the throng. 'Are those Raleigh's men?' he asked several times and pushed on without waiting for an answer. With Sydney and Gasgoigne stumbling along in the rapidly closing space made by his great shoulders Raleigh's half-brother came out before Leicester's tent and there, diffident as always, he halted. At the same moment the flap of the tent lifted and Raleigh stood in the opening. By the light of the lanterns that swung from poles on either side of the tent they could see his face, white with fatigue and shining with rain, the bright eyes and slightly parted lips.

'Hullo, Humphrey, Philip, George,' he greeted them in turn. 'Have you seen what we've brought in?'

'Are you all right?' Gilbert demanded.

'Never better. Tired. But will you guess what we've brought in?'

'Ten Spanish grandees, richly attired, and ten steeds caparisoned in gold,' said Gasgoigne: and for the second time that evening Sydney said, 'Don't mock.' For he knew that this was the boy's hour, when his friends should stand quietly by and listen, even to his boasting.

15

'This isn't mockery for once. Only there are nineteen of them and Alva's bullion wagon, with the Spanish army's pay for six months on it.'

Now indeed all three of these hearers were shaken. 'What?' they said and then as the great news sank in they clasped his hands, thumped his back, kissed him on both cheeks.

'It is the bullion, I suppose?' Gilbert asked seriously. 'I mean, the Spaniards are crafty. They didn't palm off with some rubbish, just to further their own ends?'

'Not they. They didn't have time. I'll tell you all about it, only I must get some dry things on me, I'm soaked.'

The four set off along the muddy track that led back to the tent. Here and there a man rushed out to ask if the news were true but Gilbert on one side and Sydney on the other pushed them away with a brief, Aye, he's brought in Alva's money bags,' and hurried Raleigh on.

'It'll end the war,' said Gilbert as they strode along. 'Our men paid and properly fed again will simply eat the Spaniards. They'll be rare and disheartened over this. Walter, my boy you're a credit to your family.' One of his rare smiles came from his lips and passed unseen in the darkness.

His feelings towards Walter were as much of gratitude as of pride. For like all the wars that are fought in the flat, wet lands, this war had dragged on and on until both sides were weary, so weary of mud and rain and discomfort that they barely cared any longer who won, if only they could go home and be warm, dry and properly fed again. Gilbert had another reason to be eager that the war should end. What Virginia and Guiana were to be to his half-brother, the North-West passage was to him? He asked no more of life than to be allowed to set out with the Queen's patent and a good ship under him to look for the way to reach the warm and spicy East through the cold straits that lay, he was certain, to the North of Newfoundland. But first he must gain the Queen's ear: and to Gilbert's simple, honest way of thinking the way to do that was to serve her. He had begun his service in Ireland but that had not sufficed; so here he was in Holland with sundry other noblemen and gentry who

16

had given their time and their substance to fight the Queen's war and now sinking in the mud; their money spent; their men unpaid and mutinous; and their hopes waning day by rainy day. Now it would end. The Spaniards would be discouraged by the blow that had fallen so suddenly and the Spanish army, never too docile in the Netherlands, would mutiny when their wages were not forthcoming. Walter was the hand that had knocked off Gilbert's fetters. Dear Walter, so rash, so headstrong and so lucky. Gilbert loved him for those qualities; they were the ones that he himself conspicuously lacked.

They regained the tent and stooping their heads one after another entered that limited space of shelter and comfort. Homecoming is as much a question of smell as of the senses of sight and hearing and Raleigh drew in deep satisfied breaths of the air scented of smoky oil lamp and wet leather. Several times during the eventful day he had wondered if he would ever smell it again. He sat down upon the stool that Gasgoigne had previously occupied, smiled upon his friends with drowsy contentment and stretched his hands over the brazier. Sydney knelt like a servant and began removing long spurred riding-boots. Gasgoigne, not to be undone in service, poured the wine into one of the horn cups and then, in mockery of Sydney, knelt as he offered it. Gilbert routed about until he found a woollen robe thickly wadded with lambs' wool and, as Sydney rose to his feet with the boots in his hands, said, 'Get off your wet clothes, Walter and put this on.'

Obediently Raleigh stood up and loosened thongs and buttons, letting the sodden garments fall heavily to the floor. For one instant he stood naked, a slender boyish figure, white as alabaster save for dark down on chest and thigh and the sudden change to brown at waist and neck where the exposed skin began. Then he drew the robe around him with a sigh of sensuous pleasure and sat down again.

Gasgoigne had been watching him closely. To the man of forty that momentary glimpse of the boy's body had been a revelation of youth and immaturity and possibility. Walter had everything in his favour. He was young, spirited, good to look upon and charming. On his single day's work, surely he would step straight into the Queen's favour. She would listen, eyes wide and lips parted to the story of how a boy of twenty, scouting at the head of a troop of tired men, had brought in the gold for which the Spanish general was waiting, aloof in his impregnable city. When that tale was told there, behind the teller, would be his dear friend George Gasgoigne, waiting his turn. Waiting until a happy twist of speech, a flash of wit or a well-timed compliment he might rivet the Queen's attention upon himself. That was why he, a man full grown, worldly, experienced, had cultivated the friendship of this boy; had listened to him and flattered him. Yes, and mocked him. For he was clever enough, this man whose cleverness had never yet gained him anything, to realise that Raleigh was no fool; he would tire easily of a friend who was all fawning spaniel. Gasgoigne's adulation was never unleavened. As Raleigh drained the cup and set it back on the box he said suddenly: 'Where are the ducats, Walter?'

'With the Earl. Where else?' asked Raleigh, who had seen and not greatly appreciated Gasgoigne's mockery of Sydney.

'God's curse on it, what a mistake!' cried Gasgoigne. 'Why didn't you come here first? I could have told you what to do.'

'What else was there to do but to hand prisoners and all over to the commander-in-chief?'

'Taken half of it, or all of it if needs were, and carried it to Whitehall or Windsor, or wherever she is, and laid it in her lap.'

'Whose? Oh, the Queen's. Much good that would do, we need it here. The men haven't been fed properly or paid for months. We're on short commons ourselves.' He flicked the empty bottle with his thumb.

'That is beside the question. You've your career to think of. Gaining the Queen's favour should mean more to you than feeling a lot of chawbacons.'

'Your course would have been desertion,' said Gilbert solemnly, 'and if the Queen is half the woman she is reputed to be, that would be no way to her favour.'

Gasgoigne curled his lip, 'If she is half the woman she is reputed to be Alva's money bags would have bought her soul

18

and body.'

Sydney leaned forward on his stool; his fine nose quivered. Perhaps here at last was a good impersonal cause for the quarrel after which his soul had been thirsting for so long.

'Take that back, Gasgoigne or by Heaven I'll make you.'

Gasgoigne looked at Raleigh, understood exactly the sly interest that had replaced the expression of tired contentment on the young face and shrugged his shoulders. He was not going to quarrel with Sydney, yet.

'Oh, certainly, if you wish it. I had no idea that your ideals extended so far.' Sydney was not appeased. He went on offensively: 'There were twenty chawbacons, as you call them, riding with Walter. They took their share in whatever danger was going and they and their ilk should have their share in any advantage that the money brings.'

'Paying the men and feeding them seems to me a way of ending the war,' put in the practical Gilbert.

'Of providing it with sinews, I should say,' said Gasgoigne but he spoke less truculently to Gilbert. There was no hope in his mind of supplanting the half-brother in Raleigh's affections.

'Well, quit the argument and let's hear Walter's story,' said Sydney. He alone of the four cared nothing for whether Raleigh had ended or prolonged the war, whether the Queen ever heard of the gold or not. Sydney's ambition, either for his friend or for himself, did not lie that way. He wanted to live, to savour life, to be where stirring deeds were done, to know the men who did them, to do them, when possible, himself. Wherever life promised not reward but action, there he followed. And when the drum beat towards the last action and the long silence, he went uncalculating with his ambition achieved and left behind the fairest name of them all. At this moment he wanted not to reckon what the day's work would bring but to hear how it had been done.

'It wasn't difficult,' Raleigh began, 'we'd seen nothing all day. A woman at a farm gave us some rye bread and then went indoors to an upstairs window to look out and watch us eat it, I suppose. From there she called out in a terrified voice for us to begone, she could see Spaniards on the road and if they saw us or guessed that she had fed us, they'd burn the farm. I ran up and looked out of the window and far away on the skyline I could see them, riding in a long line with the wagon in the middle. I guessed that it must be valuable or they'd have put such a slow thing at the rear. We finished the bread, there wasn't much, and then rode in a half-circle until we struck the road. There happened to be a bridge over the canal at one point and near by some stacks. We hid ourselves behind those and waited. The road was very bad and the horsemen in front didn't expect an attack, they rode easily and crossed the bridge first, about thirty of them. Then came the wagon, wallowing along in the mud, and about thirty more men strung out behind it. I got my fellows ready and as the wagon drew level I said, "Now, you chaps, here's tomorrow's dinner, come out and get it." We'd got the wagon and mastered the men behind it before the others ahead heard the row and came back. A few of them bolted when they saw the mess we'd made already; the rest fought but they weren't ready or anything. So we brought the wagon and a prisoner apiece and that's all.' He yawned and stretched his arms as he finished the unvarnished story.

'A splendid piece of strategy,' said Gilbert.

'Three to one is pretty good odds,' added Sydney.

'Oh, they weren't actually three to one at any moment,' said Raleigh, literally from the midst of another yawn.

'I hope Leicester gets it all down in his report and doesn't forget that it was your job, not his,' said Gasgoigne. He rose as spoke and pulled aside the tent flap. 'Not raining now,' he said and stepped outside. As soon as the canvas had fallen behind him Sydney stretched out his hands and grabbed Raleigh's wrist. It was slender and his fingers closed around it.

'Don't let him preach his poison into you, Walter,' he said quickly, for Gasgoigne would be back in a moment. 'So long as a thing is done, what does the report matter? Once let the worm bite you and you'll never be at ease again.' He withdrew his hand hastily as Gasgoigne's step sounded outside.

'I'm going to bed,' said Raleigh, pressing his fingers to his eyes.

In bed, however, with the tent darkened, he was unable to sleep. His mind was like a mirror in which changing scenes were shown. He saw the affair of the bridge again, saw himself reporting to Leicester. He saw what he would have done had he seen Gasgoigne first and taken his counsel. He crossed the sea, being horribly sick as he always was; he reached the Queen and poured the gold into her lap; she was pleased. No, she was angered at his desertion, as Humphrey had said. Which of the pictures were true? He thought of Sydney's hastily given warning. At that thought he sighed and turned over. Probably Sydney was right; joy lay in the action, not in the reward. But already something was stirring in him, something entirely alien to Sydney's high ideal's of chivalry. He loved Sydney, perhaps best of all the three who were now sleeping within the reach of his hands. Sydney's nature, his calm and his fire, his ideals and his poetry all attracted the boy who was so like him in many ways. But George attracted him too. Just as part of him was kin to Philip, so part of him acknowledged a secret, subtler kinship with that other bitter, restless, worldly nature. Perhaps on this very night, as he tossed restlessly on his straw pallet and listened to the rain that splashed on the stretched tent cloth above him, the duel between the two parts of his make-up, the duel that was to end only at his death, had its beginnings. At one moment he was Sydney's man and cared nothing for what Leicester might or might not write. The next, Gasgoigne's discipline, he was sweating with agitation lest his name should be omitted from the report. All the time he was aware that he had no choice or will in the matter. Two men, the poet and the sophist, were within him, fighting for mastery and neither would give up in the struggle without injuring the soul for which he fought. 'Which am I?' he asked himself. 'Sydney,' cried the poet. 'Gasgoigne,' shouted the sophist. 'Both,' moaned Raleigh.

The two symbols of the spiritual protagonists slept unheeding.

And meantime Leicester had called for new candles and as they flared and bowed in the draughty tent he bent over his report. It was heartening news for a general to send to the Queen and the Council. Sixty-odd Spaniards beaten off, nineteen and the bullion wagon captured. How the Queen would gloat! But the muddy boy who had led the men out to capture "tomorrow's dinner" was not mentioned therein. Years were to pass before that name was to reach the Queen's jewelled ears. When Raleigh heard of the omission, he knew by the sick disappointment in his stomach that the Sophist had gained the first victory.

Chapter 3

Bally-in-Harsh, Ireland
10 October 1581

Toujours de l'audace.

Lord Roche of Bally was, in a double sense, paying attention to his guest. He plied him with meat and kept his glass well filled. He hardly took his eyes from his face, trying to read what lay behind that steep white forehead and those narrow shining black eyes. He had heard a good deal about this Captain Raleigh who had once, not long ago, with a pistol in one hand and a pike in the other, stood off the redoubtable Fitz-Edmonds and twenty more at the ford between Youghal and Cork.

He had been thrilled by the story, even though Fitz-Edmonds was his friend and this Captain Raleigh one of the tyrant English, for a likely deed is a likely deed by whomever performed and the sly old Irish rebel honoured it as such. Now, with the hero of the story seated at his table, he was not quite comfortable. There were a few actions of his that would not bear much examination and once or twice the conversation had taken a risky turn. So, under the bushy eyebrows, the old man watched the young one and as he watched he wondered, and as he wondered he filled up the wineglass and started a new conversational hare.

Lady Roche had put on all the jewels that remained to her. There were few, for rebellions are expensive and the Bally-in-Harsh estates were never wealthy. She watched the young man too, for every now and then the black eyes would turn towards her and there was something in them that made the sleeping coquette in the old woman's breast stir and dream. She kept her hands, her one remaining beauty, well in view and the rings winked and twinkled in the light of the candles.

There was a third watcher, too, and in her the handsome young Captain had stirred deeper than her father's wary instinct or her mother's buried coquetry. Janis could hardly hold her knife for the trembling of her hands or swallow for the hammering of her heart in her throat. Once and once only as they had taken their places at the table had he looked at her and into that slow calculating stare she had read all that she had wanted to and it had set the seal on her beauty and desirability forever, it seemed.

'And after the Spanish campaign,' Lord Roche was saying, what then, Captain Raleigh?'

'I settled in London. I'm a man of peace really. I like reading books, writing and talking with my friends. There are some splendid talkers in London now. Kit Marlowe and Thomas Nashe and Tom Lodge...' His voice trailed off as he thought of them, his fellows up to a point but content, content with ink and paper and the little fame that might be gained by those peaceful tools. He was at home with them, he could enjoy Marlowe's verses and write answers to them, he could discuss humanity and history with Fletcher, he could be, as he had just said, "a man of peace"; but all the time he knew these were not enough. His dreams would never lie neatly bound in leather for all to read. Nor did they lie, he admitted it to himself, in the clash and clangour of arms. In both worlds he was well enough but neither sufficed him. What would? Then, suddenly at that lighted table, before three people who had been strangers two hours ago, would certainly in an hour or two be enemies, he found himself saying things that neither Kit nor Tom had ever heard.

'... while I was in London the Queen gave my half-brother a commission to seek for the North-West Passage to the East. I went with him, commanding the Queen's ship, the *Falcon*. We ran into bad weather and were separated from the rest. And I made a dash for the mainland of America. The future lies that way. The other nations know it, Spain with her Mexico,

Portugal with Brazil, they all go West as the sun does. There must be lands there, cool lands where the sun falls gently, where Englishmen might live and till the soil and build the cities that could make an empire for England. I didn't reach it. Food ran out and the men, particularly the ship's master, were against it from the beginning. But an old sailor whom I use to know, Harkess was his name, swore that westwards and the north of the Indies there is a land of pines and pheasants and rich virgin soil where all our landless men, yours too, for that matter, Lord Roche, might have fields of their own... I'm but a poor sailor but I hope to reach it yet, to see the tillage spreading, the towns building house by house. I'd like to start the first colony for England and govern it.' And as the words fell on the quiet air Raleigh knew that his dreams and ambitions had taken the form of words upon them. No longer were they a shadowy lack of ease, a blind drifting. He wanted to govern.

The shock of that discovery recalled him to the matter in hand. The meal was over, night had fallen and the business that had brought him the twenty miles from Cork could wait no longer.

'Meantime,' he said, inclining courteously towards his host, 'I am sent to take you back with me to Cork. There are questions regarding the last rising that only you can answer.'

Lord Roche smiled, even while that hidden instinct that had been burrowing uneasily all the evening came into the light and cried, 'Danger!'

'There are no questions with regard to the last rising that I can answer,' he said calmly, 'and moreover I refuse, utterly, to go with you to Cork.'

'In that case, I regret it but I shall have no choice but to use compulsion.'

'Use it and be damned. I'm in my own castle. The town outside is mine and the townsfolk are mine, too, to a man. I'm afraid that your threats carry little weight, Captain Raleigh,'

'Threats? I have made none. If you know nothing of the rising, with what could I threaten you? I invite you come down with me to Cork; if you refuse, I take you'

25

'Take me? How?'

Raleigh rose and pulled aside the heavy curtain that draped the window overlooking the courtyard. Leaning over his shoulder the old man could look down on the serried pikes shining in the lantern light. He might even see, as a man turned his back to the lanterns, the rose of England embroidered on the tunic. What he could not see was that every one of Raleigh's men was in that little group under the window. There were exactly fifty but they stood like an army and looked like one. Five hundred of Lord Roche's townsfolk had met them earlier in the day but Raleigh, with calm effrontery, had treated that five hundred as if they had been already defeated. Not offering battle, he had set his fifty to policing the streets and the Irish, unmanned by this unusual behaviour, had allowed themselves to be shepherded into their houses with promises of security if they behaved. They had behaved so well that the fifty "policemen" had been able, one by one, to steal into the castle yard and get ready the tableau at which Lord Roche was now staring.

'They are all doubly armed,' said the Captain quietly, 'but in case you should think the force small to protect you against any who may have a grudge against you on the road, call out your townsfolk. They are all stout fellows, as I saw this morning and they may escort you to Cork.'

Lord Roche, who had been busy for five minutes wondering how he was to summon his forces and dismiss this impertinent Englishman, was staggered at this invitation. Quite evidently, then, Captain Raleigh had seen the townsfolk and feared them not at all.

Accepting his fate, he went to make ready for the journey.

Raleigh turned to Lady Roche. 'I am sorry to requite your hospitality by taking your husband from you,' he said, 'but if, as he says, he knows nothing he has nothing to fear. And if on the other hand he does, sooner or later the full troops would have arrived and the odds are they would have burned your castle.'

Lady Roche accepted the truth of that and managed to smile at the speaker. The townsfolk, in obedience to the summons, ranged themselves into an escort. Lord and Lady Roche embraced one another. Raleigh bent his black head over Janis's hand and brushed it with his lips. He was smiling then, for there was a tremor in that hand whose meaning there was no mistaking, Janis said, with commendable coolness, 'I suppose your business having been dispatched we shall never see you again, Captain Raleigh?' and giving her a second long stare, the Captain said, 'Never is a long time.'

The strange cavalcade moved off into the darkness, Raleigh now here, now there, footing it with the rest. Away up in the castle a girl was holding one hand to her breast as though it were very precious and she was repeating over and over, 'Never is a long time.' Was she foolish to hear in those few words just the budding hint of a promise?

Raleigh walked into Cork with his captives. There was not only Lord Roche, there were all his adherents, too, and there was a chance that some of those impending questions might get answered. No blood had been shed, or bad feeling caused, and surely even the least sanguine young man might have hoped for praise and promotion from the day's doings but Lord Grey, the Governor, was not pleased with Captain Raleigh. For Raleigh had been, as he was often to be, less discreet with his pen than with his tongue and he had been in the habit of writing home, for anyone to read, his opinion that his half-brother, now Sir Humphrey Gilbert, had ended a rebellion in this very district in two months with a third of the forces which Grey had at his command. This rebellion was far from ended. Whispers of these disloyal writings had reached the Governor's ears but he had disregarded them. Who was Raleigh, who were his correspondents and so he continued coolly tolerant to this opinionated young man, unfair to him, even, where he could be, until he awoke one day to find that Raleigh's name was in everyone's mouth and that his letters were reaching Leicester and Burghley? He would be better out of the way, he and his busy pen. In December he dispatched Raleigh to London with letters for the Queen. He could not have devised a more certain way of being rid of him.

Chapter 4

Whitehall
30 January 1582

Queen Bess was in her chamber, and she was middling old…

He was thirty. Even his age served him where she was concerned for Elizabeth the Queen, now forty-nine years old, would have found the boy Raleigh too young; and she had not reached that indiscriminate dotage where only a boy was tolerable to her. For ten years he had lived in places where hardship and often danger were always present and the experience had marked him. His forehead, where his helmet had shaded, was still startlingly white; below it the black eyes and weathered cheeks showed the darker by the contrast. He was tall and slender but slender with hard riding and living, no gangling boy. He was dressed as she liked her men to be, richly and brilliantly with jewels in his ears and on his fingers and perfume on his hair.

He knelt before her, stooping his black head; and her heart turned over.

Once, long, long ago, before she turned her thoughts to statecraft or come to regard her body as a pawn in a game of politics, there had been such another. A hard, grown man who had come into a girl's bedroom to romp with her and stayed to play a more serious game. He had died for it, stalwart Thomas Seymour. The kisses that she laid upon that hard smiling mouth were as fatal as Medusa's; for the council, headed by poor anaemic Edward, had had foresight enough to see even then the value of Elizabeth's virginity. He had gone to the block and his last thought had been of her. He had sent her a letter, telling her how best to meet the suspicions of her half-brother and his ministers. She followed the dead man's counsel and, being clever, had triumphed. Now she sat in Edward's place and if a man pleased her, who could say her nay?

Raleigh pleased her with his presence, with his likeness of that long dead lover, with his air of having come straight to her from some manly doing. She waved that exquisite hand, the hand that had been painted on poor Gasgoigne's card, doomed never to be seen by him, and her attendants vanished. The curtains covered the door with a heavy swishing of velvet.

She bade Raleigh rise, he seated and talked to her. She gave him no idea of how he pleased her. That was not her way. Moving her lips but slightly, for she was aware of those blackening teeth, she began asking him questions. What was wrong with Ireland? What did the Irish really want? It disturbed her that a section of her people should be so stubbornly discontent. How was the crushing of the rebellion proceeding? In what was Sir Humphrey so much better than Lord Grey? Raleigh had answers for them all. He described to her the country with its contrasting scenery, its flatness, its hills, and the amazing green. He told her of the people. They were treacherous even to their own, superstitious, ignorant, poor and bigoted but amazing fighters when the spirit moved them. Of his own exploits he said no word. There was tomorrow, and tomorrow, and tomorrow. Presently Elizabeth twisted the talk in her masterly fashion round to the man himself. Had there been twenty Irish at that ford? How exactly had he arranged that fifty men should arrest five hundred? Raleigh, without humility as without bragging, told her about that too. The air grew close in the room. Raleigh, at her order, pulled back the curtain from the window and opened the lattice a trifle. He stood a little away from her and looked at her. And in less than a moment the Queen was one with the slut at the inn and the languishing girl at Bally Harsh. She hung, dark as velvet, beyond the pane that gave back their reflection. The blood raced in the Queen's veins. Here was a man to whom she wanted to be all woman; and here, oh paradox, was the man that she should have been herself, the stuff which legends are made.

He was moving his hands across the window, something was scratching the pane. Elizabeth watched. Against the darkness the scratched words showed white. 'Fain would I climb but that I fear to fall.' That was the kind of thing the Queen loved and constantly used, the veiled speech that might mean anything. She dragged her hand over the window on the pane below, 'If thy heart fail thee, then climb not at all.' What did it mean?

Late, Raleigh took his leave. The girl at the inn had said, 'Come again.' Janis had said, 'We shall never see you again.' How many women in between had parted with him with some word of hope or despair? Elizabeth was Queen of England; she said, 'Attend me tomorrow.'

The white scratches remained on the window to tell whoever drew back the curtain next morning that a new star had fallen.

*

Chapter 5

Hatfield
10 April 1583

A lady whom Time hath surprised.

Elizabeth was walking the terrace at Hatfield. It was a bright April day. Over the pale sky the young wind drove the clouds. They floated like galleons across the sun, so that the Queen stepped from the sun into shadow and back into the sun again. Below her the grass was bright with daffodils, bowing to the wind, and the hawthorns were covered with a mist of green. She was waiting for Raleigh whom she had not seen for two months; she was feeling well; there was nothing unusual in the affairs of state to worry her; and yet every now and then she paused in her walking, and thought, and then went forward, biting her lips and knocking her hands together with a little peevish movement that set her rings clinking. This was no morning to be old on. That was the trouble. All youth was in the air. The very wind was coming from the young lands in the west. The morning and the knowledge that Raleigh was this moment riding towards her sent a thrilling quiver through her below her jewelled stomacher. She was honest and clear headed enough to recognise in that quiver something utterly alien to her age and her state.

Besides, she had been reading that morning. Sometimes it was an advantage to process that kind of brain that needed only one glance at a paper to absorb the very heart of the writing upon it; but when one is fifty and spring is abroad one would sooner not understand or, having understood, easily forget that one had read—

31

Beauty is but a flower
Which wrinkles will devour;
Brightness falls from the air;
Queens have died young and fair;
Dust hath filled Helen's eye...

The verse saddened her. 'Young and fair,' she had been that once. Now, before they had dressed her, she dared not look into the silver mirror. Not all her sophistry, her wit, not all her glory, her white-sailed ships ruffling it around the world, could stave off the ultimate disaster that she was overtaking the woman in her. Poor women and dull women of this age were sinking themselves in the lives of others, their children, their grandchildren. She was a barren stock, the flower that had hung too long unvisited by the bee, and she would fall, leaving nothing behind.

That April morning was the beginning of a long train of thought that was to darken the remainder of her days and result in behaviour that was to lay for ever the shadow of caricature upon her age.

Then, quite suddenly with no announcement, Raleigh stepped on to the terrace. A cloud had just travelled over the sun and its shadow remained at her end while he stood with the light upon him. And the cloud moved as he did, so that coming towards her he brought the sunshine with him. She stood quite still and held out both hands. Not all her will or dignity could hide their betraying tremor but, stooping over them, Raleigh did not smile as he had smiled at Bally Harsh. Something of her sadness had, without his knowing, struck at his soul and as if his soul had been a harp lightly touched, it had given off a pure note, not in music but of word. 'A lady whom time has surprised,' he thought. Neither he nor any other, faced with that real but common tragedy, ever bettered the phrase.

He had a great deal to tell her for he had been on an errand of some importance. He had been part of the escort that had conducted the Duke of Alençon and Anjou to his new post as Governor of The Netherlands. The Duke had paid a lengthy visit to the land of his ex-fiancée, now his 'good sister of England,' and she had done all she could to please and impress him, even to sparing Leicester, Sydney and Raleigh to go with him to the Netherlands and attend his investiture. Perhaps that had started her melancholy, the thought of the days when she had toyed with the idea of an engagement, though God knew that she was glad enough not to be married to Alençon; still it had made her conscious of Time's passing. She had missed her gentlemen. She led Raleigh to the stone seat at the end of the terrace and she heard all about the journey and the investiture.

He sat with his hands lightly clasped, hanging between his knees; his eyes were fixed, as he talked, on the beechwoods faintly purple against the sky. He talked well, drawing the Netherlands for her as he had drawn Ireland at their first meeting. He dared to poke a little fun at Alençon's pompous fat dignity in his glorious trappings. Elizabeth was pleased to laugh at the fun. 'I always called him a little frog,' she said.

Raleigh finished the description and remained silent, staring at the trees. He never looked at people unless he intended his glance to be significant: why waste a vital force? Presently he was going to ask her something but he was not quite sure yet of her mood.

She informed him quite soon.

'I am glad you are back, Walter. I have been lonely without you and I was sad this morning, until you made me laugh.'

Here Raleigh showed his difference. Instead of offering her some outrageous flattery upon the impossibility of Gloriana being sad, as the others would have done, he asked simply and seriously, 'Why sad on such a lovely morning?'

She told him a little, quoting Nashe's verse. She had the power of using her voice as an instrument. She could swear in a voice remarkably like her father's, she could bark out her orders or croon a light endearment. She could, if needed, make her voice a trumpet call to arms but the voice in which she repeated 'Brightness falls from the air' was one few ever heard. She, no less than Raleigh, hated waste.

Raleigh continued to stare at the trees as he said, 'That is

33

no new thought. You remember the Latin "There are no fields of Amaranth on the side of the grave, O Euterpe. There are no voices that are not soon silent..." That was written before Christ was born. It is the heart cry of every of every thinking person.'

'No less saddening for that.'

'No less for that but better than being blind to it. People who do not feel Time's passing can never value it properly. To see each day as a gift that will be gone in the evening... there is something of inspiration in that.'

'Valued or not, these days lead us all to the grave. Coward I am not, Walter. I have faced many things in my day. There are those that would profit by my death, yet I never see guards against them. But the grave, I fear. No more England. No more pitting of my wits against the crafty. Other ships on other seas and no little pirate to bring me tidings of great deeds greatly done. Another on my very throne; my yeomen stripping the E from the coats and I alone with the worms.'

'There is Heaven, we are told.'

'Ah, Heaven, but shall I be Queen of England there? Come, Walter, let us walk.'

The talks had disturbed her so that she could no longer sit still. Setting her narrow feet down with the brittle delicacy that had replaced her old wild grace she went down the steps of the terrace and they began to pace the paths.

Talk of life's brevity had disturbed Raleigh, too. He must press on, ask her today.

'Gilbert is sailing shortly,' he began, 'and I crave your gracious permission to accompany him.'

There, the bolt was fired.

Elizabeth stiffened. 'I shall never grant it, Walter. Gilbert is unlucky at sea. Everyone knows that. You are no sailor. You stay here,'

'I beg your Grace only to hear me. This thing means much to me. Gilbert has been unfortunate because he has been searching for something that isn't there. Drake knows that it isn't. He tried to find the entrance to the passage. If it had been

34

there, he was the man to find it. He didn't and had to come home by the Cape. Gilbert isn't trying for that now. He's out to explore America for some place where Englishmen can found a colony. You talk to death and oblivion, your Majesty. What better memorial could you have than English-speaking people thousands of miles away, thousands of years, should say, "Our land was colonised when Elizabeth was Queen." Or, if that doesn't move you, think of the immediate, material advantages. Settlers there, with the riches wrung from the virgin soil in their hands, will look to us for goods. Why, in ten years our exports to the new lands in woollen cloth alone would exceed our export to the Netherlands.'

Now he looked at her. Gone was the woman who feared the grave; the statesman looked out from Elizabeth's narrow eyes and spoke through her tightened lips.

'I will consider of this thing,' she said, 'but I forbid you to go with Gilbert, or anywhere else, without my permission. You understand?'

'Perfectly, your Grace.'

'That is well.'

They walked on, both angered. Raleigh because he had been baulked again. There was no use in defying her and setting out to find the country without her permission. She would never let him govern it after that. And time, time was passing. Elizabeth because he had been willing, nay anxious, to leave her again, having just returned. Oh, for one moment of youth, one flash of the beauty that had been hers, so that she might subdue him as she had Thomas Seymour, so that he grovelled at her feet begging her favour at whatever cost. She struck her hands together in her fury, glared angrily at the black head above her and stalked on, silent.

So, they came to the place in the path where the bricks had sunken and a pool of last night's rain had gathered and stayed. Elizabeth, mindful of her satin shoes and the precious rare silk stockings, halted and would have turned back. But Raleigh, with no thought of the host of silly stories that the action was to start winging through the years, swept off his cloak and laid it

35

over the bricks. It was a stout riding-cloak of velvet lined with chamois and the Queen went over dry-shod. Raleigh stopped and picking up the cloak gave it a little shake and spread it out on the dry part of the path. Then looked up. Elizabeth was looking down at him with unmistakable adoration in her eyes. That had been a gesture after her own heart, sudden and suitable. As Raleigh rose to his feet and smiled down at her, she was, again, not only Queen of England but Queen of Hearts.

After supper she gave him the estates of Stolney and Newlands which had fallen into her hands from an Oxford College and promised that when the wine monopoly fell vacant on 4 May, it should be his.

Raleigh galloped back to London and set on foot preparations for the barque *Raleigh* which should carry his hopes, if not his person, to America with Gilbert.

Not Time alone had surprised Elizabeth.

Chapter 6

The Mermaid Tavern
February 1585

Such a night in England ne'er has been…

The mermaid stared out over the narrow-cobbled street at the tall, twisted chimneys of the house opposite. Sea salt still gleamed in the cracks of her and the curve of her neck lifted in a way that proved that she had been intended to grace the prow of a ship, not the door of an inn. Above her head was the pale, washed February sky, barred with thin smoky clouds and decorated with one bright star. Drake lifted his eyes to her as his feet came to a standstill on the cobbles and his surly expression lightened. Her eyes stared out as if she was watching for a new land or a strange sail to break the flat line where sea met sky. She was as ill at ease here in this narrow street as he was. Once she had ridden at the prow of who knew how old a ship. She might have known Columbus.

Drake's bent head as he entered the door was almost a reverence of her, for his lack of inches rendered it unnecessary. He was not very pleased with his rendezvous and his feet were heavy and reluctant on the stairs. He'd heard of this Mermaid Club but had little thought to visit it; a place full of chattering poets, babbling about books. In his opinion there was but one good book, full of good stories of Gideon and David and meaty phrases about smiting your enemy hip and thigh. That was where Raleigh puzzled him. He was as sane and knowledgeable as one could wish about ships and yet he could spend his spare time stringing verses or reading other people's.

But Drake had come at Raleigh's invitation because Sir

Philip Sydney had asked Raleigh to invite him. It was Sydney's last night in England; tomorrow the English, under Leicester again, were sailing to the Netherlands. Drake was always willing to wish anyone 'Godspeed' in the fight against the Spaniards. For, just as the bible satisfied his taste for books, so the motto, "Down with the Spaniards," epitomised his political beliefs. All else was foolishness, a beating of the air. Eventually his reluctant feet brought him to the doorway of a room from which came the sound of men's voices. Half-defiantly he threw open the door and, stepping into the opening which he filled with his study body, surveyed the room. It was panelled with oak, already darkening with age and reflecting warmly the light of the enormous fire that roared on the open hearth. Candles stood amongst the wine bottles on the bare table and on the chimney breast and lent their rays to the firelight to show up the four men seated in cushioned chairs around the hearth and the table. They rose as he entered and greeted him with an enthusiasm that, by pleasing his childish vanity, banished the last of his ill-humour. He greeted the little company with much affability—Sir Philip Sydney, Kit Marlowe, Will Shakespeare and Sir Walter Raleigh.

'Tonight,' said Sydney, smiling at Drake, 'my five-year-old wish is granted. Why have we never met you before, Sir Francis?'

'I've been busy,' Drake answered, 'and I come to London only on business. They've made me Mayor of Plymouth. I don't mind telling you that I find a Town Council harder to manage than a ship in a gale.'

'Why is that?' The question came from Shakespeare. Drake was to discover that evening that the quiet man with the big head never let a statement go unquestioned.

'God knows,' he replied. 'All the dolts of the town seem to get on to the Council and once there they're no longer Tom, Dick and Harry that can be talked to as such or shouted down; they're Mister this and Mister that, a little power swells their poor thick heads.' There was great scorn in the loud booming voice. The sound of it died away but the sense, a little altered,

38

would appear again, 'dressed in a little brief authority.' 'This naval commission, with friend Walter here, has been a holiday after the fight I've been having about the new conduit. Wouldn't you have thought that the fools have been glad of the good water brought to their door? They talked as though I was going to drink it all myself. As for the red robes I made them wear, you should have heard them! But there, once let the war get going in Holland again and this navy business through and I'll leave the Councillors to paddle in the conduit with the red robes tucked up round their rumps if they've a mind that way.'

'You'll go west again?' Raleigh asked.

'Maybe,' said Drake, gazing into his tankard as though he expected to read his plans there. 'But I've a fancy to take a peep at that harbour at Cadiz. I hear that there's a sight of building going forward there. I might run down to see if I can lend them a hand. Sir Walter and I know all the latest fashions in sailcloth. Eh?'

''Tis a tedious business, rigging up good ships to be shot at and sunk when you have another use for them,' said Raleigh.

'Ah, those colonies of yours. Many a good ship will go to the bottom before the seas are safe for your passenger ships or the West a home for your colonies. You don't hate the Dons as I do, Sir Walter. I put that hatred into every sail, plank, rope or cask of herrings that I order.'

'Why do you hate them so?' asked Shakespeare, reaching out for a bottle.

Drake shifted his chair to face the questioner.

'It would take me all night to tell you that. To begin with they're Papists. I don't hate them for that; only where their religion is concerned, they're neither sane nor human. I'll tell you something. Once I had to put five of my men ashore. We'd had bad luck and lost a ship and somebody had to stay behind. Five of them volunteered. They were single men and the rest were married, that was the reason. I picked out what I thought was a safe place, nowhere near any Spanish settlement, and promised to get back as fast as the wind would serve me. The Spaniards found them and handed them over to their damned holy Inquisition. Not as enemies, mark you. They weren't honest enough to treat them as prisoners of war. They took them as Protestants and whipped them through the streets of Vera Cruz; then they hung them up by the thumbs till they went mad and died. One was cut down for dead before he was and escaped to the woods. I found him, a mad wreck, all that was left of my sturdy young men that had offered to stay behind...' The strong gruff voice broke with feeling. Drake followed hard and added, 'You can't want more than that.'

'But' said Marlowe, who loved an argument, 'they say that they sacrificed the body in an attempt to save the soul.'

Drake turned round fiercely. 'Sacrifice my backside! They're cruel, they like cruelty for its own sake. I hate the whole lot of the Devil's spawn.'

He announced that as he always announced his opinions, as if there were only that view in all the world and all the sane men must accept it.

'They hate you too, by all accounts,' said Sydney.

'Oh doubtless, but not for the way I mistreat prisoners. Man, I've had hundreds and never killed but two. And that was the swine's own fault.' He drank deeply and then without a pause continued: 'I'll tell you about that. I'd taken the town but not the fort outside it. The Spaniards sent an officer with a white flag to parley about the town's ransom. I had a little nigger with me, dear little chap with curly hair, and I sent him out to bring the fellow in. I suppose he wasn't good enough conduct for his lordship; anyway, the bastard lowered the spear that the flag was tied to and ran him through the guts. The poor little devil crawled back to me and died at my feet. I'd sent him, mark you, and he looked at me with eyes like a dog's, not understanding why that has happened to him. I was savage as Satan but the lousy brute was back in the fort, safe. So, I took one of the Spanish friars that I captured and hanged him just on that spot, in full view of the fort. Then I sent another up with a message to say that I'd hang another there, night and morning, until that murderous dog was given up. There was no sign in the morning that he was coming out, so I hanged my second friar,

40

after explaining that his people, not I, bore the blame for it. My lord came out at night and I hanged him, too, and he didn't get the short sharp jerk that I'd given the friars, either.'

Shakespeare had turned away and was staring into the fire. There was no doubt that here was a man. Rough to his foes and tender to his friends. Unsubtle, maybe, but sure of himself and with a tongue for a homespun tale. A woman might fall in love with such a one. Everything might be against her loving him. Should he be ugly, diseased, poor? What could be the great disadvantage that should be overcome by the way that he told a tale? Ah, he had it! Let him be black. A man of action, a black man, who won a white woman by the tale of stirring deeds. And then? Yes, then, because he was unsubtle and only a man of action, he should lose her again.

Almost slyly Shakespeare glanced at Drake, noted the firm, well-rounded face, the blunt, aggressive nose, cocked at a sharp angle. That curly hair, growing smoothly from the forehead, would not be amiss on a black man if only it were dark instead of brown, bleached almost to straw colour. He turned back to the fire again. What fun life was! What interest it offered to the watching eye!

Drake, never silent for long in congenial company, was talking again.

'I'm forgetting. I've a little token for you, Sir Walter. Just a memento of our work together. Little did I ever think to work easily with a poet.' He fumbled with a soft leather bag that he had brought in and laid on the floor beside him. If he had found Raleigh surrounded by talking men of letters and had been silenced himself, as he had expected to be, by the wisdom and foolery of their talk, that bag would have gone away unopened and the gift would never have been made. But now, mellowed by the Canary wine and the sound of his own voice, he forgot that there had ever been an aspect of Raleigh that he had distrusted.

With unusual care he lifted with his thick fingers a jade figure out of the bag and set it on the table, just where the candlelight fell on it.

41

Imperturbable and ungraceful, with his arms folded over his bulging stomach, the Buddha sat and surveyed them.

'It's an idol,' said Drake. 'The eyes are rubies and this thing he's sitting on'—he flicked the pedestal with one finger—'is uncut opal. Not that I want you to think that it's valuable. But it's curious. They worship these in the East.'

'It's beautiful,' said Raleigh. He picked it up, surprised at its weight and the finished workmanship. 'I'm very grateful to you and shall value it forever. I've never had such a costly present before.'

Drake smiled, well pleased.

'Things like that are easily picked up in some places. I've about exhausted my store of them. But I'll remember all the rest of you when I go out again.' He would have liked, suddenly, to have had some presents for them all. Pleasant fellows who listened so attentively to his stories. He turned to Sydney.

'You sail to the Netherlands tomorrow, sir?'

'I do. And it will go hard but I'll strike a blow for the memory of your little nigger and the other sturdy fellows.'

'Oh, not for them alone. That's a fleabite. I'll tell you...'

He embarked on another story.

Raleigh sat with one hand on the cold hard knees of the Buddha and the other around his wine cup. His attention drifted. There was no need for him to listen to Drake's stories. He had heard them before. And just now, although he admired the little pirate and was touched by his gift, he was disappointed in the man. He had tried to interest him in his plans for colonising and laying the foundations of an empire. But Drake only scoffed. Buccaneering and exploring were his games. And Raleigh, outwardly so successful as to have aroused bitter enmity in many breasts, flashing through the court in his wonderful silver armour that he had ordered when the Queen appointed him Captain of the Guard, was inwardly enduring a period of intense depression and frustrated hope. The favours of Elizabeth, the ear of the Council, the money he was making from his wine and trade monopolies, what were all these but the means to an end? And that end was as far off as ever. Of his latest attempts at colonising Virginia, as he already called that land in compliment to the Queen, he had heard no word. One hundred and seven colonists he had sent out at his own expense, in five ships, led by Grenville. That should have been sure enough. Grenville was the most stubborn soul ever made by God, but he was a brilliant seaman and a sound leader. News should have come by now. If only he should have gone himself. He sat, well friended, in the cosy firelit room and ached for the far places, the hardship and the dangers of the pioneer life. This pretence of the Queen's that he, and only he, could serve her upon this navy business, how it irked him. Probably, with one excuse after another, she would tie him down for ever. All the others in this room would have a chance to use their talents. He alone must wait and wait. Perhaps Drake was right too. Maybe the seas must be safer and the political world more settled before any dream of Empire could flower.

Sydney and Drake were still talking. Marlowe and Shakespeare were hanging on their words, Drake's description of the exhilaration that took him as he made for the open sea or closed for action were being stored away in Shakespeare's mind; not in the words the sailor used but in phrases peculiar to himself. 'Once more into the breach, dear friends... stiffen the sinews, summon up the blood.' The playwright, into whose peaceful life only one bloody quarrel was to intrude, and that with his poet friend now sipping his wine across the hearth, was fired by Drake's lust for battle. Sydney, on the eve of a war in which he had no personal interest but to whose call he had responded like one of Arthur's Knights to a challenge, was glad to listen to a tale of wrongs endured that he could help to right. It gave purpose to his going.

Sydney, most sensitive and the greatest lover of Raleigh in that little company, was the first to break from Drake's spell and notice his friend's attention.

'Wishing that you were sailing with us tomorrow, Walter?' he asked.

'God knows I do. If I once got permission to leave England I'd mutiny but the ship would turn westwards. If I only knew what had become of them all...'

43

As if in answer a knock fell upon the door. Raleigh rose and in three strides reached and flung it open, expecting he knew not whom to be standing without. But not, most certainly he did not expect to see Master Cavendish who had sailed with Grenville all those months ago.

Cavendish stood in the doorway utterly speechless with excitement. In his thin young face, marked with dirt and sweat and haggard with fatigue, his blue eyes blazed. Raleigh seized both hands and dragged him into the room, kicking the door shut with his foot.

'This is Master Cavendish with some news of Virginia,' he said.

'Some news? Wondrous good news as you shall hear,' said Cavendish in a voice shaking with emotion.

'They landed? They stayed there? Is it all right?' With equal excitement Raleigh bent over the young man, plucking at his sleeve, his collar, his shoulder.

Cavendish nodded and suddenly Raleigh's manner changed.

'Poor lad, you are overtired. Sit quietly for a moment. Good tidings can wait.'

He filled his own cup with wine and handed it to the boy. With gentle hands he loosened his cloak and laid it over the back of the chair.

Cavendish drank the wine and sat silent until the room began to fade before his eyes and he was afraid that he would fall asleep there with his story untold. He was weary to the bone; he had wasted not a moment. The instant that his ship had anchored at Plymouth he had thrown himself on horseback and, except to change horses and gulp a pot of ale, had not paused in his headlong journey. He must be first, before Grenville, before Fernando, to tell Raleigh the news. For to this young man of two-and-twenty, so soon to have fame and to spare of his own, Raleigh was a creature of almost fabulous brilliance. For him the feats of the young Raleigh in Holland, Youghal and Bally, dimmed in the minds of others by envy or familiarity, were as real and inspiring as the stories of ancient heroes. Side by side with them was the charm of the man as he now was, a scholar, a poet, a courtier, best of all a dreamer of vast and glorious dreams. As Cavendish had brought his tiny, deserted ship to join the others through a storm in the Bay of Portugal and faced the crossing alone, no mean feat for one of his experience, "Raleigh" had been his watchword. While Grenville settled the colonists and quarrelled with the Indians, laying thereby the foundations of many a feud to come, Cavendish had been scouring the countryside for specimens and information that would interest his master. And now here he was, half-dead with fatigue but with Raleigh staring at him with delight and surprise, waiting for his story. And not Raleigh alone. There was the legendary Sir Francis adding his gruff word of praise and the noble Sir Philip aglow with enthusiasm, talking of what they together would do for the colony when he came back from the wars.

With his vitality restored by the wine, and that headier draught, praise, Cavendish began to pour out his explanations and descriptions.

'They were going to make their headquarters there,' he said, marking the spot with the candlestick. 'The river runs thus.' He traced its course between the tankard, a wine bottle and the jade Buddha. 'The Indian country lies this way. There has been a little trouble there already. Oh, nothing,' he added hastily as Drake sat back with an expression that said, 'I told you so.' 'It'll blow over now that Lane is left in charge. Sir Richard is so rash...' He stopped abruptly as he realised that he was criticising his superior.

'What was the trouble, exactly?' Raleigh asked smoothly.

'It'll all be in the report,' countered Cavendish uneasily.

'You tell me now.'

'It was only that Sir Richard missed a silver cup and suspected the Indians. When they refused, being unable or unwilling, we never knew which, so give it up, he burned a village and some standing corn... It made some ill feeling but Lane will patch it up.'

'If I could only have gone myself.' It was a cry from his heart.

45

Cavendish hastened to change the subject. From his pocket he drew three long clay pipes decorated in simple pleasing patterns.

'The Indians make these of clay and press on the patterns in clay of other colours.' Fumbling again, he brought forth a bundle of leaves, dried pointed leaves that gave off a new and fragrant scent.

'They make smoke; thus, I will show you. It is one of their customs, and a pleasing one.'

He filled the bowl of one of the pipes with the leaves, pressing them down with the ball of his thumb.

They watched him place the stem of the pipe in his mouth, with the bowl inverted over the candle-flame, and draw steadily until the leaves were burning and giving off blue smoke. When it was going well, he wiped the mouthpiece almost reverently on his sleeve and offered it to Raleigh.

'Never mind if it chokes you. It does so at first but later 'tis most comforting.'

One after the other he lighted the remaining pipes and offered them in turn to Sydney and Drake. How was he to reckon the importance of the quiet man seated upon the left of the stove? The pipes were refilled and passed about. The room, the first in England to do so, became blue with smoke. The men coughed and choked. Master Cavendish mentioned the pines and the pheasant that old Harkess had talked of long ago; and described roots that the Indians dug out of the soil and ate. He added that he had great store of them upon his ship and that they had proved a veritable cure for the scurvy. He talked of the great birds that lived in the Virginian forest. They had speckled feathers and red jowls that unfolded when they were angry; their flesh was like that of a chicken but richer and there was more of it. ''Twould oust the goose at Martinmas if we could rear it here.'

They talked, or listened as their mind was, until the last bottle lay upon its side and the last leaf in Master Cavendish's packet had yielded up its fragrant soul and everyone except that young sailor was feeling sick and dizzy. Then they clattered down the stairs, still talking. Sydney renewed his promise to strike a blow at the Spaniards in Drake's name and Drake promised that he would call on the new colony and leave stores directly the Queen gave him permission to sail. Beneath the mermaid's seaward stare they parted with handshakes and good wishes. Raleigh asked Cavendish home with him and took his arm, thereby making the young man the proudest soul on earth for the moment. Drake swaggered off, planning his raid on Cadiz. Sydney walked slowly, thinking of Drake and Cavendish and chiselling out a sentence that was to live, 'With a tale he cometh, a tale that holdeth children from play and old men from the chimney corner.' Marlowe hurried home to write an account of all these doings to the dark lady who was more than half in love with Will. Shakespeare himself walked heavily, pregnant with *Othello*.

Raleigh, dragging more of the story of Grenville's doing from Cavendish's unwilling tongue, swung on a seesaw of the mind. Now high and elated because his dream had a form and a name at last, now low and in despair lest, like an unskippered ship, it should founder.

Chapter 7

London
1586

Raleigh was on his way to visit Lettice Knollys. That was why his hat was drawn low on his brow and the collar of his plain dark cloak turned up to touch his nose. Too many of the Queen's men had visited Lettice. Raleigh was not going to lose favour that way.

It was not a love tryst.

Two days before had come the news of Philip Sydney's death at Zutphen. That bright flame was quenched forever. Raleigh had lost the only friend who had really understood his dreams or sympathised with his aims. And Raleigh felt a need to talk with someone who had loved him; besides, it was fitting that he should proffer his sympathy to the lady who had lost, not a friend but a lover. He did not approach the front door—servants were always gossips—but skirted the house until he saw that a lamp was burning in her room at the back. He tapped discreetly upon the window and the gap in the curtain widened and Lettice herself looked out at him. 'Side door,' she said quietly and a moment later he was in her room. An old woman who was working by the fireside rose and shuffled away without so much as a glance his way. Raleigh and the lady stood alone looking at one another. He was astounded to see her looking as usual. There were no traces of tears in her bright, delicately shaped eyes or of abandoned grief in the neat hair or clothes. It ran through Raleigh that if he died now, no one would grieve; but if he had laid his love at any woman's feet, he would wish her to appear just a little altered by his death. In what way he did not know but just a little changed, as if Sorrow had touched her.

Lettice Knollys bade him to be seated and herself sat opposite. She had hoped for two long days that he would come. Something had assured her that it was likely. And for two days she had wondered what, when she met Raleigh again, her attitude should be. Would you more readily arrest a man's attention by a show of unbridled grief for another or by demonstrating in every word and action that your interest lay in the future, not the past? She had decided upon the latter course and in that she had misjudged Raleigh.

All his doings had borne evidence of an essential hardness and selfishness in the man. His behaviour to the Queen, so outwardly discreet and cool must, all London was assured, cover a great deal of something that was neither discreet nor cool. Else why she favour him so? It was not likely, argued Lettice to herself, that a man so hard and calculating would have any use for sentiment. Those pouched and cynical eyelids, too, deceived her and many other people. Such wise eyes, already lined at the corners with the memories of rather unkind laughter. A man with eyes like that would have no use for a woman who snivelled like an untried schoolgirl over a dead lover. And that was why her hair was neat in its elaborate wreaths, plaits and curls, her face untamed by tears, her dress perfect in detail. That was where she had made her mistake. All that was hard in Raleigh, except his courage, had been acquired and carefully fostered and was alien to the man himself, although vital to his schemes. Elizabeth's foolish and pathetic attempts at youthfulness moved him to pity and poetry, not to laughter, as all the Court, laughing themselves, supposed. And had Lettice Knollys appeared before him distraught with tears he would have done his best to comfort her and probably, in mutual sorrow, come very near to her. She realised that too late.

They talked for a little of the dead man. Of his grace, his poetry, his chivalry; of the bright promise of his youth which had been put out for ever. Lettice sat unmoved. Presently she offered him wine and took some herself, looking at him over the edge of the beaker as she drank. She agreed all that he said about Philip but it was obvious that to her he had been only one of a string of lovers and would be easily replaced. And then, just as Raleigh, sickened and disappointed with his visit, was rising to go, she burst into tears, covering her face with her full-laced sleeve and turning her slender, shaking shoulders towards him.

They were tears of chagrin and disappointment but he could not know that. He had come to see her, she had had her one golden opportunity and now it was gone. Raleigh would go back to the Queen and, with Sydney dead, their paths would never pass again.

Raleigh instantly imagined that he had been misjudging her and that was the result not of indifference but of great control which had now broken. He left his seat and came and stood by her with his hand on her shoulder. Through the warm, satin-covered flesh he could feel frail bones, small as a child's and, like a child, she seemed herself helpless and sorrowful. Raleigh slid his arm farther around her and pressed the shaking body to his shoulder, soothing her with gentle words and rather awkward pattings. There was no desire in his touch: he would have said that he was past the age to be moved easily to desire, least of all by a woman whom he had until this evening regarded as belonging to his friend.

He held her calmly for a moment and was then aware suddenly that a change had come over her. She was no longer crying and had turned in his arms, pressing her face and breast towards him. He became conscious of her scent, her warmth and softness, and that unnameable force which emanates from a desirous woman and which the Hindus hold will cause a date tree to become fruitful if clasped by such a one. Uneasy caution drove out his pity, he loosened his clasp and stood up and she leaped up and faced him, her secret written plainly in her heaving bosom, moist lips and veiled eyes. Disgust shook him. He said slowly, 'Philip is lucky to have died before he knew your looseness.' With his cloak over his arm and his hat in his hand he went quickly out of her presence. He did not see the hatred and fury gather in her face and had no idea that he had made, with that simple sentence, an enemy that would work him infinite harm.

Chapter 8

The Ring Meadow
Spring 1588

Elizabeth brought her fan down sharply on the arm of her chair and some of the fragile sticks snapped, which added to her annoyance. God's death! Hadn't she enough to bother about without this confounded fellow always being at her to let him go to Virginia?

'I forbid it, absolutely and finally,' she snapped. 'Bide here where your duty is. With the Spaniards at our door, it is a time to waste ships and men on another of your wild-goose schemes?'

'That's just why,' said Raleigh urgently. 'Very soon the Armada will be upon us and we shall be able to spare no thought for other things. My ships are ready; with your permission I can embark in three days, visit the colony, leave them stores, hearten them and be back before the first galleon leaves Cadiz.'

'So you say. And I would have you know, Walter Raleigh, that there are those who tell me that there is no colony in Virginia. That the whole thing is a cock-and-bull story to bolster your reputation and there be others' — she lowered her voice venomously — 'who say that your eagerness to be away is because you are at heart a friend of Spain.'

'Who ever says that lies in his teeth. Tell me his name and before God he shall eat his words.'

'Many say it, Walter.' She was feeling better after her outburst. 'You could hardly fight a hundred of them. I don't believe it...'

'I thank your Grace for that, at least.'

'... but I am weary of your nagging at me. Within my realm, within my court, within my room, I would have peace.' She punctuated the list of her possessions with blows of a broken fan.

51

The years that she dreaded were laying heavy hands upon the Queen. Time had overtaken her. Her own red-gold hair had recently given place to a wig, the first of a collection that was to number six hundred at her death. Her face was frankly painted but it now had the charm of a well-executed mask and no longer hurt the sensitive observer by its pretence to youth. Her hands were still beautiful, unbelievably frail of bone and white and wrinkled enough to justify the story that, imitating the grandees of Spain, she slept in gloves dripping with olive oil and honey.

Having rebuked Raleigh, she was anxious to charm him, so she brought her hands into play by stripping the painted satin from the broken sticks of the fan. 'I've ordered a Pageant,' she began in a gay voice.

'Indeed?' said Raleigh sullenly. For the moment disappointment made him careless whether he offended her. To be a favourite meant nothing, the favours he asked were not granted. This year he would be thirty-six; more than half his life was spent; and here he was, dependent upon the will of an ageing autocrat who not listen to reason.

'A Pageant will put the people in a good humour and liven up the Court, besides showing the Spaniards how little we care for their threats,' went on the gay voice.

Raleigh thought, I'll go without her leave and yet what good would that do? She would never let him govern after that. Nevertheless, it was worth trying. If he were on the spot ruling well, he might brazen it out.

He roused from his thoughts to discover that he was no longer alone with Elizabeth. Breaking off her monologue about the Pageant she cried, 'Ha, Robert! What a treat to see a smiling face! Walter here is sulking because I will not let him go racing off to America just as Philip is launching his Armada.'

Essex eyed Raleigh with covert hatred.

'Why not let him go, your Majesty?'

'He's a sailor and we shall need such,' said the Queen.

'There are sailors enough and to spare,' said Essex. The tone added, 'and better ones than he.'

Raleigh looked at Essex as if he were seeing that stalwart form and bright ruddy face for the first time. He had never taken Essex seriously, certainly never seen in him anything to fear. Partly this blindness resulted from assurance. Rail at him as she might, the Queen was glad of his counsel, grateful for his philosophy when the dark mood was on her, as it had been on that April day at Hatfield. What could a callow boy do to stave off the morbid thoughts that overlook an aged and intelligent woman? Partly it came from indifference. For the playful moods of Elizabeth always bored and often distressed the Captain of her Guard. Let the Queen have another lap-dog to kiss and fondle and slap. It gave her older and rather tired toy a chance to attend to the things that he really cared about.

But now, as he saw them exchanging bright glances as they planned the coming Pageant, he saw his mistake. He saw that Essex would be glad to get him out of the way. He threw off his sullenness quickly and joined in the planning, improving upon any suggestion that Essex made, catching the Queen's eye, playing the courtier. And while Elizabeth smiled and listened and sided now with one and now with the other, the two men eyed one another with sidelong glances of jealousy like two dogs spoiling for a fight.

II

They faced one another across the paced-out space of turf in the Ring Meadow. It had been the scene of many famous duels. It was quiet and flat, ringed with trees and within easy reach of the city. The sun struck warm on Raleigh's shoulders through the yellow silk shirt and struck fire from the blade in his hand as he tucked up his frilled cuff. High overheard a lark, early disturbed from her nest, was singing. It might be a death song. Waiting for Blount to give the signal, Raleigh looked at the man he had come out to kill. Big solid body and long legs in a shirt of blue and breeches of the same colour slashed with scarlet, there was yet something curiously immature about Essex. Raleigh no longer wished to strike him; something in him had been satisfied when he had slashed his glove across that sanguine young face. But of course, this had been inevitable: there remained only to go in and win. Virginia and all his hopes must not be wiped out by a thrust of a puppy's sword.

Blount raised his arm, the handkerchief dangled. Young Cavendish, Raleigh's second, drew a hissing breath between his teeth. Raleigh, with his eyes on the handkerchief, saw that Blount, instead of dropping it, had stepped over to Essex and, seizing him by the elbow, pointed back towards the river. A page was running at full speed up the path by which they had come, waving both his arms and, as he drew within earshot, shouting with the full force of his lungs. And behind the page there was a woman, moving swiftly, though with difficulty, across the dewy pasture. She leaned upon a cane. It was the Queen. Not contented with the efforts of the page, as soon as she saw that she had their attention she lifted her cane and bellowed, 'Stop!' in a voice that went ringing away amongst the trees.

Essex strode towards Raleigh. 'Did you plan this?' he asked. There was a world of baffled hatred in his voice.

'No. Did you?' said Raleigh.

Then, moved by a common impulse, they sheathed their swords and began to run towards the Queen who, as soon as she saw them moving, stopped and leaned on the cane again.

The early sun was pitiless to that unpainted face. Her wig, over which a scarf was tied in a clumsy knot beneath her chin, had slipped sideways to that one red curl rested rakishly on a black eyebrow. But she never looked more truly regal. When they were within six paces, each striving to reach her and get his word in first, she said in a voice as crisp and cold as hail, 'Down on your knees, both of you. So! This is how you obey my orders about duelling.'

Down in the dewy grass knelt the two big men. The Queen took a step or two forward and seemed to wait for them to recover their breath.

'What is this all about?' she demanded.

They began to speak together, babbling of insults and mockery.

54

'Stop,' said Elizabeth. 'Walter, as elder, speak first.'

'It was about a small thing,' Raleigh began. 'He chose my colour for the Pageant, so that I and my men appeared like his followers. When I taxed him with it he insulted me.'

'How?'

'He said he thought I should have chosen a more Spanish colour, whatever that may mean.'

'Then,' said Essex, speaking without leave, 'he flung his glove in my face and challenged me.'

'So should I, so would any man,' said the Queen. 'That was an insult for which you will apologise. And you will apologise for making such a coil about nothing,' she added turning to Raleigh. 'We all know of your monopolies, Walter, but I hate yet to hear that a man has a monopoly on the right to wear russet-red clothing.'

'It was done deliberately to shame me, to make me look like his man...'

'That will do. You were both wrong. What is worse, you are both disobedient. Haven't I forbidden duelling about the Court? A fine thing it would be if I lost Walter by your hand, Robert, or Robert by yours. Finer still if you each disabled the other upon the eve of the day when England needs every able-bodied man. Save your blows and your spleen for the Dons.' She drew a deep breath.

'A fine thing it is, too, when I must be dragged from my bed at crack of dawn and stand in a wet meadow, catching my death of cold to keep two grown men from letting the daylight into one another's worthless carcasses.'

At this the pair stirred uneasily. They were both aware that in her state of health it was a risky thing for the Queen to do. But Elizabeth had not finished. She had enjoyed standing in her younger days, as many a tottering Ambassador had discovered to his cost. And now, her back might be aching, her hand resting heavily on the cane, the wet soaking into her thin shoes, she would not move until she was ready.

'Stay where you are and listen to me.' She lifted the cane and gave them both a poke, no playful one either, in the ribs.

'If you two ever quarrel about anything, anything whatever, I'll banish you both. That I swear by God above me. If one of you had killed the other this morning I'd have hanged the other, as Christ's my judge. Disobedience to me is treason that I will punish as such. Remember that, both of you. Now you may get up. Robert, you will apologise for saying what you did. Walter, you will apologise for striking Robert.' She ignored the origin of the quarrel, 'Go on! I am waiting.'

They got up sheepishly, with absurd wet patches on their breeches' knees. 'I apologise, your Lordship,' said Raleigh.

'I apologise, Sir Walter,' said Essex.

Then, solemnly, both together,' 'I accept your apology.'

They stood waiting for the next order.

'Dress yourselves. Boy! Bring those doublets.'

They struggled into their clothes feeling, and somehow looking, like naughty children.

The Queen had spent her fury and was now only anxious to fill their hearts with concern for her. With a typically Elizabethan change of manner she beckoned to Blount.

'Bear you my cane,' she said in a voice that had little more than a whisper. 'You two must give me an arm each to the boat.'

She slipped one of those pale hands through each crooked silken elbow and bore with all her weight.

Whether her exhaustion was as great as she implied neither wondered. They walked along, supporting her tenderly; and although no blood-letting had eased the pains of their rivalry, each was conscious of a half-humorous fellow-feeling. They had looked, and felt, so ridiculous kneeling there in the grass and cracking their tight doublet seams in the haste.

Elizabeth, who had been acutely conscious of the gathering storm, was just an acutely conscious of the truce. She walked between them and every now and then a sharp rheumaticky crack was heard. She had been a martyr to auricular rheumatism since her youth and now, giving her ankle a twist before she set down her foot, she found that she could regularly produce the reproachful sound. She enjoyed seeing Raleigh wince at each evidence of her abused infirmity.

Chapter 9

Whitehall
August 1588

How so great man's strength be reckoned?
There are two things he cannot flee,
Love is the first...

Within the room he could hear the tinkling sound of the virginals and a voice singing to the thin notes of the simple, plaintive tune.

'When we two are parted.
All the world is dim.
Stars and moon and sunshine
Absent are with him.

Not a flower will blossom,
Not a bird will sing,
Lacking the sweet summer
He alone can bring.

When we two are parted
All my heart is numb,
And it will not waken
Till again he come.

Come, love, bring the summer,
Bid my heart awake.
And for all the guerdon,
My devotion take.'

The song ended with four little notes that fainted on the air.

Raleigh opened the door and entered just as the Queen said, 'The music is well enough. But you will have to learn a new song. It is the fashion here for the men to solicit the maid not, as you sang, the other way about.'

Most of Elizabeth's ladies would have reduced to silence, if not to tears, by this crushing snub but the girl who had been singing, though she coloured to the eyes, said lightly, 'Next time, your Majesty, I will sing it the other way about.'

'You'll have difficulty with the "dim" and "him",' said the Queen shortly. 'Not at all,' said the girl, 'listen.' And lifting her chin she sang to the same tinkling little tune but without accompaniment:

> *'When we two are parted*
> *All the world is grey,*
> *Star and moon and sunshine*
> *Go with her away.*

'The rest needs but the changing word.'

Some of the people around the Queen smiled but the ladies stood aghast at the girl's temerity. Elizabeth, who liked spirit and had admired the assurance and the swift twist of the little verse, said merely, 'Well, see that you sing it so,' and turned aside to speak to someone else.

It was one of those semi-formal gatherings in which her soul delighted. Three great chandeliers, each bright with twenty candles, hung from the painted roof and spilled their light on her gown of creamy silk and the great jewels that blazed on her fingers, in her ears and at her throat. A table laden with fruit and sweetmeats and wine stood by the wall and nimble, lithe pages weighed forward by great silver salvers ran in and out amongst the guests.

Raleigh pushed through the crowd and bowed over the Queen's hand. She touched his shoulder with one finger and inquired, 'Is your wound healed?'

'Perfectly. It was only a scratch.'

'And do you like the medals?'

'It was generous of you to give your ally all the credit,' Raleigh said, smiling. He referred to the motto on the medal which Elizabeth had had struck to commemorate the defeat of the Armada, 'God blew with his breath, and they were scattered.'

Elizabeth laughed.

'I wanted to point that out for all their holy water and their priests on every galleon, they hadn't the monopoly of God.' Lowering her voice, she added, 'I will dance with you presently, I must talk awhile with Crofts and Cecil.'

During the conversation Raleigh had been looking around covertly for the girl who had sung and upon his dismissal he stepped aside so that he had a clear view of her. He watched her, reckoning her beauty point by point. She was tall, but not as tall as the Queen, very slender but with high full bosom that betokened pride. Her cheekbones were high and prominent so that her cheeks were hallowed, she was young, one-and-twenty at most. Her hair was fair, almost silverish gold and, instead of being tortured into curls and wreaths, was parted in the middle and plaited into a coronet across the top of her head. Her gown of night-blue velvet emphasised the pallor of her skin and the blue of her wide eyes. Amongst the ladies with hennaed hair and painted cheeks that imitated the Queen she looked simple and natural but when Raleigh, yielding to his curiosity, went nearer to her he wondered whether lips could be so red or a fair-haired woman own such black lashes.

The man and woman with whom she was speaking walked away and, with attention adrift for a moment, she became conscious of Raleigh's penetrating state. She turned so that she faced him fully and thrust out her under lip and flung up her head with defiance that said, 'Here I am, stare at me if that is your pleasure.' Black eyes met blue across the moving throng of people. She took the full force of a gaze that had stirred many a heart better armoured than hers. She saw the narrow, tanned face with the high white brow, the black hair and the neat little pointed beard. Unable to withdraw her eyes, she did not appreciate the elegance of his white satin doublet and breeches or the jewelled sword belt. She saw only his face; and suddenly her heart began to hammer. A warm wave of discomfort crept up from the low edge of her corsage and drowned her face. Slowly and reluctantly, she lowered her eyes and turned away.

Raleigh sought out Arthur Throckmorton.

'Who is the girl who was singing, the one who answered the Queen so boldly?'

'My sister Elizabeth,' said Throckmorton furiously; 'I shall have something to say to her anon. She is new to the Court but she could have known better.'

'She has a lovely voice,' said Raleigh casually.

'Well, enough, if she knew when to silence it.'

Raleigh walked away. The busy affairs of the past and the attendance that he had danced upon the Queen, besides something in his own nature, had kept him from philandering. But tonight, as he moved about in the bright, crowded room, he knew that his hour had come. He looked upon the new Maid of Honour and told himself, 'That is my woman.'

The fiddlers and the flautists appeared suddenly in the gallery and struck up a lively air. Raleigh had the caution to look round for the Queen but she was dancing already, holding the French Ambassador by the hand and stepping with such verve and spirit that it was impossible to recognise in her the old woman who had needed two strong men to help her across a meadow. Seeing her thus occupied Raleigh began to search for the lady in the night-blue gown. She was standing with her brother in a far corner of the room. Arthur Throckmorton was evidently having his say. His sister, with her lower lip outthrust and bright scarlet face, was listening to him in a rage that he would not let her voice. Twice, as Raleigh threaded his way towards them, he saw her open her mouth to protest or to defend herself but each time Arthur, striking the palm of his left hand with his right clenched fist, silenced her. Unobserved Raleigh stole up beside them and then suddenly catching her by the hand, whirled her into the dance. She gave a little gasp, turned even brighter scarlet in the face as she recognised him and then laughed.

'I thought it was time to end the lecture,' said Raleigh as they stepped and twirled, parted and bowed and clasped hands again.

'A moment more of it and I should have boxed his ears and then gone home, in disgrace, for good.'

'Aren't you enjoying the Court life?'

'I wasn't,' she said, and shot him with a glance which renewed his doubt whether she were as unsophisticated as at first sight she appeared. He was glad of the doubt, however, it was much easier to play with someone who knew and understood the rules of the game. He tightened his fingers over hers. She had a surprisingly hard firm little hand, bony but not in the least fragile.

'Did you think my behaviour so shocking?' she asked.

'Not shocking, unwise perhaps.'

'You adore her, don't you?'

'That's an unwise question.'

'But you do, don't you?'

'I told you the question was unwise. Don't you?'

'I hate her.'

'Sh! You must never say that.'

'Why not? It's the truth.'

'That is why you mustn't say it.'

'I can say what I choose tonight. I'm going home tomorrow. This time next week I'll be on the moors where I can sing and say I choose.'

'Oh no.' said Raleigh smoothly, 'tomorrow there is a meeting of the Council at eight. You will be free then and you'll meet me by the south gate in the garden.'

They parted just then for the final turn single and as they joined hands again she looked him in the face and laughed, showing her short, white, rather childish teeth.

'Shall I?' she asked.

Raleigh dropped his voice.

'Please,' he said urgently.

The music ceased suddenly and there was the Queen beckoning him with her fan.

*

The August evening brooded over the garden. Along the wall
the red and white hollyhocks were merely dark and pale in the
gathering twilight. At their feet the stocks poured forth their
hearts in sweetness; looking up Raleigh saw the first star prick
through. It was almost half-past eight, he had been waiting for
more than half an hour for he had been early, like a lad at his
first rendezvous. He began to fear that she kept her threat and
gone home. She was quite capable of it, he knew that much
about her already.

He paced up and down and soon the one star was joined by a
million others. A bat came swooping past and a white owl went
by on a noiseless wing.

He tried to drag himself away. He told himself that she was
young and gauche. What did it matter whether she had gone
back to her moors or no? In two days, he would have forgotten
the feel of those firm little fingers, the sound of that immature,
tinkling voice.

It was foolish, anyway, to wait here any longer. He swung
round on his heel; and faced her. She had come up so softly
over the grass that he had had no idea of her nearness until she
was there, within reach of his hand.

Tonight she wore a dress of shining white satin patterned
with black fleurs-de-lys. It fitted her closely to the waist and
then billowed out stiffly in folds that covered her feet. Round
her neck and shoulders she had draped some misty white stuff
and above it her face was a pale blur in gathering light. The
thought that she had come set his heart racing. It was one of the
most thrilling moments of his life. He had never dreamed that
he would find himself so violently attracted to a woman. As he
greeted her his very voice was unsure.

'So, you stayed. I had given up hope.'

'I've been hanging up dresses,' said Mistress Throckmorton
dryly. 'We tried on twelve dresses and all that goes with them
before she was fit to appear at the Council. Then of course
Mary Fitton and I had almost an hour's work to put them back.'

There was a stone bench between two buttresses in the wall

and they sat down there, side by side. Her nearness was a joy and a pain and a miracle, all in one.

'You're Sir Walter Raleigh, aren't you?' she began as she settled her dress around her on the seat. 'Do you know, I didn't know that last night until afterwards. I've only been at Court a week. You've been away, haven't you?'

'Yes. A splinter went into my shoulder, during the fighting. I've been down to Bath to get rid of the stiffness. You'll see a great deal of me now. I'm Captain of the Guard.'

'I know. You wear a suit of silver armour and all the ladies lose their hearts to you. But you are very remote and hard to please. You're clever, too, and very, very brave. Once in Holland you captured Alva's money train and in Ireland you arrested a whole village single-handed. Also, you're a poet. In addition to that you are interested in colonies and introduced tobacco and potatoes into England. You are thirty-six years old, a great favourite with her Majesty, Essex hates you and Cecil is your friend. There! Isn't that a lot of information for one night's gleaning?' She paused, rather breathless with the rapid recital, and looked at him with sparkling eyes.

'Wonderful. Why were you so interested? Did you guess at the one thing you haven't mentioned, that there is one lady who will find me neither remote nor hard to please?'

She nodded.

'I guessed it. You haven't made a tryst with any other woman than the Queen since you came to Court. I found that out without telling anyone that you'd made one with me.' Her flippant manner gave way to gravity. 'And you mustn't make another. She would be more angry than you can imagine. You might not guess it but I'm terrified of her. I won't show it but my bones melt when she looks at me. She's a terrible woman.'

'You exaggerate. She's terrible for a moment but it blows over. She can't help her temper, she inherited it with her throne. As for seeing you again, I must. I love you.'

The harvest moon, rising big and golden over the trees of the garden, swam into view as Raleigh made his declaration and by its light her face became visible again. It was set and hard and the unearthly light had the look of a marble face exquisitely carved.

'Even if that were true, we mustn't meet again. She'd probably throw me into a dungeon. I couldn't abide that. I love the air and the open spaces. And it would ruin you. I'll tell you for your own good that I am a perfectly ordinary woman, not clever, not brave. I'm stubborn and selfish and have a quick temper. And, to complete the disillusion, my family call me Bess.'

'I'll call you Bess, too,' said Raleigh.

'I'd rather that you didn't, except in fun. But there'll be no need to call me anything. Think over what I've said and don't imperil your favour with her for me.'

'You've had your say, now listen to me. I'm stubborn, too. And I've never seen anyone so beautiful or charming or honest as you. That one succeeds at Court does not necessarily mean that he is either a hypocrite or a sycophant. I hope I'm neither. I love you. You may not love me yet but I'll show you the way. And if you do neither man nor devil nor Queen shall come between us.'

He had spoken with his eyes on the hollow at the base of her white young throat. A sweet place to kiss, he thought, and he kissed her. She gave a little gasp and then suddenly put up her little hard hands on either side of the face and kissed him on the mouth.

There is no coyness in her and not a grain of falseness, he thought, as he clasped her to his breast. She is unique and wonderful and adorable. She is the mate for me.

Six months went by on the dizzy wheels of enchantment. Under the sixty candles they danced discreetly and as the fiddles reached for the crescendo whispered arrangements for future meetings. Across a crowded room their eyes would meet, heavy with secrets. The darkness of the winter nights hid them as they met in the chilly garden and kissed one another with cold stiff lips.

They lived in the present and the future held only one word for them; "Virginia."

A thousand times, at Hampton and Windsor and Whitehall whither they had followed the Queen, as the hour for parting came, saddening them with the thought of imminent separation and unappeased passion, Raleigh said: 'I must have news soon. If the settlers are content and she will send me to govern them. You'd come, wouldn't you?'

And a thousand times Lisbeth, as he had named her, had answered, 'I'd go anywhere with you, Walter, out of her reach.'

In the late spring of 1589, the news that they awaited so eagerly came. A letter from Grenville was handed in at Durham House.

> '... I regret to have to report to you that the colony of Virginia is no more. When we landed to leave the stores which you had sent, there were only a few rusting tools and a crumbling hut, to mark the spot. Whether they have wandered away, or fallen victim to the Indians or Spaniards, there is no telling. We fired the guns and lighted a beacon, which we kept going day and night for two days, and conducted a search over a wide area, but we received no sign. I fear this will be very heavy news to you, but I assure you that every effort that you could have made yourself was made. In token of which I sign myself.
>
> Your Servant,
> Richard Grenville

Raleigh groaned as he laid down the sheet. In his mind he could the thunder of Grenville's guns, dying over the waste land; see the bonfire's futile light reddening the tall dark pines. Another dream had ended. The timbered house covered with blazing creeper that had been built in his mind for Lisbeth crumbled before his eyes. Tonight he must meet her and tell that there was but one way to end these miserable brief meetings, the brave way, the open way before the Queen's jealous eye.

Even at that moment he spared a thought and a sigh for his colonists. What end had they met? So, few, so far away.

65

That at least was quickly answered, for as he set out for the Palace grounds, where in the bare garden he would break the news to Lisbeth, a messenger came with a second letter.

He turned into the house to read it and sent the bearer down to the kitchen for refreshment.

Good Sir Walter (the letter began), I write in all haste to relieve your mind regarding the well-being of your late colony. Upon my arrival in Plymouth, two days after Grenville, I find all manner of rumours rife. The truth is that I arrived there some months ago on my way to Cartagena and found them in sore distress. The Indian chief who had been well disposed to them died and his son had been raising the tribes against them. They were on the eve of a war in which they were outnumbered. They were also short of food. I heartened them against the Indians by offering them guns and ammunition and one of my pinnaces. Also, I loaded four boats with food. But we got a taste of Hatteras weather and the boats and the food were swept away. By that time they were much discouraged, and upon my offering them their passage home, all accepted eagerly.

Already I have heard, since anchoring, that there was never such a colony. The survivors have scattered amongst their friends, but if any trouble you with their disbelief, send them to me. I will mend their manners. If seamen do not stand together, who should? Let me know when you ship out the next lot. I will call upon them, and if needful bring them home.

Yours ever,
FRA. DRAKE

Even in his distress and anger Raleigh found his heart warming towards the writer of that letter. He had added the last sentence with a smile, certainly, but it was a smile in which there was no malice. And although Drake, with his pirate mind, obviously disbelieved that there would ever be a colony there in the future, he would shout down anyone who dared say in his presence that there had not been one there in the past. Raleigh envied Drake. He waited for no one. Whatever he wanted he took with his own hands. But Drake wanted so little, he mused, folding the letter. A good ship, an adventure that any other man would regard as impossible folly, a Spanish ship to take or town to sack: nothing that would have been of the slightest use to Raleigh. And other aims must be obtained with other weapons.

He set off in the raw March evening to meet Lisbeth.

The delay of reading the letter had made him late at the stone seat that had been their most frequent meeting-place, and Lisbeth was walking rapidly to and fro with her arms clasped round her shoulders against the cold. It was too cold for sitting still and, slipping his arm around her so that she was half enveloped in his cloak, he fell into step beside her.

'I've got the worst possible news,' he said almost at once.

He felt her stiffen and thaw away from him. 'She knows?' she asked, voicing her ever-present dread.

'Oh no, not that. The colony is a failure. Grenville found the land deserted because Drake had picked up the colonists on his voyage out. I had letters from both of them today.'

'Is that all?' There was a world of relief in her voice. To her mind they were no worse off than they had been yesterday.

'All? Isn't it sufficient? You know what it means? Endless meetings like this, in rain and fog and frost, when I can't even kiss you properly.'

They turned sharply at the end of the path and began to walk back, automatic as sentries.

Lisbeth did not speak for a moment and when she did it was to go, with her usual forthrightness, to the heart of the matter.

'I don't share a room with Agnes now. I've been moved to the one at the very end of the balcony. It should be very easy to climb into.'

'Darling, you don't know what you are saying. You, who have always been so careful.'

NORAH LOFTS

'We can still be careful. Make it midnight or a little later.'

'I couldn't do it. Oh God, I wanted it so different; open and honest. Can't it be so, Lisbeth?'

'Think of Mary Fitton.'

Raleigh thought. Both Mary and her lover were in the Tower. Hardly a fate to risk.

'I'll see you tonight, there,' said Lisbeth suddenly and, throwing off the fold of his cloak, she broke and went running into darkness.

Four hours later he swung himself silently on to the balcony and crept across to the last window where a dim light was burning as a sign and a welcome. Lisbeth came to meet him with the candle in her hand and in the upthrown light he saw the shadows of her lashes tremble on her upper eyelids. With her pale hair pouring over her shoulders, she looked childish and strangely touching. With no great joy in his errand he put his arms around her. But divested of its whalebone and muffling petticoats her body was soft and supple and desirable and lit in him a passion which the years might darken but only death could quench.

68

Chapter 10

London
1589

He finished speaking and stood with the letters from Drake and Grenville in his hands, offering them for the Queen's inspection. She pushed them away angrily and, never minding the blackened teeth that the sneer exposed, said:

'So, and this was the colony that was to rival the Netherlands in its demand for woollen goods. Swaddling clothes more like. A fine exploit indeed if your object was to provide the world with a good joke.'

Stung out of the politeness that was never too easy in the face of her unreason, he said;

''Twas as much your fault as mine. I begged of you last year to let me go and see to it. Once there, with it under my hand not all the Indians, all the Spaniards in the world, nor the devil himself should have taken it from me.'

'You talk big, Sir Walter. Large talkers are ever little doers.'

'You alone of all people in this world can say that to me. The colony was there, as you can read for yourself, and with a little care and nursing such as I could have given it, it would be there now. On you who denied it support such an attitude sits ill. Large talker I may be but I shall yet to see it an English nation.'

'You count on a long life,' said Elizabeth.

She had worked herself up into a fine rage and the sight of him, staring at her with hard black eyes, white lips and high-held head, did nothing to assuage it.

'I count on the English coming one day to their senses. Spain bought all the new world with three ships and a few gaol birds that England denied to Columbus.'

The jibe at her grandfather's meanness, of which she had inherited so large a share, decided the Queen. True, his courageous words and brave face in the hour of failure thrilled her. But he must learn; he must not answer her so; she had endured his pride and insolence for long enough. Some perversity, sprung from who knows what source of memory, frustration or physical ill-being, made her delight in administering the lesson.

'Since your brilliance matches so ill our sloth and dullness, we will excuse your presence from the Court. And in order that you may devote the whole of your valuable time and indispensable attention to this Phoenix that rises every year, I will have you relieved of your duties as Captain of the Guard.'

'As your Majesty wills,' said Raleigh, cut to the quick; 'have I your permission to go to Ireland?'

'Ireland or Hell, wherever you please.'

'I thank you.'

He bowed very low, then rose up very straight and tall and went to the door. Something in Elizabeth cried, 'Come back, I didn't mean the half of it.' But she gave it no voice.

Had she been a little younger, a little less schooled in control, she would have run after him and brought him back with her hand on his arm. As it was, she thought, 'Confound the fellow. What is it that gives him this power?' Was it, she wondered, that he always carried off a situation with high hand, the way she liked to use herself?

She sat quite still for a long time and then realised, with some amazement and some dismay, that her scanty eyelashes were gemmed with tears.

II

'Come with me, Lisbeth. She's angry already; a little more would hurt neither her nor me and in Ireland we'll be out of her reach.'

'The grave is the only place where we'd be that.'

'I'll join with the rebels. All they've needed along is a man to lead them.'

70

'Do you think I'd make you a traitor?'

'Anything, if you'll only come with me.'

'No.'

'Not if I plead you in the name of our love?'

'No.'

'In God's name, why not?'

'In the Tower we should not be together.'

'We should not be in the Tower.'

'Why should we be luckier than the Pembrokes?'

'Risk it, Lisbeth. Risk it for me.'

'No.'

'We may not meet for six months or more.'

'From the Tower we might not meet again. A little separation may be good for us. It will harden us, at least.'

'You're hard now, Lisbeth.'

'One has to be, in my place. A soft woman would have ruined you ere now.'

'At least, you'll think of me and wait.'

'Always. There's no other Raleigh at Court and you need fear no lesser man.'

'For the last time, come with me, love.'

'For the last time, no.'

Chapter 11

Ireland; London
1590—1592

'She's fair and proud; ice to the world and fire to me, Spenser. I've never known her to lie or quibble. There are few women of whom a man could say that.'

'Only one, I should imagine. Did your first pipe make you feel sick?'

Raleigh came out of his dreams of Lisbeth to stare at the young poet.

'Damnably. Sydney and Marlowe and Drake and Shakespeare and I reeled home as if we were drunken.'

'So should I have been, in such a company.'

'You'd better come back with me if I ever go. We'll make you a member of the *Mermaid*. You'd be at home there.'

'If I only could. But you've read of the crow that consorted with the peacocks, haven't you?'

'My dear fellow, you are too modest. I see genius in you and I do not use the word lightly.'

Edmund Spenser flushed darkly. Was Raleigh sincere in his praise or did he just flatter? Or again, was he so pleased to find one congenial soul in this Irish wilderness that enthusiasm biased his judgement? He laid aside the half-smoked pipe and unfolded the papers that he brought with him and feared to show before.

'It's the beginning of my new poem,' he said diffidently. 'I wondered if you would read it and give me your opinion.'

'It would give me the greatest pleasure. And in return you shall read this that I've just written for Marlowe. You've read that thing of his, *Come Live With Me And Be My Love*, haven't you? Well, this is a reply to it.'

He handed the sheet to Spenser, who took it reverently. Indeed, in all his intercourse with Raleigh the young poet was like an acolyte before the altar fire. This man knew Shakespeare as 'Will', called Marlowe 'Kit', had once, long ago shared a tent with Sydney. He was himself a poet of no mean order. And some fate had sent him to Youghal, next door to Kilcolman where Spenser had served the Muse alone. It was a thought to fill a humble heart with awe.

Raleigh pored over the pages. There was no mistake about it, Spenser was a poet of the first water. A find indeed. To Raleigh's complex nature the discovery was as exciting as the sight of a galleon ploughing heavily from the Isthmus would be to Drake. For a moment or two he enjoyed his pure artist's pleasure in a superb artist's work. And then suddenly, as he sat there, expediency crept in as it seemed fated to do upon everything that he had touched. He caught a glance of his own verse which Spenser had laid aside on the table. There was that last verse:

But could youth last, could love still breed;
Had joys no date, had age no need;
Then these delights my mind might move
To live with thee and be thy love.

The idea of joys passing with youth set his mind travelling along two roads at once. His own youth was passing and there was nothing to show for it. He had dabbled in poetry but he was not amongst the poets. A politician, he had no seat on the Council. A coloniser who had spent money lavishly upon his foundling, he had been compelled to watch it die for want of care. His youth was going. Elizabeth's was past. 'Had age no need.' What did she need, this ageing woman? Assurance, doubled and trebled, that she was the Gloriana of her own imaginings. Simple! Fool that he'd been to argue with her, to try to convince her as he would another man. Fool to have countered her complaints of age with reasonable philosophy. What she had wanted, and had wanted all along, was flattery, extravagant flattery such as others

73

gave. By God, she should have it! Out of his exile he would bring her such an oblation as no Queen had ever had before. When Raleigh turned his mind to adulation what extravagance, what art, what consummate subtlety should go to its making!

He leaned forward and tapped the unsuspecting Spenser on the knee. Spenser, with a picture in his mind of Raleigh, Shakespeare and the rest conversing amid clouds of smoke at the *Mermaid*, had made another attempt to master the pipe and was now feeling more sick than he would have cared to own.

'What are you going to do with this, Edmund?'

'I had nothing planned. I had wondered whether, when you're restored to favour, would you ask the Queen to allow me to dedicate it to her.'

Raleigh smiled.

'As I have said before, you are too modest. Not only shall you dedicate it to her, with it you shall render her immortal. All you have to do...'

The night was warm and the stars came out and glowed and paled again over Raleigh's myrtles and cherry and cedar trees, before he had finished telling Spenser what to do. An alteration here, an addition there and Elizabeth was the Faerie Queen, vivid, indestructible, immortal.

The young man hung upon Raleigh's words, thanked him for his interest, welcomed his suggestions and never, never suspected that upon the wings of the *Faerie Queen*, Raleigh was planning to fly back to the Court and to Lisbeth's embrace.

Morning was brightening over the bay when Raleigh walked to the gate with him and watched him, in the unreal light, depart with his manuscript under his arm, his hair ruffled and his collar askew.

The older man turned back and walked through his rows of blossoming potatoes, hating himself. Tonight, he had twisted a lovely thing into a tool for his hand. It might be lovely still but the bloom was gone. And the boy suspected nothing. Poets accepted him as a fellow; sailors trusted him as one of themselves; only the politicians dealt warily with the third man that was in him. A chilling thought.

From that hour he began to watch his moment for reappearing at Court. Spenser's manuscript would be beneath his arm and other, even sweeter compliments upon his tongue. But even he, dreaming under his young mulberry trees, never guessed that Lettice Knollys, robbed by death of Sydney, baulked by Raleigh had enthralled and captured young Essex. The news came to him in one line of writing, unsigned, only in its brevity revealed as Lisbeth's. 'Essex is married. Come back.'

It was the only word that Lisbeth had sent him in all the time of his exile; but exile ended with its coming.

II

Once again he lay beside Lisbeth in the narrow little bed and her pale hair streamed over his breast. Only now, when the first cock crowing had warned him that it was time to go, did they find words. Apart from a few incoherent endearments their reunion had been as silent and simple as the spring mating of birds whom the winter had parted.

'She was pleased to see you, I suppose?' Lisbeth said languidly.

'Amazingly, considering how we parted, consigning one another to Hell. Essex and his wife are not in the Tower, you know. She may grow lenient with the years.'

'She daren't try Essex too far. There is royal blood in him and he is immensely popular. She is never lenient without a cause.'

'Your distrust is deeply rooted.'

'I saw her face when you came in. She wore the look I dared not wear. With Essex she was finding life dull. Cecil is so cautious; Burghley is old and sane. She is facing a loneliness that I have known all these months. And then suddenly you were there. When she stretched out her hand and called your name, I could have killed her.'

'For envy of a word? Why? You have something of me, sweet, for what it is worth, that she can never have. A queen is a lonely thing.'

'I suppose so. What a queer mind yours is, Walter. I look

75

at her and see a tyrant, a greedy mistress of slaves. You see a lonely woman who should be pitied, not feared or hated. Nothing is simple to you.'

'One thing is, that must begone.'

He clasped her again, kissing her with a passion that must be leashed as he stole from the window; that must give no sign tomorrow when they meet in the Queen's presence.

The months went by. The nights brought the stolen hours of pleasure; the days new evidence of the Queen's favour. Spenser received a pension of fifty pounds a year.

But over it all there hung that faint mist that hangs over a golden day in autumn when the year has looked into the eyes of winter and turns from the sight, trying to blind herself with the bright banners of bracken and rowan, and wakes to find that overnight the first frost has turned the banners to cerements.

He left the Queen late one evening. The fighting mood was on her. For the tenth time she had worked herself into a passion of belligerent zeal by talking of Grenville's death. With eyes flashing under her red wig, she told Raleigh the story that he already knew word for word. How Grenville had accounted for a thousand Spaniards before his flagship, with her masts, her guns, her very decks cut away, surrendered. How he had lain, mortally wounded, for three days and at the end, calling for wine, had swallowed it and crushed the glass into his mouth and swallowed that, too, to show the stuff of which the English were made.

'... And when I send out an expedition, you shall lead it,' she promised him, at the end of the recital. 'There is no other man around me so fitted to follow such an example.'

'To die abroad my flagship with my gullet full of glass?'

The Queen shuddered.

'I did not mean that. Grenville was cut off and did his best in that position, as you would, Walter, despite your sneers. But you shall have a young force with you and run no risk of that.'

It was late and the drowsy women, waiting to undress the

Queen, yawned and fidgeted in the anteroom. But when Raleigh took his leave and had reached the door, Elizabeth called him back.

'I have something for you, Walter.'

He choked back his own yawn and returned to her side.

'What would you say to Sherborne?' she asked, peering up at him archly.

'Sherborne?'

'That Dorset place that I've had such trouble about. I've got the lease in my hands at last, ninety-nine years. You can have it.'

'You are too kind. How can I thank you?'

'I jeered you once about your expectation of longevity. You see I have provided for your extremest old age.'

She smiled upon him in pure affection. Her light mention of words that had been spoken in the heat of an angry moment was touching, as the reminder of some trivial cause of a quarrel is to lovers who have been reconciled. And the present was indeed a queenly one, one that poor Burghley or Walsingham would have been grateful for after a lifetime of service. On his knees before her, Raleigh determined that the expedition upon which she had promised to send him should be successful. He would not fail her.

It was late, Lisbeth would not be expecting him. Yet he felt a desire to tell her the good news. He longed to point out to her that the Queen had a kind and generous side to her nature. Leaving the Palace door, he skirted cautiously along the side of the garden and sat down within sight of Lisbeth's window. When it was lighted, he would know that she had returned from the disrobing. When it and the other windows were darkened, it would be safe to climb to the balcony and step inside. Sitting there in the darkness and utter quiet he found his head nodding forward with sleep and presently awoke with a start to find his clothes damp with dew and all the windows dark save the one at the end of the balcony. He waited for a long time, in case Lisbeth might be the first back to her room, but no light appeared in the other windows, so presently, moving like a cat, he mounted the balcony and tiptoed to the window. As he did so he could hear the squeak of a furiously driven and ill-cut quill. It arrested him. To whom could Lisbeth be writing, she who had once sent him five words on an unsigned page? He stopped outside the window and peeped around the curtain. She was sitting at the table and the candles just astir in the draught cast their light on the page and on her cheek, deepening the hollow in it. Her hair hung in a heavy plait over one shoulder. Her left hand supported her head while the right scribbled away with the scratching pen. He stood and watched her for a moment or so and then said, very softly, 'Lisbeth,' That would not alarm her, for he was the only one who used that name and she was accustomed to his sudden and stealthy comings.

Nevertheless, she jumped up at the sound and the pen rolled away on the floor as she put her hands on either side of the table as though to hide the paper and stood so, facing the window.

He stepped over the sill and drew the curtains behind him with a practised hand before he held out his arms to her. She left the table reluctantly and came towards him. He saw that the hollowness of her face had not been merely due to the shadow, she looked drawn and haggard as though she had just gone through some shattering experience.

'What is it, love? To whom are you writing?'

'Nobody, just writing,' she said, and tried to draw him towards the bed, away from the table.

'But you look so pale. Are you ill?'

'I was surprised to see you. I thought for a moment 'twas your ghost.'

'You have no need to fear my ghost than you have to fear me. Something must have upset you to keep you out of bed, writing so late. And why is that valise out and half-packed? You're not going to Hampton?'

A sojourn at Hampton always meant separation, for there Lisbeth shared a room with Agnes Lawley and Raleigh could neither visit her nor meet her late in the garden.

'Oh no,' said Lisbeth, 'I just wanted something from it.'

78

Her manner was so strange, and she held him down on the edge of the bed so fiercely, that he was convinced that she was lying.

'You are hiding something from me,' he said. And the look of alarm that flashed into her eyes confirmed his belief.

'I'm going to look at that letter.'

'Walter, please. You can see it tomorrow. It is for you. Just a silly little letter, just to say... that I... love you.'

He pushed off her detaining hand. The idea of cautious Lisbeth writing so unnecessary a thing was absurd.

She jumped up immediately. 'Please, Walter. I beg you not to. I couldn't bear you to read it before my eyes.'

'It isn't to say that you are tired of all this?'

She was silent and he thought that he had hit upon the truth. His first reaction was a pang of self-reproach. Of course, she was tired of it. Any woman would be. He had never put her first. The Queen, Virginia, his ambitions, had all come before her. He left the table without attempting to touch the papers and drew her to the bed where they sat down, side by side. The decision that he had just taken made his heart race. It was like standing at the top of a cliff of unknown height and preparing to throw yourself over.

'Lisbeth,' he said. 'I have been thinking I'd rather live with you, out of the Queen's favour, obscure and poor if needs be. Will you marry me, sweet, and let's have done with parting?'

There, it was over. He looked at her, prepared for protest, perhaps, or surprise but not for the stony, white, stricken face that she turned towards him. For one shattering moment he feared that it was too late, that she had already married someone else in secret. Scarcely moving her blanched lips, she asked:

'What makes you ask me that, tonight?'

'Do you need a reason. Didn't I ask you the same thing before I went to Ireland?'

'You never mentioned marriage! Or braving the Queen on her very doorstep. And I told you no. You wouldn't have mentioned it again so soon, with everything unchanged, unless you'd guessed. God, and if you have, others may too.'

79

'Well, if I have, what of it?' He had no idea of what she was talking about but he was crafty enough to see that by an assumption of knowledge, he would get the truth sooner than by questioning.

Lisbeth stuck out her chin, the stricken look was replaced by one of obstinacy.

'Well, even so, I shan't marry you. There be plenty of bastards in this world and no one the worse. You shan't throw up everything because of an ill-timed babe.'

So that was it. With complete truth he was able to say:

'I had no intention of so doing. I had no knowledge of that when I spoke.'

'You said you'd guessed.'

'Not at all. If you remember my words were, "If I have, what of it?" I thought that would draw out the mystery and thank God it did.'

Tears of anger filled her eyes and brimmed over her lids.

'You're too clever for me,' she said stormily, 'but with all your cleverness you can't make me marry you. And never will I do it of my own will.'

'Very well. I may not be able to make you, though such things have been known, but I shall go straight to the Queen in the morning and tell her that her Maid of Honour is a maid no more and point to myself as the seducer. A fine stir that will make. Can't you picture brother Arthur's state?'

'You wouldn't dare.'

'Would I not? You've something to learn of me yet. Listen, Lisbeth, before I go from this room tonight, you give me your solemn promise to marry me, secretly, as soon as may be. We'll wait then until after the expedition against Spain. It will bear so much?' He waited for her affirmative nod. 'When I return, I aim to be so high in favour that the Sultan's harem could not undo me! And after all, she has well-nigh forgiven Essex.'

'I'd rather go home. I should have gone tomorrow if you hadn't come tonight.'

'And you profess to love me.'

'I do love you. That's why I would not ruin you.'

'I ruin myself tomorrow unless I have your promise.'

'In return, then, promise me one thing.'

'And that is?'

'Never to tell her, or anyone else, if it means the Tower. Banishment I could bear, if you bring it on yourself, but imprisonment never.'

'I give you my word, that so far as I can prevent it I will.'

'As far as you can prevent it! Oh Walter, one breath of her anger and you would be like a straw in the wind. Oh, that a woman who has never known love should have the power to prevent others from enjoying it. Well may Burghley say to his son, "Fear to be Raleigh". I'd sooner you were a humble herdsman.'

'All privilege has its price, dear heart. The humble herdsman who lifted his eyes to you would lose his ears. We must, as the new Prayer book says, do our best to grapple with "the state to which it has pleased God to call us". So, you have my promise and I have yours. And I hope the boy will forgive you for trying to make a by-blow of him.'

'Is there a priest you can trust?' Lisbeth was already regarding the practical aspect.

'Four or five who look to me for preferment. Fret no more about that or anything. Only wish me a fair wind and a sight of the Spanish plate ships. And now good night. Do you know that all this hour has gone by with never an endearment?'

'Better this dearth before than afterwards. I wonder how many times you will wish that you had gone straight home this night.'

'Jehovah!' cried Raleigh, ignoring this thrust, 'that reminds me of what I came to tell you. She has given me Sherborne.'

'Sherborne?' asked Lisbeth as Raleigh himself had done some hours earlier.

'It's an estate in Dorset. Very pretty, I believe. A fine place for the boy. I shall love being a father, darling.'

'You'll have bought the privilege dearly enough,' said Lisbeth dryly.

He parted the curtains without drawing them and put a long

81

leg over the sill; and then, with a wave of the hand, was gone. Slowly Lisbeth tore the letter into strips and held them one by one in the flame of the candle. Then she unpacked the valise and went to bed and dreamed that the Queen came to her with a wailing babe in her arms and said, 'Take it, it is yours by right, I stole it from you.' She pushed it away and screamed, I don't want it. It has a look of you. Take it away!'

She woke to find Agnes in her long white nightdress bending over her.

'I had to come,' said the girl apologetically, for Lisbeth was not a person who welcomed even a charitable visitor to her room, 'You were screaming so. You've been mumbling to yourself for a long time, too.'

Lisbeth realised that in her agitation she and Walter had forgotten their usual caution.

'I've been dreaming such dreadful things. It was kind of you to come to me, Agnes.'

She felt momentary affection for the unsuspecting neighbour.

'It's those stupid potatoes that they make such a fuss about,' said Agnes. 'Enough to give any one nightmare. Pigs' food I call them but if that Raleigh started eating acorns, I suppose we should all have to eat them too.'

Lisbeth laughed and Mistress Lawley thought that she was not such a dull stick after all.

Chapter 12

The Tower
1592

He bade Lisbeth yet another hurried and secret farewell, took leave of the Queen all atremble lest she should change her mind again as she had done before and hurried down to Gravesend. He was forty years old and had endured disappointment in almost every department of his life, yet his heart was as high with hope in this bright May as it had ever been. Once more, as in the matter of Spenser's poetry and Essex's marriage, Fortune was on his side. One good smashing raid on the Spanish treasure town and Lisbeth would be his. In this new chance he forgot his previous disasters, all the things that had made havoc of his hopes. He saw each rope, each barrel in its place, and early on the morning of May the sixth dropped down the river outward bound.

It was the first time that he had been in command of a fleet. Old dreams of Virginia troubled him a little as the white sail lifted and the *Roebuck*, his own contribution to the fleet, rose and fell to the swing of the sea. He put them away. What was forty? It was only after one had finished making mistakes that one could begin to build: and what better pledge of ability in age could one wish for than the Queen? Thinking of her darkened his brow a little, she had been shilly-shallying about this expedition ever since March and then, when the season for a successful raid on Panama was over, had let it go. The one hope now was to run into the plate on their way back to Spain.

Already the choppy Channel waters were making the Roebuck dance and cavort as nimbly as her namesake; and Raleigh felt the old, familiar retching of his queasy stomach.

He forced himself to make the last round of his vessel, saw that others were holding their distance and went down to his cabin. There were his books and the jade idol that Drake had brought back from the East and given to him in memory of their work together on the Navy Commission six or seven years ago; and there too was a great blue bowl of primroses that he had bought from a small boy at the dock, early that morning. It was his last purchase for his fleet and in the eyes of Drake or Frobisher or Grenville that bowl of pale flowers, slopping water at every heave of the ship, would have been another proof of his queerness.

He looked round at his treasures with a sigh of satisfaction and then cast himself flat on his bunk. For some hours he was deadly sick and towards morning fell into an uneasy sleep of exhaustion. Arthur Throckmorton haunted his dreams. Lisbeth's brother was furious with him but would not say why. He stood him with a club in his hand, a thick knotted bludgeon such as the Irish had carried along the road from Bally-in-Harsh to Cork, and he said, 'You'll pay. Fear to be Raleigh. You'll pay.' He struggled up from the depths of sleep to defend himself and opened his eyes. A sailor stood by the bunkside.

'Ship trying to overtake us, sir. Shall we stand to?'

'Yes, I'll be up in a moment.'

He stood up, confidently enough, but the heaving of the *Roebuck* as the slackened speed and took the full of the waves set him retching again and it was only by hanging on the furniture that he was able to drag himself about sufficiently to perform a hurried and incomplete toilet. He was still at the foot of the companionway, grasping the rope that hung there to keep himself from swaying when a burly figure, accompanied by the sailor, appeared at the top.

'Sir Martin Frobisher come aboard, sir,' said the sailor.

Raleigh raised his sick eyes and nodded to Frobisher, who set his sure feet on the steps, came down swiftly and thrust his hand under Raleigh's arm. Moving so, they went into his cabin.

'You're sick,' said Frobisher, his hard voice as sympathetic as he could make it.

84

'Not more than usual. I'm always like this for an hour or two at first. I'll be all right as the day grows. What's brought you here?'

'Queen's orders. I'm to take charge of this expedition and you to go straight back to Hampton!'

'In God's name, why?'

'That she didn't say. She sent for me an hour before noon yesterday, gave me my orders and bade me haste; and that's all. I don't mind telling you I've had the Devil's own job overhauling you. You look as if you'd be better ashore, too.'

'I'm all right, I tell you: and I'm not going back.'

'Not going?—but those were the orders.'

'Maybe. My orders were to go ahead until I sighted the Spanish ships and engage them. And by those I hold.'

'But I tell you...'

'It's a waste of your breath, Frobisher. Here I am and here I stay until I see fit to turn back.'

'And what do I do?'

'Please yourself. If you think your orders justify you in joining us, we'll be very glad of your company.'

'My orders were to take charge of this expedition.'

'And so were mine but earlier. When I turn back you may take on. Perhaps as you go up, you'd be so good as to carry an order for me. Straight ahead, with every inch of canvas she'll carry. Thank you. I'll see you presently.'

As Frobisher retired Raleigh turned aside and was sicker than ever. Evidently something was amiss and with the single-mindedness of a man in love he could only think that it was something to do with Lisbeth. That she was ill did not occur to him; for the Queen would never have recalled him for that. She would have delighted in the thought that he should be serving her while the woman he loved sickened or died. They had been discovered, that was the cause of the upset. And there was nothing that could offset that crime now, save that he should go back laden with treasure.

So, the *Roebuck* held on in the van of the fleet and Frobisher, fuming and impatient, brought up the rear and for four days they pushed on until, in the evening, Cape Finisterre lifted its dark bulk out of the darkened sea.

They cruised about, within sight of the coast, for two interminable days but there was no sight of a Spanish sail. Then Raleigh sent for Frobisher. 'There's one more chance,' he began; 'we can halve the fleet, half can stay here and the other half sail on to the Azores—we may fall in with them so.'

'In God's name, I hope so. If you go back empty-handed after this piece of disobedience it will go hard on you, Sir Walter.'

'Who should know better than I?' said Raleigh: and proceeded to discuss which vessels should go and which stay.

But it was all of no use. The fleet sailed back from the Azores without having seen anything more formidable or promising than a fishing smack. And by this time Raleigh had worked himself into a fever of anxiety about Lisbeth and was willing to return. He had his books and clothing and the jade carried aboard Frobisher's boat, saw that burly seaman installed in the *Roebuck* as General of the fleet, wished him luck and took his leave; all with a calmness and coolness that brought unwilling admiration to Frobisher's mind.

Once, when the order to sail for Gravesend had been given, he did have a moment of uncertainty. The ship, though smaller and less seaworthy than the *Roebuck*, was good enough. Why not turn pirate? Why not sail West and spend years if needs were rivalling Drake's early exploits? Why go meekly back to face some unknown unpleasantness, intensified now by his defiance of orders? But it was no good. Somewhere in England Lisbeth was waiting for him to redeem that promise that never, if he could prevent it, should they be parted. And Elizabeth was quite capable of venting her spite upon that defenceless head. He sailed back on the trail from Finisterre empty-handed and heavy-hearted.

He waited only to wash, redress and perfume himself before presenting himself before Elizabeth at Hampton, whither she had betaken herself for the warm weather. It was a formal reception which made it harder and augured ill for him. Scarcely had he paid his respects and reported the ill-success of his mission, to which the Queen barely listened, than she turned to a waiting woman, saying, 'Call in Sir Arthur Throckmorton.' Lisbeth's brother appeared from the ante-room and though he bore no shillelah, his face was threat enough.

'Sir Walter,' said the Queen sternly, 'this man swears that you have seduced his sister. What, after this long time, have you to say to that?'

'Merely...'

'No lies now.' Did she, even in this extremity, even in this cold rage, so much more deadly than her raging furies, wish to save him the shame of lying before them all? 'He has his witness. And though the girl herself is as dumb as the dead, it is evident that part, at least, of his story is true.'

'I was going to say, merely, that he lies. Elizabeth Throckmorton is my wife.'

Those who were watching Elizabeth saw the patches of rouge stand out starkly from her cheeks as every vestige of normal colour drained out of her face, leaving her chin, her nose and her forehead white as bone. It was the face of a woman who had received a mortal blow, though she would strive to conceal it.

'You have proof of that?' she said at last, and her voice betrayed nothing. The movement of her blood was beyond her control but she had had a long and hard training in making her voice obey her.

'Ample,' said Raleigh.

Elizabeth beckoned to one of the women who had drawn a little apart, though not out of earshot. One never knew when the Queen might repent of making a public scene of this and drive them out with spiteful blows if they stood too close.

'Sir Walter's cousin waits below; fetch him here and be speedy.'

Nobody spoke in the room until George Carew appeared at the door with the flustered woman behind him. The Queen's breathing was plainly audible.

The Queen had no time for George Carew, though for once she had found a use for him. She said shortly:

'I give you this man into your charge. Take two of the guards and conduct him to the Tower. Hold him there in the Brick Tower until further orders and consider yourself responsible, your life for his.'

Raleigh bowed again before her, turned, hesitated and turned back again.

'I beg of you, grant me of your mercy one favour. Tell me where she is?'

'In equally good keeping but not in the Brick Tower,' said the Queen, and turned away her head.

The gardens at Hampton and along the river were bright with the first flowers of June. The hawthorns stood, pink and white in the meadows, refuges for the cuckoos that went calling across the space between the green of earth and the blue of Heaven, as Raleigh turned his face towards the Tower. The Queen's last words had implied that Lisbeth was under guard. Incarcerated somewhere in a place chosen by a jealous woman, now, when more than ever she needed the fresh air, needed friends around her, needed her husband's comforting presence. He groaned inwardly; such havoc had love made of their lives; so little had he prepared for this catastrophe.

Carew, who knew, surely, he knew, being Master of Ordnance at the Tower, could have told him that every step was taking him, if not to her, towards her. But as is often the case, there was little love lost between the cousins, Elizabeth could not have chosen a better gaoler. Carew would tell him nothing. And there was nothing to let him guess as he went under the gateway of the Tower that Lisbeth was languishing in the North Bastion. He could see it from the window of the room they assigned him, it closed in his view and he hated it. Doubtless Lisbeth, if she looked from her narrow window, saw the Brick Tower and hated it too, though not for the reason that she might have done. He wondered when Lisbeth's hour would be. He had come back in January; she had been sure, she would never have started to write that letter if she had not been sure, at the beginning of April. May was gone and here was June beginning. Would four months or five see him out of this? Out of this and, if not restored to favour, at least a free man with the right and the power to seek out his wife. How long would Gloriana's anger last? He realised quite soon that there was no way out save through the Queen. There was no record made of his imprisonment, Carew told him so much; there were no charges preferred against him that he might be called upon to answer and, by answering, clear himself. Nothing but the Queen's displeasure had put him into this place, nothing but her forgiveness would ever get him out.

The longest day passed. Evening by evening the light lingered a little less long on the sides of the North Bastion; morning by morning the sun was a little later in creeping across the bed and waking him. August ended and the morning came when looking from his window he saw the first veils of autumn mist obscuring his view. The sight shook him. He assured himself that it was nothing. Summer was not yet over. One mist could no more make the autumn than one swallow the spring; but he was shaken, he had reached an age when that first foreshadowing of the year's decay set him dreaming of other years that had gone downward into the oblivion of winter. He was a poet, too, and for such the first things, the first snowdrops, the first wild-rose on the wayside hedge, the first mist of autumn or the first frost of winter, are ever troubling things; eloquent of the many dead who have noted and loved them in past years and now do so no more.

Throughout his imprisonment he never wrote to Lisbeth or mentioned her name in any of the letters that he wrote. Any mention of her would have been fuel to the flame of the Queen's anger and there was no hope that any letter meant for Lisbeth would have reached her hands unbroken. His caution showed him not yet unhopeful.

His appeals to the Queen had been many, couched in the most flattering terms at his command. When she prepared to go on one of her Royal progresses he wrote:

*'My heart was never broken till this day, that I hear
the queen goes away so far off, whom I have followed
for so many years with so great love and desire in
so many journeys, and am now left behind in a dark
prison all alone...'*

Would her vanity lead her to swallow 'love and desire' from a
man whom she had imprisoned for loving another? There was
no sign that she had ever received that or any other letter from
him.

Then there was the day when the Queen was reported to
be on the river in her barge. Raleigh flung himself upon his
cousin beseeching him to let him go, disguised, upon that
same river, only to look for a moment upon that loveliness,
so long forbidden to him. Carew protested that he dared not.
Then Raleigh, half-acting and half-despairing, drew out his
dagger and tried to persuade George that way. It was absurd,
of course, and who knew it better than Raleigh? But it looked
well in Carew's report, especially as he added that he feared
that his prisoner would go demented if the Queen persisted in
her anger.

Elizabeth, however, was for once insusceptible to flattery and
drama alike. She reinstalled Essex in her favour. His crime was
the same as Raleigh's but he was only a boy. There lay the rub.
Essex might in a moment of youthful passion be led away into
folly and yet remain heart-true to her, as he protested. Raleigh
was a man of forty, old enough to withstand a bright eye and a
natural curl, had his heart been fixed. His intrigue, which she
might have forgiven, his marriage, which was unforgivable,
were insults to her because she had never felt motherly towards
him. He was almost her contemporary and he had slighted her.
So, in the end it was not concern for her heart, though she was
sore enough, but for her pocket that made her send to Carew to
set the prisoner free.

PART TWO

Chapter 13

Dartmouth
September 1592

With a cargo of ivory
And apes and peacocks,
Sandalwood, cedarwood, and sweet, white wine.

All along the roadside the gorse was blazing and the hedgerows were gemmed with reddening hips and haws. Children busy in the blackberry thickets, their hands and mouths stained with the purple juice, looked around at the sound of hooves and stared at the two horsemen spurring past. One of the riders was finely dressed and his cloak, the colour of the blackberry stains, streamed away behind him and showed its lining of silver grey. Sometimes he smiled as he rode and the children who saw him then were inspired by the finery and the joviality to wave their grubby little hands. Then the gay rider waved back to them and the sun brought out all the colours that were embroidered on his gauntlet. The other rider neither smiled nor waved but rode sternly and looked sullen.

And sullen Raleigh was finding him. Early that morning he had come to the Tower and said, 'The Queen bids you get ready and ride with me to Dartmouth. She has work there; but you are still a prisoner and are to regard me as your keeper.'

'How you will enjoy that, Blount,' Raleigh had said, smiling. 'What is the work?'

'That we shall know anon. The horses are ready.'

'And so shall I be when I am dressed. I should hate to bring disgrace upon any keeper.'

Blount, notoriously mean and plain in his clothing, had frowned and waited impatiently while Raleigh put on his finest doublet, his stiffest ruff and his riding boots of Russian leather. Blount's impatience was unwarranted, for Raleigh's hands were shaking with eagerness and in less than ten minutes he had slung the purple and silver cloak over his shoulders with a jaunty movement that in itself was an offence to the watcher and said, 'There, I am ready.'

And so here he was, clattering down to Dartmouth on some errand for which, of all her servants, the Queen had deemed him most fitting; and he was riding the highway, breathing the free air. Well might he wave and smile.

The scent of wood smoke sharpened the air and quickened his blood. Flocks of small birds gathering for their journey to the South chattered on barns and stacks. He smiled at them, too. They were adventurers, they were free. He knew a sudden pang of pity for birds in cages. It was a sight upon which he would never look unmoved again.

The day broadened to warm gold and then dimmed so the grape-bloom and cyclamen of evening and in the next small town they stopped and sought an inn. There somebody recognised that narrow face with the beard that stood out unusually black against the prison pallor: and after that, though Blount tried to maintain his status as Sir Walter's keeper, it became impossible to do so. People crowded to the doors and windows of the little hostelry just to have a look at the famous man. He was enjoying one of his brief recurrent periods of intense popularity. He was the man who had married his love and bidden the Queen do her worst. Stout burghers peered at him admiringly; red-faced women gazed yearningly in at the

window. Somebody saw fit to run to the house of the Mayor
and inform that a distinguished guest was staying at the *One
Bull*. The Mayor had been sitting at ease in his slippers, with
a tankard in his hand. He 'shushed' his visitor to silence, for
the Mayoress was in the next room and would wish to be in
the forefront of any civic stir. He called to her, 'Going out on a
matter of business, my love,' and tiptoed upstairs for his chain
and hat of office. He donned them in the street and fastened
his shoes and doublet then, with his informant at his heels, he
hastened to the *One Bull*. The landlord respectfully greeted him
and pointed to the door of the room where Raleigh sat eating
his supper. To Blount's annoyance he had ordered candles and
refused to pull the curtains, so that any citizen of Tenmore who
cared to do could watch the great man feeding. Those who
were nearest the window now had the additional pleasure of
seeing their Mayor, his gold chain gleaming and his doublet
buttons forced into the wrong buttonholes, peep round the
door and then squeeze his portly figure into the little room.
He bowed hastily several times and said (but unfortunately the
citizens could not hear this), 'Your servant, Sir Walter, your
servant. I'm the Mayor. I bid you welcome, Sir Walter, very
heartily welcome in the name of all the citizens of this ancient
Borough.'

'That's very kind of you, your Worship,' said Raleigh,
smiling at the comical little figure. 'Very kind. Won't you sit
down and have a cup of wine with us? My—friend and I are at
supper, as you see.'

There was no cup for the Mayor but before Raleigh could
call for one his Worship had gone to the door and shouted. And
when the cup came and the wine was poured the first citizen
of Tenmore placed himself in full view of the window so that
others, less exalted, might see him at his ease with the great.
This might teach them that their Mayor was no common man, it
might even inspire that stubborn Town Council to give him his
way about the refuse dump in Cook Street. He drank his wine
and bobbed and smiled broadly every time Raleigh looked at
him.

93

Raleigh, tired after a glorious hard day of riding in the unaccustomed country air, pleased with his treatment at the *One Bull*, delighted with his supper and with the world in general, was so courteous that the little stout man was beside himself with pleasure.

'If only we had known, Sir Walter, if only we had known, we would have given you a proper welcome and offered you the hospitality of my poor house. My wife would have been delighted, delighted indeed.'

'I should have been delighted too.' Oh, if only Edmund or Will or Lisbeth or one of them had been there to have caught his eye and appreciated the fun of this. Or the Queen herself; she would have enjoyed it as much as anyone. Presently, fortified by his wine, the little man allowed his curiosity to speak.

'And what, Sir Walter, if I may ask you, has brought you to these parts?'

'The Queen's business, your Worship. I ride to Dartmouth first thing in the morning.'

'And would it be anything to do with the "Mother of God"?'

'The Mother of God?' repeated Raleigh, genuinely puzzled.

'The great ship that came into Dartmouth two weeks ago. That's her name, at least that's the English for it. I'm sorry but the Spanish name is beyond me.'

'The *Madre de Dios*?' asked Raleigh at a venture.

'That's it, Sir Walter, that's it. A great ship with a wonderful cargo that no one seems to know what to do with. I wondered whether they might have sent to ask you about some of the goods on her or about paying off the men. They're in a fine pickle. I don't telling you that I heard that Sir Robert Cecil came through this way. I didn't see him myself but I heard that he stayed for a change of horses at this very inn and took away two silver forks that our host had bought from a seaman the day before. Sir Robert, so I'm told, said that they part of the cargo and the sailor had no right to them. But the sailor had had the money and the host was the loser. That was what made me wonder if you were going on the same business.'

Raleigh looked towards Blount; surely if he knew he would

94

give some sign now. There could be no harm in telling this little man whether or not his guess was right, it would be known soon enough if that were the errand. Raleigh himself was inclined to think that it was. But Blount was still sullen and drank his wine with his eyes lowered.

'Well, your Worship, you know what public business is. One must be discreet.'

'To be sure, indeed yes,' agreed that public figure.

'So, we won't talk of my errand, if you don't mind.'

Convinced that he had hit the right nail on the head, his Worship smilingly agreed.

After a moment or two he saw Raleigh smother a yawn and with exquisite tact rose to take his leave.

'This has been a delightful meeting, Sir Walter, delightful. And if you intend to come back this way, I do beg of you to be my guest. As it is, pray do not settle your score here, that shall be a civic charge if you will allow Tenmore the honour.'

'I shall be delighted. It was very gracious of you to call on us. I will certainly let you know next time I pass this way. Good night.'

The little man bobbed himself out and went home with a vastly good opinion of himself that the sight of his maladjusted buttons did but little to diminish. He had material for stories to his cronies for years to come, and for his children and his grandchildren after that. And Raleigh, in an odd moment of easy good humour, had gained an adherent who would have gone a long way on his fat little legs to serve him.

Much of the same kind of scene was enacted at each place they stayed at and so, followed by good wishes and curious questions, they came at last to the *Falcon* at Dartmouth. They rode into the *Falcon* yard at midday and as soon as their horses' hooves sounded on the cobbles a plump woman in a great white apron ran out to meet them.

'Is it Sir Walter Raleigh?' she asked in a voice hushed with reverence.

Raleigh nodded and swung himself rather stiffly from the saddle. The early exhilaration had left him. He was still in good

95

spirits but he was sick to death of Blount and his saddle had galled him.

'Sir John Hawkins is within, waiting for you,' said the woman.

'Is he indeed? Splendid. Show me to him and then follow with a bottle of Canary.'

'That's there a 'ready, Sir Walter. Sir John saw to all that.'

Hawkins was beginning to feel the weight of his sixty-seven years; he prised himself out of his great chair with some difficulty and came with his rolling sailor's step to meet Raleigh, who went towards him with hand outstretched. The old man wrung his hand and thumped him upon the back.

'God, man, but it's grand to see you. Come and sit down and let's drink to your freedom.' Then, seeing Blount in the passage, he added in a voice as low as he could make it, though even so it was plainly audible half-way down the passage, 'That gloomy fellow is Essex's man, isn't he? Must he come in here?'

'I'm afraid so. You see he's my keeper for the nonce.'

'Keeper be damned, I want to talk to you, Walter.'

Hawkins never used a courtesy title if he could avoid it. It was only the infrequency and formality of his visits to the Queen that saved him from addressing her as 'Elizabeth' or even 'Lass'. He turned to Blount now and said, in a voice that had out-bellowed many a gale:

'There's a good room at the end of the passage, sir, where you can sit in comfort and see that your charge does not escape you. He and I have much to talk of.'

Raleigh smiled as Blount turned huffily and retraced his steps along the passage. Blount had been deliberately dumb all through the journey, it served him right that he should sit alone now while Raleigh heard all the news.

As soon as the door was closed and the wine poured, he said:

'Now tell me all about it. Yon fellow gave me no idea of what I was brought here for, save that it was the Queen's business.'

'He wouldn't. He's Essex's friend. They're all as sick as mud because I've got you out of the Tower.'

'You did?'

Hawkins nodded with intense self-satisfaction.

'I'll tell you all about it,' he promised, lifting his wine. 'On the eighth—I remember the date, for it was the Queen's birthday—Frobisher came home with the *Madre de Dios* in tow. She was coming from Malabar and she carried the best cargo these shores have ever seen. They had a hard job to get her. She was manned by eight hundred and they put up a fight for sixteen hours. But you know what an old bulldog Martin is, once he gets his teeth into anything he won't leave go, so in the end the Portuguese gave in. But that wasn't the end of the row. Frobisher and Burgh—that's his second-in-command—fought about the treasure all the way back and the minute the crews landed they carried on the fight. Most of the stuff was landed on the quay, satin and ivory, pearls and rubies, you never saw such a haul, and the sailors who hadn't been paid began to help themselves. By that time word got through to the Queen and as she'd lent ships for money for the expedition—.' Hawkins pulled himself up and said in a different voice. 'But of course you know all that, you were in charge of it, weren't you, till she sent for you... well, you see, she was after her share, as who wouldn't be. She sent that Cecil fellow down to say that nothing was to be touched. That's where I came in. I happened to stroll down to the harbour, just to have a look, you know, and there I saw about a hundred tons of spices lying about in the sun and the spray as if they were dirt. All the sailors and the merchants cared about was the jewels or the silver stuff. And all round there were people clamouring for their shares and sailors roaring that they hadn't been paid. You never saw such a pandemonium. So I wrote a letter; you know how I hate writing, so I made it good and strong that there might be no mistake and I shouldn't have to write twice, and I said there was only one man in England that knew the value of those spices or the silk or those little ornament things and only one man whose judgement the sailors and the merchants will accept, and that man was you.' He poked Raleigh with a stubby forefinger. 'So here you are, you see.'

'Then I owe you more than I can ever repay,' declared Raleigh solemnly.

'Don't say that until you see what lies in the harbour. There's enough there to repay many debts and I'm a share-holder,' said the crafty old pirate. 'Not that I did it for that,' he went on earnestly, catching Raleigh's glance. He poured out more wine and drank some, smacking his lips with pleasure. 'Oh no, it wasn't for that. You'd never guess what made me write that letter.' He leaned back in his chair, the picture of good nature. And yet, thought his companion, this is a man with few friends and many enemies and a reputation for foul temper.

'Do you mean a reason apart from thinking it my job?'

'Aye, quite apart from that. Man, if I hadn't liked you wild horses wouldn't have got your name out of me. I'll tell you...' He leaned forward as if he were about to confide some enormous secret. 'You may not remember it but one time when I came back from a voyage, I told you that I'd heard of a tree where oysters grew instead of leaves and a land where men had their heads growing out of their chests instead of their shoulders. And you didn't laugh. I've told the same tale to people that are ignorant of you and they jeered me. But you said you'd tell some play-writing friend of yours that it was good enough for one of his plays. And I'd like well for a word of mine to get into print. I'd write a book myself if I ever had time and didn't have such a lubber's hand with a pen.'

'You've the best hand with a pen of any part of Europe, in my opinion,' said Raleigh seriously. And the thought, what a book that would be. Full of incredible tales and bloody doings and courageous deeds. Good reading, though.

A passing figure darkened the window and Hawkins gave a snort. 'Here's that cursed lawyer Cecil. You arrange things your own way, Walter, never mind him.'

Sir Robert Cecil opened the door and Raleigh rose to greet him. Hawkins remained seated and thanked God that he was a sailor, not a statesman, he did not have to feign a politeness that he did not feel and he didn't mind a sail-needle if Cecil guessed how much he disliked and despised him.

Raleigh and Cecil had not met since the Queen's discovery of Raleigh's affair with Lisbeth. In the early part of the uproar when Arthur Throckmorton had accused Raleigh of seducing his sister, Cecil had faced about and joined in the outcry against Raleigh and called his conduct "brutish". The word had been repeated to Raleigh and hurt him. He had imagined that Cecil would have stood his friend in any crisis, if not through love, then through his distrust for Essex. Cecil had written to him in the Tower, assuring him that his feelings were unchanged, that the word had been used of the seduction, not the marriage about which he knew nothing at the time. Raleigh had accepted the apology and said that he had understood but now he eyed Burghley's son narrowly. He recalled Lisbeth's words, 'Well may Burghley say to his son, "Shun to be Raleigh,"' and he wished that he could read the mind that lay within that long fox-like head, behind the eyes of which one was so much smaller than the other.

But Cecil's greeting left nothing to be desired.

'I am indeed glad to see you, Sir Walter,' he began, 'glad for you and for myself. This task is completely beyond me. There are goods whose very names are unfamiliar to me. And the chests are all labelled in Portuguese, which makes it more difficult. The labour of Hercules, that's what we're faced with, the labour of Hercules.'

Hawkins looked at Raleigh, smiled and lifted his bushy eyebrows and Raleigh smiled back, 'Fussy little fool,' the glance said.

But although Raleigh smiled, he did not accept the glance's meaning. Upon the surface the Treasurer's son might appear to be fussy and inefficient, nervous of responsibility he certainly was, but he was also clever and crafty, as Burghley's breed could hardly help being.

Hard upon Cecil's heels came Sir John Gilbert, Deputy for Devon, and he gave Raleigh the most eloquent welcome of them all. He came in, speechless, and they could all see how the working of his throat shook his ill-pleated ruff. He stretched out both hands towards his kinsman, tried to speak and then fell forward with his arms around his shoulders, shamelessly in tears. Raleigh patted his shoulder and kissed him on the cheek.

'Strange times we live in,' said the Deputy when he had recovered from his burst of emotion, 'when a man can be imprisoned for marrying a wench. 'Tis worse than the Inquisition!'

'Sh,' said Hawkins in as near a whisper as he could manage, 'there are long ears in this room and a long tongue tacked to them. We don't want you in the Tower.'

'We'd better get down to the harbour,' said Cecil, who had heard every word of the last speech. Uncouth old ruffian, he thought to himself, we'll be rid of him then, he isn't on the Commission and he shan't interfere. But as they moved down the passage Hawkins waddled after him after them and he alone remembered Blount in the little room at the end.

'Come you along if you want to keep your prisoner in sight,' he shouted as he threw open the door, 'we're just off to the harbour.' And as no one suggested to Sir John that he was unwanted, he accompanied them all the way and no one would have guessed that he was not head of the Commission himself. The harbour of the simple little sea-faring town was strewn with all the riches that Herod once offered Salome. The sandalwood chests gave out a fragrance of their own and mingled with it was the scent of a thousand spices. Some of the chests had been roughly handled and the contents were spilling out on the stones.

Here were the treasures of the East. Fabled wealth that had set Columbus's sails wearing westwards. Treasures for which every crime in the catalogue of Satan had been committed at some time or another.

'Smell the spices?' asked Hawkins; 'they're what the ignorant hogs left out in the full sun. There're are carpets, too, that'll be heirlooms long after we're all sodded. They weren't even covered up from the rain.'

The five men walked through the barriers that Cecil had ordered to be erected and began to view the spoils. There were precious stones that had been dug by whipped slaves from the secret places of the earth: embroideries over which women had bent until they were blind: carpets woven by children who never played and whose limbs would never grow out of the cramped positions that their labour had demanded. There was ivory for which men had hunted the elephant and brought him down pierced with a hundred arrows, each with a slow death in its tip; and nutmegs that had been carried from the inland groves to the coast upon the raw backs of patient little donkeys.

Raleigh booked them all. He was the one man of that little company who could have read into them all their tragic stories, understood the sweat and blood and pain and danger that had gone to their gathering. But he had no time. For him they were merely the price of favour, the ransom of his pride. He handled the pearls, snatched by some dark diver from the depths of the shark-ridden sea. He remembered that Drake had told him once how the pearl divers died after three years of the work, coughing up lumps of their misused lungs. But did not see the dusky ghosts, only the shining orbs that would gleam on the neck and fingers and ears of the Queen for whom he instantly reserved them.

The merchants who had rushed down from London at the first news of the cargo came up to make their bids after their long impatient waiting under Cecil's embargo. To them Raleigh sold the more ordinary and well-known wares. One hundred thousand pounds' worth of pepper he auctioned off in one day. Then he paid the seamen. They came up one by one, men with brown leathery faces and strange tattoo marks on their arms and chests, to take their pay. He spent the whole day standing at the gate of the barrier with the ships' lists in his hand calling out the men's names, the sums due to them and crossing off each as it was paid. Then he made a careful list of all the other goods. Frankincense, crystal, porcelain and amber, tapestry, satin, cinnamon, pearls and ambergris, carpets, ivory, cloves and sandalwood. With this list and another upon which figured the name and proportion of every shareholder. Raleigh retired on the third night to the *Falcon*, ordered his supper and a bottle of wine, closed the door to all comers, even Hawkins, and set himself to work out a very interesting sum.

The evening had grown chilly and there was a little fire

crackling upon the hearth and augmenting the light of the candles. Raleigh laid the two lists before him, lighted his long pipe and, chin on hand, gave himself up to the thought. The Queen's share came to twenty thousand pounds. A pretty sum: but she would not be exactly delighted to receive her just dues, however high the interest that they represented. He must find some way of increasing her share; and that was damned difficult with this Commission looking into everything. He cursed Frobisher for a fool. If he could have managed to control what he had so cleverly captured, there would have been no Commission. Good God, no, and Raleigh would not be here, he'd be in the Tower still. Slight perspiration broke out on his forehead at the thought and he hastily substituted a blessing upon Frobisher's thick stubborn head. He knocked out his pipe and rubbed his nose with a puzzled air.

There was his own share due on the loan of his *Roebuck* but if he sacrificed that to the Queen it would cripple his future plans. He might give her half, of course. Then there was Hawkins, he had lent his *Stallion* and was entitled to thirty-six thousand pounds. But that couldn't be docked, partly because Hawkins knew exactly what his share should be but also because Hawkins had stood his friend and certainly mustn't be robbed by the man whom he had commended to make the division... but...

Hawkins...

Clear in his mind as in his ears three days before rang that booming bass voice, 'You're the one man in England that knows the value of the spices and the silk and those little ornament things.'

Dear God! What fortune.

He refilled his pipe and set to work on the first list. The porcelain, the satin and silk, the ambergris and the frankincense he priced at rather less than their value. The more marketable commodities, ivory and carpets, jewels and cloves and nutmegs, he wrote down at their actual worth. Then he apportioned the goods amongst the shareholders. When he had finished the Queen had, upon the paper, her bare twenty thousand pounds but the true value of her share, as Raleigh realised with delight, was eighty thousand, just four times her due.

A crafty smile that made his face almost as foxy as Cecil's curved Raleigh's lips. He poured wine for himself and drank to his own wit.

Then he drew towards him a clean sheet of paper, headed it, "Dartmouth this twenty-eight of September 1592", and began to write to the Queen. He told her of the labours of the past days. He wrote down the true value of her share and explained exactly how he had arranged it. It would have been a waste of his effort to leave her to imagine that any other man could have given her so much; and he concluded...

> *'This is more than ever man presented to her Majesty as yet. If God have sent it for my ransom, I hope her Majesty, of her abundant goodness, will accept it. If her Majesty cannot beat me from her affection, I hope her sweet nature will think it no conquest to afflict me...'*

Next day the other members signed the list of shares and John Hawkins rolled off with his thirty-six thousand pounds, blessing Sir Walter and the happy thoughts that had come into his old head on that September day.

'If ever the doctors order me a leech, I'll send for you, man,' was his parting shot at Blount, who had hung on Raleigh's heels through all the busy days.

The speech made Raleigh wonder what he should do when the work here was finished. Should he return to the Tower? Or risk it and go to Sherborne?

The Queen had received his letter by this time and she must, she must have softened towards him. Yet, if he rode meekly back with Blount to the Tower, there he might stay, forgotten. Better risk it.

At breakfast on the day after all was in order for their departure he said to Blount, 'Well, do you intend to do with me?'

103

'I took you from the Tower and to the Tower it is my duty to return you.'

Raleigh laughed. 'You'll have to get someone to help you then, for my dead body will be heavy. I'm going to Sherborne.'

'And I shall bear the brunt of letting you go,' said Blount bitterly.

'You need not. You can come to Sherborne, too. I offer you the hospitality of my poor house. My wife will be delighted, delighted.'

Blount refused to smile at Raleigh's imitation of the fussy little Mayor of Tenmore. He'd had quite enough of Raleigh's airs and graces and more than enough of his company.

They parted in the courtyard of the *Falcon*. 'You've attended me splendidly. Thank you. Good-bye,' cried Raleigh as he mounted.

Blount grunted and mounted himself, to ride back and report as viciously as possible to the Queen. And to tell Essex that Raleigh was more dangerous than they had feared; he had a way with the common people that his common enemies could only deplore.

Raleigh rode to Sherborne. He was deeply disappointed at the Queen's silence; but the thrill of flouting the authority of Blount and those behind him lightened his volatile spirits and he sang as he rode. The mocking mention of his wife had set him hungering for Lisbeth; soon she would be with him. Eighty thousand pounds was surely ransom for two.

Autumn was striding over the country now. His horse set clouds of dry leaves flying: the elms blazed pure yellow against the pale blue of the sky. As he neared Sherborne the bonfire of his beeches burned to welcome him and his heart rose. The weary horse trotted down the drive to the door with the white flight of steps before it. And as he came to a standstill the miracle happened. The door was flung open and Lisbeth, with a new heavy step came, hastily yet carefully, down the stone stairs to throw herself into his arms. He held her closely for a moment, and then took her face in his hands and looked at her.

'How in the name of wonder did you get here?'

'I was sent. Oh Walter, how marvellous to see you again.'

'Isn't it? But who sent you?'

'It's four months since I saw you. Oh, the Queen. There was a message or something that you'd be here anon. I couldn't really attend properly. Oh Walter, we're together. We're free.'

'We're together and we're free,' he repeated, but his mind was elsewhere.

The Queen had released Lisbeth upon the receipt of his letter. That was fine, of course, but (he stroked his beard thoughtfully) were freedom and Lisbeth and Sherborne to be his sole reward? That would be so exactly the Queen's gesture... 'You wanted this woman, take her and live with her and keep out of my sight.'

He felt that Lisbeth was looking at him. He discarded the thoughts that had been, in essence, so disloyal to her. 'I am stunned,' he said, to excuse his momentary abstraction. Then in a sudden burst of wild spirits he swung her into his arms and ran up the steps over the doorsill.

'I should have been here to do this some days ago,' he said.

Lisbeth, in the midst of her laughing protest that the two of them were too heavy for him, forgot for a little that queer shadow on his face and her instant's suspicion that the welcome had not been quite so joyous as she had imagined it.

Chapter 14

Sherborne
1594-95

Lisbeth, running down the stairs with her slender figure braced to balance the weight of the child, saw the brown stranger admitted at the door and stopped as if she had been shot. She knew in an instant, by his clothes, his gait and his voice, that he was a sailor and a sailor could have but one errand in that house.

'More, more run,' cried young Walter, who enjoyed being carried downstairs; but beyond saying sharply, 'Be quiet,' she took no notice of him. And when she did make the descent, she came slowly and thoughtfully. She set the child on a chest in the hall and said, 'If you sit there and don't stir till, I come back, I'll play with you then. If you make a sound, you'll go straight to bed.'

Walter, who was used to his mother's uncompromising manner, was quite uncrushed by this speech, gazed at her wide-eyed, and said, 'Walter sit.'

Lisbeth went through the main door and turned sharp left on the terrace. She did not hear the drumming that Walter had already discovered the way to produce with the heels of his little red shoes on the hollow side of the chest. At the end of the terrace was the window of Raleigh's room. A climbing rose-bush, now unflowered and bronzed of leaf, grew beside it and standing in its shelter she could see into the room without risk of being seen. During the spring and summer, just past, she had stood there often, watching her husband bowed over map or book or intent upon some letter to Elizabeth or Cecil.

The sailor, whose name, though she did not then know it,

was Whiddon, sat on one side of the table in a high-backed chair. Upon the opposite side her husband was sitting on a stool which he tilted on its front legs as he leaned forward to take some papers that Whiddon was holding towards him. Through the closed window she could hear no word of their conversation but she could see Whiddon emphasise some point with a jab of a brown forefinger. Raleigh jumped up from his stool and went to a shelf for a book. Flicking over the pages he returned to Whiddon and laid the book before him; as he did so he leaned one hand upon the back of the sailor's chair. The two heads, one square and reddish, the other black and narrow, came together as the two men scanned the page and Lisbeth was conscious of a sickness at her heart. Something was being planned within that shining room, something in which she had no part. At this moment Whiddon was all to Raleigh and she was nothing. She put out her hand and a trailing branch of the rose-bush brushed across the back of it, breaking the skin. She put her hand to her mouth and was surprised as its icy cold. She realised that she had been standing in the November air, uncloaked and hatless, for a quarter of an hour; and that made her remember Walter, perched in the hall. Anyway, she was doing no good here. She turned away and went with her light, supple step back to where the child waited. He chattered all that time that she dressed him and put on her cloak and gloves; she said 'Yes' and 'No' at intervals but she neither heard, nor actually answered, his questions.

This morning was the culmination of something that she had suspected and dreaded all through the past year. She had been aware of Walter's growing discontent and uneasiness but she hoped that Sherborne would lay its spell upon him as it had upon her. He had seemed interested in his experiments with potatoes and tobacco, was pleased when the former throve and disappointed with the latter turned out to lack the sweetness of the more sun-soaked Virginian kind. He had bred horses and falcons and ruled his estates well. Surely, thought Lisbeth, striding rapidly about the garden, here was a life that would have contented most men. Even those who had been bitten by the germ of ambition in their younger days could have settled here at the age of forty-three and looked back on the dreams of their youth as mere boyish folly. Comfort and dignity within doors, exercise, authority and interest without, what more could anyone want? But she realised that in her mind she was preaching to the converted; she was content at Sherborne, Walter wasn't. She had seen him push away his food untasted at some mention of the Queen or of Essex. She had lain beside him, feigning sleep, through many long night hours when he tossed from side to side and groaned with agony no less bitter for being secret. And now there was this sailor with his emphasising forefinger and his charts and he was persuading Walter into something. Of that, she was sure.

Furiously she drove her heels into the soft turf, peevishly she called to young Walter, who had run to a distance, to come and walk beside her. He came obediently, his hands full of beech nuts, and looked up into her face wonderingly. She was always firm but seldom cross with him and he knew quite well that he had not been naughty this morning. His eyes reproached her and with a sudden revulsion of feeling she stopped and lifted him in her arms. With his soft body against her shoulder and the sweet baby smell of him in her nostrils she was overcome by tenderness and that made her the more annoyed at the circumstances that had mad her snappish a moment before. She thrust out her red under-lip and her eyes narrowed. Whatever scheme Walter was hatching should not mature without some opposition. If he could write to Cecil, so could she. It remained for her to find out, if that were possible, what exactly the scheme was.

Young Walter was bored by the close embrace and the silence; he struggled in her arms. She swung him round so fast that he was riding on her shoulders and, bouncing in imitation of a restive steed, galloped with him into the house.

Whiddon stayed through the night and all through the next day but the only clue that his hostess gained of his business was the chance-dropped word, "Guiana". But she was there, by intent, sweetly innocent and smiling when Raleigh saw him off, and she heard her husband say, 'I'll apply for the patent at once and I'll get it, never fear. Cecil hasn't forgotten Dartmouth...'

For half an hour or so after Whiddon's going they played with young Walter and Raleigh, rampant on the furry bearskin rug with the child astride his shoulders, did not appear the kind of husband to cause his wife any undue anxiety. But presently he rose, dusted his breeches and brushed back his hair.

'I have several letters to write,' he said, don't wait up for me.'

He kissed Lisbeth in a kind, husbandly fashion, ruffled Walter's curls, as he passed and went to his study.

Quick as thought Lisbeth handed the child to his nurse and sped to her room. She was not in the habit of writing many letters and it took her some minutes to collect her materials but presently they were ready beside the extra candles and she sat down to address herself to Cecil. Her father and his father had been good friends, her brother Arthur was one of his cronies, she did not imagine that her appeal would be wasted. In her cramped, pointed handwriting she drove line after line across the page, '... *if any respect to me or love to him be not forgotten I humbly beseech you rather to stay than to further him. I know your persuasions are of effect with him...*' On and on and on, beseeching, reminding, coaxing... '... *by the which you shall bind me forever*'.

Below her, a little to the south, in a room whose light she could see cast on the terrace as she drew back her curtains, Raleigh was penning, for the same eye, an urgent appeal for Cecil's good offices for him with the Queen. He too was beseeching, reminding, coaxing.

And Cecil, deep in his own tortuous schemes, read both the letters and thought, like a certain King of Israel, 'Am I God?'

II

The patent came in the following January, as Raleigh had known it would. The Queen had been unable to resist his importunity. The new word, "Guiana", had caught her fancy. He had discarded Virginia; it was too late now, both he and

109

Elizabeth were too old to stake any hope on a venture in a country that would have to grow slowly, as a child grows. And the Queen was not so much in love with her successor, whichever he might be, as to wish to spend time or money on enhancing his inheritance.

Gold was Raleigh's newest cry. His letters to Elizabeth and to Cecil did but repeat the promise of those strange old charts that lure men to destruction, 'Here be much gold.' He was wise enough to know that when that last Tudor heart was adamant to sentiment and reason, those ears deaf to poetry and prayer, the one would quicken and the other prick to the parrot promise of gold.

And he had been right. He held the precious document in his hand at last. It gave him permission to penetrate into the lands of the Orinoco, to explore and, if possible, to settle, any such lands not already in the procession of a Christian monarch. It was made out to 'Our Servant, Walter Raleigh'. The deliberate omission of the conventional 'trusty' or 'well-beloved' gave him to understand that to the Queen he was neither. The insult was a sharp blow to his pride, already chafed raw by his months of impatient waiting. He would waste no time now. It must be broken to Lisbeth at once. With the patent in hand, he went in search of her.

Lisbeth was sitting in the parlour with her embroidery frame drawn close to the blaze of the logs on the stone hearth. Outside the short winter day was already dying redly behind the dark-grey boles of the beeches. The firelight turned one side of her golden head to copper and struck warm dancing lights from her gown of amber-coloured velvet. On the stretched embroidery a peacock, bright in blue and green, walked on a daisied lawn. He was fourth of his kind, destined for chair covers in Lisbeth's dining-hall.

She looked up as Raleigh entered and she knew by the parchment in his hand, and the expression on his face, what he had come to tell her. But she gave him no opening. After one glance she returned to her frame and went on drawing the needle in and out. Her heart was beating madly high in her throat and her fingers trembled but she seemed composed enough.

Raleigh fidgeted around the frame for a moment or two, pulling the loose threads to the back of the embroidery. Then he went to the fire and stirred it with his foot. A log fell forward and he replaced it, looking at Lisbeth as he did so. But although the clatter had made her jump, she did not turn her head. In and out, in and out went the needle.

'Lisbeth,' said Raleigh at last.

'Uh-huh,' she murmured, bending her neck to peer earnestly at the last stitch.

'I've just received the Queen's patent to go to Guiana.'

'Guiana?'

'You must have heard me mention it. It's in South America. They say that Eldorado is there.'

'Do you believe it?'

'Of course I do. So does the Queen. She wouldn't have sent me this else.'

'May I see?'

'Of course.' He unfolded the crackling sheet and handed it to her. She left the frame after carefully digging in the needle and with the patent in her hand sat down on a low stool near the fire.

For a long time she said nothing and the way she leaned to the light of the flames prevented him from seeing her face. Then she laid it back on his knee.

'A politely worded death sentence,' she said, frigidly calm.

'You exaggerate the danger, sweet.'

'Do I?' She turned towards him and raised her blue eyes to his face. There was neither fear nor anger nor surprise in them; only an expression that he had never seen before, a kind of mocking pity, born of a peculiar wisdom.

'Do I? What happened to Oreliana? What to Diego Ordace? What to Pedro de Osua and Agiri? There be four that we know of. How many more whose names are not even recorded have gone out to that far land to die of fever or wounds or treachery?'

Balaam, when his ass turned and spoke to him, was not

111

more surprised than Raleigh at hearing these familiar and long-brooded-over names fall from Lisbeth's lips.

'What do you know of all these?' he asked.

'As much as you do. All that can be learned from those books that you read.'

Raleigh jumped up from his chair. This interview was taking an unexpected turn. He had imagined that Lisbeth would cry and that he would clasp and comfort her. For calm, dry-eyed argument he was not prepared. He began to walk around the room and talk in jerky sentences as if he were addressing another man.

'Grant that they died. The road to every successful venture is paved with the dead. Magellan set out to sail around the world; he was killed. Did that deter Drake? Not in an instant. If men stopped to consider what fate had overtaken other men, they would leave their food for the thought of those who had been poisoned at the table. Men die of scratches every day, a nail in the foot, a breath of contagion. Those whom you named died at least more worthily, in Adventure's name.'

'All for what, Walter. Can you tell me that?'

Raleigh stood still and paused for a moment before he answered.

'It's a call,' he said at last, 'and only those who hear it can understand. There are in England thousands of men who can live as I have living. What does it need? A mouth that can be stuffed with food, two legs to grip a horse. Life should demand more of a man. Here amid this security and comfort I'm like a dog that has followed a stranger who has offered it a bone. The master whistles and though it knows that it will get no bone there, but rather a rebuke, back to his side it goes.'

'So, our life here, our home, our child, are no more to you than the stranger's bone,'

Raleigh realised that he was talking to a woman, one of those to whom everything is personal.

'Oh Lisbeth,' he said, 'that was an unfortunate simile. Women can't be talked with. They are so literal-minded. And the woman has yet to be born who can believe that a man can love her yet leave her; or understand that the world would have ended long ago if, when love and action clash, action didn't sometimes win.'

'Being but a woman I can understand that once, when love warred with ambition, for that was what you meant by action, it was young and strong and so won for a season. Now is ambition's turn. Someday, when you are old, if you live to be old, you'll know ambition for the hollow thing it is. You'll be glad, then, that love outlived it.'

'I love you now, Lisbeth. I always shall. But there's something too strong for me in this matter. And now that the Queen has written so coldly and contemptuously to me I would go to Guiana though I knew that death, in all the forms men fear most, awaited me.'

'I know. To appear well in her eyes, you would make me a widow and the boy fatherless. You need not protest, Walter, it is true. Let us accept the truth.'

She was silent for a moment. If it had only been some ordinary, pretty woman who had threatened to supplant her! A woman could have been fought with women's weapons. But against this insidious enemy, this ambition for honour and the Queen's favour, she had no defence. Golden hair, soft skin, plaint body were all alike, worthless.

When she spoke next her voice had changed. It was with genuine interest that she asked:

'What is it about her that makes her opinion of such moment? Too old for love, too false and vain and heartless to be idealised, yet she must be served and flattered. What is it about her?'

Could it be learned, this secret of attraction? Could Walter, who was so clever with words, give it a form that might be studied and followed?

'I can't tell you, Lisbeth, I doubt whether any man could. You may be angry with her but it is like being angry with the Almighty, it recoils on your own head. You may offer her extravagant flattery and scorn her that she accepts it yet, in your heart, you know that she is not deceived. She can make herself ridiculous by her flirtations and her parsimony and a byword by

113

her prevarication. And yet, beyond it all she has a dignity that nothing, not even her own behaviour, can impart. She is the Queen. She is, in essence, England. And if I could only wring one smile from her, hear her say, "Well done," I would not count what the words had cost me... All this has nothing to do with you, my sweet. That I tell you this proves it. You are me, therefore you must understand.'

He fixed her with one of the direct, long looks that had, in the past, had the power to turn her heart to water but she withstood it.

'I understand. I understand, too, how right are the Papists to demand celibacy of their priests. A *dévote*, whether to God, Queen or mere adventure, is not fitted for traffic with simple things like hearth and home.'

He said sadly, 'Your bitterness betrays your anger with me.'

'On the contrary I pity you as I would a man who was sick. You are sick. You leave a woman who loves you to serve one who despises you. You leave Sherborne for a country where death lurks in every bush. If that isn't sickness... Let's talk of it no more.'

She lighted the candles and seated herself at her work. In and out, in and out flashed the needle. And in and out flashed the thoughts of the woman who was learning the lightness of the anchor of love. It was the unknown that called to men. That was why once Raleigh had gone to the Tower for her, while now he could not rest with her in Sherborne. Four years of intimacy had worn away the charm. Perhaps that was the Queens secret. Lisbeth sat with her needle poised as she contemplated it. Nobody knew the Queen, really. Strange tales afloat proved that her body was as mysterious as her mind. Lisbeth was, for a moment, a firm believer in Elizabeth's virginity.

Suppose, mused Lisbeth, the Queen had desired one man to stay with her and had been unable to command him. What would she do then? The answer came at once. What had Elizabeth's sister done to keep Philip of Spain in England? Tied him to her with stories of her pregnancy; and he had believed them and waited and waited for the child who had never been conceived to be born. Would that be worth trying? Would that story hold Raleigh? It might, for a time. And it would ruin his plans. Not his plans only but his faith in her and her own joy in their union. Too high a price to pay.

She felt exhausted as well as unhappy. Rising slowly, she pushed the frame into the corner and went to bed.

An hour or so later Raleigh stretched out his hand to draw her towards him. He was eager for reconciliation and for love in the little time that remained to him. But Lisbeth turned away and lay on the edge of the big bed, silent. He was too proud, too fastidious to make further advance.

Next day he left Sherborne, early, to get together his ships and stores and to find men willing to set out with him.

On the third of February, through a blinding snowstorm, he rode back to say good-bye. Lisbeth, who had spent the three lonely weeks between loving and hating him, and remembered their parting, hesitated for an imperceptible second before she kissed him on his arrival. Raleigh was cold and weary; he had imagined that she would be pleased to see him; he noticed the hesitation and was suddenly and furiously angry. Throwing off his cloak he said harshly, 'Send me some food along here. Meere is coming in for his last orders.' He went rapidly along the passage to his study and remained closeted there with the overseer for the whole of the evening.

Lisbeth wandered about disconsolately, looking at the clothes and the books that were to go with him and which she had packed as efficiently as she did everything. She lifted the jade Buddha out of his box of shavings and stared down at his inscrutable smile. We're all idolaters, she thought. Walter was my idol and he hasn't been as indestructible as this hard green stuff. She realised, perhaps for the for the first time, that she was the weaker of the two and that unless she managed a reconciliation, and identified herself with his aims and interests, her life was going to be marred forever. There were so many interests in his life; she had only three, Walter, the child and

115

Sherborne. And of these the first was much the most important. She had learned that this afternoon when he had dropped his arms and the smile had left him. She would have given much to have that moment back again. That was impossible but the night was still young.

She paid her final visit to Walter the younger and tucked in the coverlet that he had disturbed. Then, slowly, she went into the bedroom. She spread out her hair and brushed it for a long time. In the quietude she heard Meere leave, heard the final good wishes and promises that Raleigh should find all in order upon the estate at his return. She heard her husband put up the bar on the door; then she listened for his steps on the stairs. It didn't come. He was putting away the books and papers and extinguishing the light, she thought at first. But the little time that that would have taken passed and there was no sound.

She had undressed for some time now and the bitter cold was striking her through her night-robe. She looked at the bed. Some remnants of the old Lisbeth urged her to get into it and sleep if that were possible or, failing that, to pretend. But the new woman who had been born that afternoon was smitten with panic at the suggestion. It might mean that Raleigh would stay downstairs all night. The last few hours must not be spent so. Tomorrow it would be impossible for her to go to him. And of how many, many tomorrows would that be true? He would be out of reach of her voice and her hand. The thought grew more poignant as she remembered his virtues. He was ever kind. In an age of public chivalry and private brutality he had always treated her with consideration and tenderness. He had never given her cause for jealousy in the usual way. He had married her and thus blighted a career that he was now taking desperate measures to restore. In the final count, indeed, it might seem that she had sent him on this perilous venture. She snatched up the candle and ran downstairs and along the passage on her bare feet.

Raleigh was sitting by the dying fire. The candles on the table were dead and the two remaining on the chimney breast were nearing their end. He was sitting with his elbows on his knees and his chin in his hands, staring at the red embers.

At the opening of the door, he turned. Before Lisbeth could say the words that she had prepared he saw her feet and rose, crying, 'My love, your poor feet!' He put an arm round her shivering shoulders and pushed her to his stool and taking her feet in his hands held them to the fire. Lisbeth could bear no more. She fell forward weeping upon his shoulder; put her hands behind his head so that her fingers felt the long prick of the strong black hairs. Raleigh clasped her so tightly that the buttons on his doublet bruised her breast through the thin stuff of her gown. Their lips clung together and he could taste the salt of her tears; there was no need for speech. Presently he carried her upstairs.

So, they spent their last night as lovers: and in the morning she stood in the snow with a shawl over her head and the boy in her arms to watch him mount. He leaned down and kissed her for the last time and took one of her hands in his warm nervous grip.

'Have no fear for me, sweetheart. A man knows somewhere within him when he goes to his death. I shall come back to you.'

He loosened his clasp and drew on his glove.

At the end of the drive, he turned in the saddle and waved. She waved the child's plump arm. 'Wave, Walter'.

Next moment the screen of leafless trees and thickly fallen snow had hidden him from her side. A bitter wind tugged at the shawl. She turned and clasping her little boy tighter went slowly up the steps into the quiet home.

Chapter 15

Guiana
1595

In just a moment they would know. The muscles in the men's chest cracked as they pulled at the oars; their naked torsos gleamed with sweat and the scent of it mingled with the stink of stale food in the barge.

Raleigh stood up and waved his arms. 'It's the great river, lads. This is the Orinoco.'

'It's thirty miles wide if it's a yard,' said Keymis in an awed voice.

'It leads straight into the heart of the Golden City,' said Raleigh.

The barge and the boats came out on the shining bosom of the greatest river and every one of them, including the leader, gave a sigh of relief. There was the actual river, now they might begin to believe in the existence of the city. For days and days they had doubted that there was any great river. They had been lost in labyrinths of streams that appeared to run in any direction, even backwards, through the flat jungle lands. They had been almost stifled as the boats crept through tunnels of green gloom where the great trees met overhead and the sky was hidden by a screen of creepers that threw their arms from branch to branch and wove a living, flowering roof. There had been places where the vegetation had met over the stream and had to be hacked before the boats could pass. But this great river flowed through more open country and the men who had wilted in the airless, uncanny silence gained heart as they rowed along.

Presently they were cheered, too, by the sight of some naked Indians paddling a canoe ahead of them.

'Overtake them,' Raleigh ordered; 'they may be able to direct us or at least sell us fresh food.'

The Indians, with expressions of terror, paddled madly and then, finding that the boats of the white strangers were gaining upon them, ran the canoe into the bank, scrambled ashore and disappeared.

The boats drew level with the abandoned canoe and the rowers could see that it was filled with flat cakes of some bread-like food and gleaming fish, still squirming together in a silver, wriggling mass.

'I shall land here,' said Raleigh, 'and look around. You can build a fire on a bank and cook the fish. I'll pay for them if I get near the natives.'

'Don't go alone,' urged Gilbert, preparing to follow, 'they may be treacherous.'

'They'll see that I intend no harm if I go alone,' said Raleigh. 'Stay here and see that the food is shared fairly. And save me some,' he added. For already the man were falling upon the bread cakes with an avidity bred by weeks of a diet of weevily biscuit and salt beef as hard as timber.

He noticed as he scrambled up the bank that the colour of the soil had changed from a dull red to a blue colour. He made a mental comment to himself that this the soil in which ore was to be found. Lightly he scaled the bank and in a hollow close by, but cunningly placed out of sight from the river, he came upon the Indian village. The little mud huts were shaped like beehives and not a great deal bigger. Before some of the low doorways smoky little fires were burning and around them coloured clay cooking-pots lay where the cooks had dropped them in terror at the alarm that the fishermen had given only five minutes before.

Raleigh looked around. Every hut was empty; but he knew that the Indians had not had time to go far and he had a feeling that every bush and tree around the clearing concealed a watcher. He sat down on the charred stump of a tree; probably, he thought, the tree that had grown there, and which had been felled by fire for lack of an axe, was now the canoe that was

119

adrift under the bank. He laid out the knives and hatchets that he had brought as goodwill offerings and lighted his pipe. Before he had smoked it a brown face, then another and another peered cautiously out from the screen of bushes.

A stone came flying through the air and caught him full on the temple. He put his hand to the place and then lowered it, bloody, and stretched out both arms to show that he was unarmed though the good hatchets glinted within reach of his hand. He managed to smile in the direction of his assailant. There was another long pause.

Presently a man stepped out into the open, timid but curious. Raleigh did not stir, though the blood from his cut temple was running, warm and sticky inside his collar.

Soon there was a ring of naked brown watchers. Raleigh spoke then, in Spanish, 'I come as a friend.' But at the sound of that dreaded tongue consternation was plain upon every face. He shook his head and repeated the words in English. He smiled stretched out his hands again, pointed to his offerings.

Nobody stirred. Slowly he stood up and retreated to a little distance, sat down again and watched them. One by one, a step at a time, the Indians crept forward and began to examine the knives and axes with signs of interest and pleasure. But when he stood up again and moved towards them, they dropped the things hastily and scampered away.

He picked up a knife and, holding it by the blade with handle outwards, offered it to the man that stood nearest. After another long hesitation the man put out a cautious hand. It hovered, closed round the handle and as Raleigh immediately released the blade, drew back. The man looked at his present curiously. His friends gathered round, chattering. He let one of them hold it and ran back to his hut.

In a moment he was back, holding a squawking hen under his arm. Within reach of Raleigh, he wrung its neck and laid it, still twitching, at his feet. Then he retreated several steps and watched. Raleigh picked it up, went through the mummery of plucking and eating it, smiling and rubbing his stomach with signs of pleasure. Then, at last, the man smiled too and made clucking noises of understanding. The others took courage and in a short time the knives and hatchets were all gone, and in their place lay a motley collection of fish, bread, cakes, chickens and lumps of pork.

The Indians then clustered together in a crowd, displaying their presents, Raleigh thought, but after a time during which their gabbling and grunting rose to a tumult two men came towards him holding a third between them by the arms. The captive was protesting volubly. One of his captors stopped and picked up the stone that had struck Raleigh a little before and he pressed it to the man's hand, then he pointed rapidly and repeatedly from the man to the stone and from the stone to the wound that it had inflicted, indicating as plainly as possible that this was the man who had flung the stone. The two warders then gave him a violent push so that he landed on his knees at Raleigh's feet. He looked up in terror, rolling his eyes and jabbering rapidly. Raleigh drew his silver-handled dagger from is belt, the man gave a terrified yell and threw up his arms but made no other effort either to escape or to protect himself. The smooth silver handle slipped into the stiff uplifted fingers; Raleigh's hand came down in a friendly smack on the shaking shoulder. The man rose nimbly to his feet and darted away just as all Indians with cries and shouts took to their heels and went haring across the open space to the other end of the clearing. There they formed a solid mass for a moment, bowing and stamping rhythmically with their bare feet. Then the mass parted and the villagers fell in behind another party who advanced steadily towards Raleigh.

At the head of the party walked an old man. He was very bowed and leaned heavily upon a gaily coloured pole as he walked. His long hair was quite white and hung down on his shoulders, forming a curious frame for a face wrinkled and brown as a two-year-old russet apple. Although the people who followed him were almost all stark naked, he wore a loin-cloth and another piece of the same material was draped over his shoulders and perched on the long white hair was a tuft of coloured feathers. He came straight towards Raleigh without

121

timidity as without curiosity and not even his thin bare shanks, caked with dust, nor his evident decrepitude could quite deny him a certain odd dignity. Raleigh stood still and looked at him. About five paces away the old man stopped and said in tolerable Spanish: 'I am Topiawari, King of Arromaia. If you come in peace, you are welcome.'

'I come in peace,' answered Raleigh gravely.

'From the Spanish?'

'Not so. I come from England.'

'Ah yes. I have heard of that land and of the Queen that rules it. She is the enemy of Spain.'

'That is so. I trust that that does not make me less welcome to you, Topiawari.'

The old man shook his head but he eyed Raleigh closely. 'The stranger who comes in peace must ever demand a welcome. Are you alone?'

'There are nigh a hundred with me but all in peace. They eat of your food, below there.'

'Bid them come up,' said the old man, looking towards the spot to which Raleigh had pointed, 'and we will eat together as is the custom among friends.'

He turned to his people who had stood quietly during the conversation and spoke in his own language. They hurried towards the huts and some of them blew upon the embers of the fire, others took the clay jars and fetched water while the rest killed and plucked chickens and spitted them on sharp sticks which they held in the fire. Soon the whole village was full of the savour of cooking food. The English sailors came up from the boats and old Topiawari, with twitching nostrils as mobile and as sensitive as those of an inquisitive dog, moved amongst them, examining their clothes, their weapons, their very money for signs of Spanish origin. He held his head on one side as they talked amongst themselves, listening for some Spanish word or phrase that might betray them. But by the time that the feast was ready, and the sun had set, he seemed satisfied and returned to Raleigh and began to speak with more confidence.

They spread the feast in the open, for there was no hut in the village that would have accommodated all the natives and their eighty guests and, although friendly feelings were prevailing, there was a tendency for both white men and brown to feel more at ease in the company of their own kind. Raleigh and Topiawari, Keymis and two of the Indians who had come with the king sat a little apart and were served first with the choicer portions. The fish and the chickens and the pork were laid upon the ground on leaves or round plate of clay. There were more of the flat cakes of bread and wine in clay jars decorated with colours as Raleigh's first pipe had been. Other smaller, flatter jars, filled with oil and with a floating wick, lighted up a strange scene.

Choosing simple Spanish words, so that the old King should understand, Raleigh told him of the taking of St. Joseph.

At the mention of Berrio's name the Indian scowled and spat into the darkness behind him. When he heard that Berrio's city had been destroyed he laughed; and when Raleigh told him that the Spaniard was now his poisoner he beat on the ground with his fists and chucked.

'Berrio is a bad man. And cruel. He killed my nephew, who was a son to me. Of course, the Indians would not fight for him. He steals their maidens, or buys them with axes that lose their heads at the first stroke, and then he sells the so young and fair ones for one hundred and fifty pesos in the islands. All the Spaniards are bad and cruel. I am, as you behold, an old man. Every day I am called for by death, yet they led me about once, like a dog on a chain, for seventeen days, three of them without water.'

Raleigh looked at the old man, so touching in his age and his simple dignity. The fine phrase, 'every day I am called for by death,' appealed to the poet in him. He thought of the treatment that had been meted out to thousands of Topiawari's kind. Harkess's old stories about the Indians who had been driven into the mines, never to emerge into the light of the sun again, returned to his mind.

Sitting there, with the leg-bone of a chicken in one hand and a flat bread cake in the other, he determined that when the land was settled and under his governance, as he was certain one day it would be, the Indians should be treated with kindness and justice.

'Have you heard of a golden city in the West?' He asked Topiawari, as the thought of his plans reminded him of his mission.

'Ah yes. The golden pleasure city of the Incas, where the leaves and flowers in the gardens are of the metal that the white man prize above all things. That is the city of Manoa which now the Spaniards hold.'

'Are you certain that is the city?'

'For myself I think so. But I have spoken with those who hold that farther still to the West there is a richer city. They say that it belongs to a tribe that is dying. But all nations have such tales. I heard while I was with the Spaniards, of a city called Heaven, where the souls of the just fly with wings like birds over flowers that never shed their petals or walk over streets paved with pearl. I heard, too, of another city where the streets are all of blazing fire and the souls of the unjust walk upon the flames of day and night and not consumed. The name of that city is Hell. You have heard of it, perhaps?'

'I have heard of them both,' said Raleigh, unsmiling. 'But our concern with them lies on the far side of death. Manoa is real. I have read what Martines wrote of it. I would fain to see it.'

'It is very far and, like Hell, it is very full of Spaniards. I would fain not see it.'

Raleigh leaned forward and threw all the persuasion of which he was capable into his voice and glance:

'Send out to all your tribes and villages, gather in all your fighting men, aye, and the women too that can hold a spear, and you and I, Topiawari, your people and mine, shall wipe out every Spaniard in Manoa. And your land shall have peace in return, I promise you.'

The old shook his head.

'It is not possible. All your men are but few and brave they may be and well-armed; yet they are but flesh and blood. My people are more in number but the spirit of them is broken. They fear the Spaniards as I do, knowing their fierceness and the hardness of their hearts. And I am an old man, fit no more for fighting, and my nephew who might have led them, Berrio killed. It is impossible.'

'Nothing is impossible for those who dare.'

'There speaks a man who has never been beaten. We dare not go against the Spaniards, even to right our wrongs. All that the Arromaia can hope for now is to avoid trouble in their lifetime and leave no children behind to suffer. Look around you, my friend. How many little ones do you see? None. Yet our men are lusty and our women kind. But the bud has not been allowed to flower, nor has this twelve year. Better never to be born, we say, than to live as slaves. By the time that he'—he pointed to one of the Indians with him—'reaches my age, there will be no more Arromaia. Yet my father's father's fathers have ruled them since the moon was no bigger than a star.'

The old voice trembled and broke. The old king turned away his head and wept. Raleigh, strangely shaken, put his hand upon the shrivelled arm.

'Take heart, man, and come with me, you and your people, I swear that you shall be free and shall see the children plentiful as stars before you die.'

Again Topiawari shook his head and this time there was a look of stubborn terror upon his face.

'It cannot be. We are a beaten people. The young nations rise in the East like the sun and like the sun the old nations die in the West. Where are the Incas or the Analis that were there before them, and the Watopi that were before the Analis? All gone. And the Arromaia go, too. You may defeat the Spaniards and rule awhile in their place. Then another younger nation will defeat the English and you will know then, in the body of your son's sons, the truth of what I say to you tonight. Urge me no more.'

'The young bud is grafted on to the old brier in my country, Topiawari, and the rose blooms. I offer you the young nation's arms and courage. With a little courage now you may buy peace for your people.'

125

But Topiawari had said his last word. 'Urge me no more.' And now there was terror in his voice. Raleigh's persistence was overwhelming him. He could see himself being dragged into a fruitless attempt that would rob his people of the little peace that their present meekness and obscurity had allowed them to retain.

Yet his feelings for Raleigh, though clouded now by fear, were still friendly. The oil had wasted in the little jars and the night advanced relentlessly upon the lighted circle. Topiawari put forth a thin brown finger and touched Raleigh upon the temple where the stone had hit him. He turned to one of the Indians and spoke in his own language. The man rose and hastened into a hut. When he returned he carried a clay jar, beautifully decorated and closed with a cork stopper. He put it carefully into the King's hand and sat down again. Topiawari drew out the stopper and sniffed the contents of the jar.

'It is a secret unguent,' he said, and passed the vessel to Raleigh. 'Smear it liberally upon that wound and upon the bites that you and your companions have so stupidly scratched until they fester. I will tell you how to make it. That is a thing we never told to a Spaniard. Gold was always their cry and they would torture any knowledge that they thought you had of that from you. But they never troubled to ask what we knew of herbs and we never told them, though it would have saved lives, being infallible for any wound that has not broken the vessel of life. There is a compound, too, that heals all the aches of the body and makes the bearing of a child no more than the plucking of a ripe fruit. That, too I will tell you, because you are disappointed with me for not going with you upon this so desperate journey; so that when, back in your own country, you remember Topiawari, it may not be altogether with contempt.'

And the man who had exhausted himself in his efforts first to promote a friendly relationship with the Indians and then to procure their alliance settled himself to write down at Topiawari's dictation the preparation of various drugs. His soul was sick with disappointment and he was utterly weary but, looking at the old man's face in the dying, flickering light, he realised that the Indian was giving him something that he evidently prized very highly; and partly in pity, partly in genuine interest, he took pains to write down the recipes with great care and to ask for an explanation of anything that he did not understand.

Even so the old king was not satisfied with his attempt to make amends. When the feast was finally ended and the Indians whose homes were in the village were lending mats and blankets to those who had come with Topiawari to view the strange white men, he came close to Raleigh and said, 'Come with me.' He led him to a hut that stood a little apart from the others and stooped under the low doorway. Within the hut three of the little lamps gave a dim light that seemed brilliant in that small place after the darkness outside. A young Indian girl was sitting on the mud floor threading a necklace of scarlet berries; she let them drop and they rolled about her feet as she stood up and came meekly before Raleigh.

'The Spaniards take our women and the taking is much resented,' said Topiawari, 'but this maiden belongs to me and I have made her ready for you. Time was when I could have offered you your choice of a dozen but virgins are scarcer now. Still, you are welcome. She is yours.' Changing from Spanish to his own tongue without a pause he spoke rapidly to the girl. She nodded her head and whispered a word or two. Topiawari lifted her head by placing his thin brown finger under her chin. 'She is fair,' he said, wondering at Raleigh's silence.

'Yes, she is fair,' Raleigh repeated. His eyes were not on her flat, brown, frightened face. In the yellow light her newly oiled body gleamed like bronze, she had slim brown legs and thighs and her breasts were like those of the girl at the inn who had stolen his virginity so many many years ago. Lisbeth was far away; it might be months before he saw her again. The scent of the oil that on the girl's skin came to him, heavy and headily aphrodisiac. He was no boy now and although his love for Lisbeth had overwhelmed even his ambition, he was not a man to whom women meant much. But here in this strange land, in the company of a king to whom the present of a virgin was as much a token of normal hospitality as the present of a meal, full of meat and strong native liquor, he was suddenly aware of the savage that lives so thinly disguised by clothes and speech and custom in civilised man. What age-old wisdom had gone to making her ready! How firm and supple would that young body be! For a moment he lusted for her in the way that Christ Himself described as adultery. It was not the memory of Lisbeth that held him back but the thought of his mission.

'I have with me eighty men, Topiawari, and our aim is to make the Indians our friends. To further that aim I have forbidden any man, however provoked, to lay a finger on one of your women. And the rule I make for others I cannot disobey myself. My gratitude for your present is not the less because I cannot take it.'

'Who would know?' asked the old man slyly.

'I should, Topiawari, and my command would lack conviction.'

'You are the stuff of which kings are made,' said the Indian simply.

The girl stood watching. She could not understand their speech but she knew somehow that the duty which Topiawari had explained to her would not have to be performed. She turned and, stooping, picked up her scarlet berries.

The slim brown back and the little stooping knees moved Raleigh to say, 'Tell her that it is my tabu, not that she is uncomely.' Topiawari translated and the girl flashed the white man a smile over her shoulder.

They went out of the tent and the king bade his guest good night.

For a long time, Raleigh did not sleep. He lay on his back on a soft skin that one of the Indians had spread for him and stared at the sky, studded with stars. The moon rose, wide and red, from the darkness of the trees at one side of the clearing, grew pale, sailed over and disappeared behind the trees on the other side. He thought of Lisbeth lying alone, white and very faint and distant like a flower drowned in a deep pool. She was not as real at that moment as the city was calling him from the reaches of the uncharted river or the Queen into whose ears he saw himself pouring the tale of its taking. He thought of Topiawari and his sad acceptance of defeat. So he might have sat at Sherborne waiting for death. What was it that drove some men? Was it hunger for the acclamation of their fellows, human and passing, as Lisbeth had so bitterly said? Or was it that they were given some part to play in the vast drama of the world? Suppose Columbus had preferred to mend nets and drink wine in the back streets of Genoa or Christ had been content in the carpenter's shop in Nazareth. That life, pattern for all human lives, had been planned from the beginning; every journey, every meal, every word spoken had been preordained and known somewhere, by someone, before ever Mary had felt the stir in her womb. If one, then why not all? And what kind of a planner could it be who arranged for some men such hard parts to play? These Indians for example; the galley slaves of Morocco; the Huguenots in France. Was it all perhaps for the entertainment of some immortal playgoer who, looking now upon this clearing in the savage forest and seeing him awake, would think; 'Raleigh soliloquises'?

The effort to understand the un-understandable made his brain reel. He gave it up, as so many had done before him, turned over and slept.

He did not hear Topiawari's men steal from hut to hut and rouse the sleepers, nor the stealthy brushing of bare feet as the Indians, loaded with their food and blankets, struck the trail that led through rock and bush to the king's village. When the first Englishman awoke the huts were completely deserted. Topiawari hated the Spaniards and was on the way to loving Raleigh, but it was not the love that casteth out fear, and not one of his Indians was going to bring disaster upon the tribe by going up the river in an English boat.

'I'm sorry, Sir Walter,' Keymis said, 'but that is how the men feel and I'm not hiding the fact that I agree with them.'

Raleigh steadied his chin on his shaking bands and said through his clattering teeth:

'Just a day more, Keymis. It can't be a day's journey farther. After all, its only rain and a little thunder. It can't hurt any of them.'

'But if we get there, what can we do? Half the men are sick and we're all starved. Besides that, think of yourself; with an ague like that you should be abed.'

'I'd have seen it. I'd have something besides a few sacks of ore to take back with me. Just a day more Keymis. I'd speak to them myself but I hate them to see me like this.'

Keymis looked at the swollen river racing past the boats that could make scarcely any headway against the flood. 'He's mad as the Gadarene swine,' he thought, 'but you have to humour the mad.'

'Very well, I'll do my best,' he said.

Raleigh hugged his arms in his hands and went on staring up the river.

Twenty-four hours later.

Keymis said, 'I'm sorry, but there it is. That last storm finished it. There's half a bread ration apiece left and if you don't give orders to turn back, I shall. We've been all crazy to let you bring us so far.'

Raleigh stood up. Above the roar of the river and the hiss of torrential rain he raised his shaking voice.

'You think you're lost and are going to starve here. I'll prove you're wrong. I'll walk into Manoa on my feet and I'll bring you food. Who'll come with me?'

No voice but those of the river and the rain. And then young Gilbert's, not quite finished breaking and cracking on a note of pity and fanaticism:

'I will.'

And the moment after old Whiddon's bass boom:

'If you're fool enough, I am.'

Six hours later.

130

'There, straight ahead of you. Can't you see it? The gates are crystal and jacinth and there are twenty-four towers of ivory full of silver bells. They're ringing to welcome us in. Manoa, Manoa!'

Whiddon said, 'Take his feet, Gilbert. God help us all now. We're done.'

They raised him from the mud that was already gurgling and sucking him under and, stumbling along, knee-deep and sometimes waist-deep in it themselves, they carried him back to the boats that were already headed down-river.

Three days later the tumbling brown river brought them level with the Indian village again.

'Drive into the bank,' said Raleigh, 'and hang on with the oars and branches and anything you can. We'll get food here at least.'

He dragged his shaking limbs out of the barge and scrambled up the bank.

In the little clearing the village lay, deserted. 'Perhaps,' he thought, 'they avoid the river during the rains.' And at the thought a pang of horror shook him. If that were so, then he had murdered eighty men who had trusted him further than any men had ever trusted any leader. For even at the mad rate at which the river was running they could never reach Trinidad before they starved. Only the torrent had saved them so far. Terrifying as it was, hurtling them from one bank to the other, momentarily threatening to engulf them, it had brought them down-river at more than a hundred miles a day. He stooped at the doorway of the first hut and lifted the edge of the thick straw mat that hung there against the rain. He could see nothing, the air inside was so thick and so sharp with smoke that it almost blinded him, but just as he was drawing back, desperate with disappointment, a woman screamed. Raleigh could have wept with relief at the sound. 'Topiawari,' said Raleigh. It was the only word of their language that he knew and would, even upon his English tongue, serve to tell her that he was not a complete stranger. But once again Fortune was with him. Without a word the woman unfastened the mat from the doorway and with it over her head like some strange square mushroom, she stepped out into the rain, beckoning to Raleigh to follow. They splashed along until, at the doorway of a hut, she stopped and pointed. Raleigh lifted the mat and was face to face with the king.

'My friend,' exclaimed the old man, 'How have you fared?'

'Damnably,' said Raleigh, 'and unless you feed us, Topiawari, I and my men must starve.'

'It is fortunate that I am here. I came down twelve days ago to settle some dispute and could not return for the rain. But tell me how you fared.'

'My men are holding the boats with utmost difficulty,' said Raleigh.

Topiawari rose at once.

'I will order that every hut contributes a handful of meal,' he said. 'I cannot ask for more. They have little enough themselves and the men cannot hunt in this weather. There will be neither flesh nor fish, I fear.'

He went to the door and shouted. A man appeared with a mat on his head and ran off on the errand.

'Now,' said the king, 'tell me, did you reach the city?'

Raleigh shook his head. 'No. The food gave out and the rains came. The men were scared—they were not to blame for that. I tried to finish on foot. I was sure of where it lay. But the ague took me and if two faithful fellows hadn't carried me back, I should have died there. But that's all over. Next year I come back with more stores and more men and then I look to you to join me, Topiawari.'

The old man shook his head. 'For an old man like me to make plans for another year would be foolishness. Next year I shall be with the dead. Nor would I make any promises for my people. The timid ox does not throw off the yoke. You even may work us harm. You may by chance say in the hearing of a Spaniard who knows your talk, "Topiawari fed us. He was poor but gave us what he had." And straightaway the Spaniards will be upon us saying, "You have food to give away? So, then give us food." Or "This hospitality betrays your wealth, Topiawari;

show us the source of your riches or we will put out your eyes."
And returning next year you may not find one of my people to
wish you well. Ah no, you must not look to us for more than
a handful of food given gladly or, perchance, a blow struck
against your enemies in the dark.'

He folded his thin hands together and seemed to sink into
himself a little as he sat on the floor. There was something
indescribably sad, to Raleigh, in his voice, his pose, his
hopelessness. To his senses, sharpened as they were by his own
sense of failure and his bodily weakness, it seemed that the
Indian King bore in his frailty the wrongs of all his people,
spoke with the voice of all the defeated the earth over. The
rain hissed down on the hut roof and leaked through into the
puddles on the floor. All the world seemed desolate and success
only the witch-light luring into the bog.

The man who had gone abegging came back with a laden
woven pannier in each hand. He set them down before Raleigh
and they gaped a little so that he could see the dingy maize
flour with which they were filled.

'I cannot express my thanks. But I will repay, if not you, then
your people,' said Raleigh.

'It is nothing,' said Topiawari; the patient downcast
expression of his face lightened in a half-smile.

In his mind's eye Raleigh saw his study at Sherborne with
the candles lighted and Lisbeth at her work and Walter playing
on the bearskin before the glowing fire. Even if the Queen
rejected his attempt and scorned his company, these could be
his still and his fields, his books, his friends, his unconquerable
hope. Topiawari had nothing. Not all his kindness, his unusual
intelligence, his natural dignity could disguise the fact that he
was an almost naked savage sitting in the mud, waiting for
death. Yet out of his poverty he had given food to strangers
who meant nothing, not even hope to him.

The most sophisticated and subtle man in England,
Elizabeth's one-time darling, habitué of the most glittering,
sceptical court on earth, looked down on the handfuls of coarse
dark meal that had fallen from the hands of people who were

poor as no one in Europe understood the word. He imagined the brown hands scooping up the treasure from the half-empty jars, the fingers closing round it, hovering above the basket and unloosing. Something ached in his throat as the ague ached in his bones. He took the ring that bore his seal from his wasted finger and lifting Topiawari's shrivelled hand he slid it on to one of those dirty ones. Then he laid his hands on the bowed shoulders and kissed him on both cheeks.

'I shall come back next year, Topiawari, my friend. And I shall bring a strong force to set you free. Live for me and for that day.'

'May every one of your hopes flourish, may every day be a joy to you and may your end be peace,' said the old man.

Picking up the sodden baskets Raleigh bowed his tall head under the low doorway of the hut. A tear, part of weakness, part of emotion, ran down his cheek. He had no free hand with which to brush it away; the rain engulfed it as he made his way back to the barge.

Watching the men as they wolfed the wet meal and resumed their wrestling with the river currents he thought, there was his maps, the specimens of ore, the friendly relationship with the Indians, to show for his labours. The expedition could not be termed an utter failure. There was always tomorrow.

The ships were where he had left them. Flowerdew met him as he came aboard.

'Everything in order and ready to sail. Nothing to report except for...'

'Except what, man? Don't keep me from my bed.'

'Berrio escaped sir. Three men lowered a boat to go fishing. A storm came up and they went below to shelter. When it was over they found the boat and the prisoner gone. I'm terribly sorry...'

'Oh well,' said Raleigh, 'it would have been difficult to know what to do with him. We're not at war officially and have no right to prisoners. Sail as soon as you're able.'

He threw himself upon the narrow bunk. No bed in all the world had been so soft.

Chapter 16

London
1595

Shakespeare rubbed the cover of *The Discovery of Guiana* with an appreciative forefinger.

'I wish my Jew would put covers like this on mine,' he said enviously. 'This is a delight to handle as well as to read.'

Raleigh gave a rueful smile; he had published the book himself and given quite as much care to the choice of binding and print as he had to the contents. The whole thing had been meant as a present to the Queen and he had had no word of acknowledgement.

'You enjoyed it?' he asked.

'Oh, very much,' said Shakespeare. I've been waiting at the *Mermaid* to tell you how much. But you never came, so I had to seek you in your lair.'

'I'm glad you did. It's been dull and lonely and I can't face the *Mermaid* anymore. I walked once as far as the door. But clubs are for young men, not for such as I am who see a ghost in every chair.'

Shakespeare looked up sharply. He imagined that Raleigh was referring to Marlowe. He had forgotten Sydney and the others whom death or business had called from the haunts of their youth. There had been a time when he, too, had avoided the *Mermaid*, a time when Marlowe's face would look out of a dim corner and his voice would ring down the dark stairway crying, 'Wait for me. Will, I'm coming your way.' For Marlowe's death had once laid as heavily upon his conscience as if it had been his hand that sped the fatal blow. He knew, though the knowledge was his alone, that he could have saved Marlowe if he had wanted to. There had been a time... But the master mind had discovered a cure for such hauntings. He would turn the horrible experience to good account and the Banquet scene in *Macbeth* had exorcised Marlowe's ghost forever.

'Avaunt and quit my sight; let the earth hide thee! Thy bones are marrowless, thy blood is cold... I am a man again,' wrote Shakespeare and straightaway was. Marlowe mocked him no more from the shadows and his voice was silent on the stairs He said now.

'You mean Marlowe? He brought his fate on himself. It was none of my business. Am I my brother's keeper? His ghost sits in no chairs for me.'

Raleigh had missed Shakespeare's glance and was struck by his instant assumption that Marlowe was under discussion. He remembered hearing of Marlowe's supposed death in a tavern brawl but the story had gone past him as a thing of little moment. He judged now from Shakespeare's manner that he had found in the sorry affair some cause for self-reproach and he was conscious of an envy for the man who had his mind under control so complete that he had not even to pretend innocence. 'His ghost sits in no chairs for me,' had about a ring of a veto. And if conscience could be so controlled why not his nagging ambition that gnawed him day and night?

'I don't know the story, Will,' he said, 'but tell me how you banish his ghost.'

Shakespeare reached out his fine hand for the wine bottle and refilled the Venetian glass that stood at his elbow before he answered.

'Get down on paper the thing that is fretting you. You, for example, if you will bear with me while I say so, are eaten up with a desire to do some great thing, a desire to excel, ambition in other words. If you pictured yourself with another name, in other circumstances, and wrote out of your own ambition the story of an ambitious man, getting at his motives, sparing nothing, your ambition would live upon that paper. And since nothing can come from nothing, your trouble would be eased thereby because some of it would have gone from you into the man you wrote of. That is a strange doctrine, maybe, but I have proved it true. A man may saw up a tree or rear a stack of corn and still be, except for a little sweat, exactly the man he was before he took saw the pitchfork in hand. But with less tangible things, things of the mind, it is otherwise. Didn't Christ Himself say, "Virtue is gone out of me," when the woman with the bloody flux touched His garment? In that case virtue had gone along some invisible channel that is yet as real as the Thames, though not so credible perhaps. And I have written of love until there was no love left in me; I was young then and regretted that it should be so; but now, at a riper age I rejoice that whatever befell me could, unless skill deserted me, be written away.'

He lifted the glass and drank deeply.

'But,' said Raleigh, 'according to that it would be possible to write yourself empty. You could rid yourself of all that made you what you are. In time you would be a cipher.'

'Not at all. The mind of a man is not like a pig's bladder that boys kick round the streets, emptied by the pulling of the string. It is rather a slate. In my case a slate that is continually being wiped clean. But experience writes anew on it and the man is restored but not in his image.'

Raleigh pondered the words, there was truth in them somewhere; there was fallacy too.

'For a clever man, Will, you are singularly unambitious,' he said at last. 'Could I write like you I would want all the world at my feet. I should want to go to Court. I should hunger day and night for recognition from the Queen. That growing pile of manuscript in my room would be a daily thorn in my flesh.'

'There's time for all that,' said Shakespeare comfortably, lifting his wine again. 'And if ever ambition bites me I'll write it away. I'll write of an ambitious man who ruined his life thereby; Wolsey perhaps. And I'll decry ambition, "by that sin fell the angels" I shall write. And the jade will look over my shoulder and say, "This man knows me too well," and flee my sight.' The first psychologist leaned to the grate and gently knocked out his pipe; then smiling he turned to his host.

137

'But I didn't come here to talk of myself. I came to say that I have read your *Discovery* with great interest and pleasure. Has the Queen acknowledged it yet?'

'No, nor never will.'

'Not openly perhaps. But there is this with which you may console yourself, if you seek consolation. If she were not still aware of you, not afraid in her bones that by setting eyes on you she would forget her anger, she would have sent for you. Be well assured that every word you wrote about the possibility of conquering Guiana and holding it with a force of three thousand men has found a home in the store-room of her brain. The doorway may be closed to you, the attics full of the fluff and fury, but let a time of need come and it is to the store-room she will go and there find your name. She'll look coldly on it, maybe, but she'll shake it and dust it and use it. Mark you my words.'

Raleigh looked at his guest. He was suddenly aware that this man knew more of the working of the minds of other men, more of the working of his own, than was common. Now he thought of it, the man had a seer's face. That full broad forehead, from which the hair was already receding, those large, clear, watchful eyes might have belonged Moses or Samuel. There was a queer comfort in the thought that Shakespeare believed that the Queen would remember Raleigh some day. Perhaps in some strange way he knew. That would explain why, with his name unknown and his pocket always empty, he could look on fame and fortune and say, 'There is time for all that.' Such a speech, such a thought would never have occurred to Raleigh's self. Why, he had been as impatient for acknowledgement at twenty as he was now at forty-three. He remembered with sour amusement the agony that Leicester's omission of his name from the account of the taking of Aiva's bullion wagon had caused him. And more or less that kind of agony had been his ever since.

'It's all very well for you, Will,' he said, answering his thought and not his guest's last speech. 'Your work is of the kind that may endure. Why, generations yet unborn may read and act your plays, enjoy your poetry, lap up your wisdom. But unless I get what I want now I shall go down in history, if I go at all, as the man who was so infatuated with Queen Elizabeth that I once put down my cloak to keep her feet dry.'

Shakespeare laughed:

'Did you indeed? Well, that is a charming story to outlive you. Particularly if the historians add, "Striking the gallant youth upon the shoulder with her walking-stick, the Queen exclaimed, 'Rise, Sir Walter.'" It didn't happen like that, I suppose?'

Despite himself Raleigh laughed.

'Hardly. Now what do you think of her, Will? The Queen I mean. There's a subject for your perspicacity to work on.'

'She's simply any ordinary intelligent woman given her head. Half what is called her Machiavellian statesmanship is mere woman's craft in a high place. A crafty woman, and she wasn't clever either, once outwitted me. Men have been very wise, Sir Walter, to keep women within doors tending the babies. If they ever get out, God help us. A woman lawyer, for instance, would outwit Satan.'

Raleigh, glancing at Shakespeare, saw a sudden change come over his face. The eyes opened wide and then veiled themselves, hiding the flash. The playwright picked up his glass and drained it quickly. Then, with no more pretence at conversation, he rose from his chair and said good night as if he was speaking in his sleep.

Raleigh was not to know that Portia had just sprung fully armed from Shakespeare's brain, as Minerva from Jupiter's.

139

Chapter 17

Cadiz and London
1596

The colourless light of the January day fell full on the polished table at which the members of the Council sat. The leaping fires at either end of the room did little to warm the air that seemed heavy and cold as water. The Queen hunched up her shoulders and furtively rubbed her hands together in her lap. Burghley was speaking and she was looking at him, listening to what he was saying about the King of Spain's sickness, but her eyes were not seeing her minister's shrewd grey old face. Instead, she saw the new raw Palace of the Escorial and in it Mary's unsatisfactory husband dying and with his last breath urging upon his people the need to haste in this latest move against renegade England, that he might not die with his vow unfulfilled. He had sworn, that slow, earnest man, that he would bring back the true Church of England and to that, thought Elizabeth, lifting her chin slightly, he had made a loveless marriage with poor Mary, and had then offered himself as a suitor to her sister and, being refused, had settled down to the role of implacable enemy. And now he was dying. For a moment the Queen was almost sorry. It was almost as if a friend had sickened, she seemed to know him so well. His hesitations, his flashes of decision, even his stubborn old-fashioned adherence to his great heavy galleons seemed for that one moment to be endearing revelations of his personality to the woman who had been ever a thorn in his side. Nevertheless, he must be fought. She threw off the feeling that she and all these living men were met here to plan a war upon one who might even now be dead. That was nonsense. Philip might die. But Medina Sidonia, and behind

140

him all the other lords of Spain, the priests and the Cardinals, behind them that Arch-enemy the Pope, were all living and potent and dangerous. She lifted her hands and clasped them upon the table as Burghley finished speaking, then in the even, passionless voice that she reserved for the Council conferences she began to speak herself.

'I agree with the point of view that Lord Burghley has so reluctantly adopted. There must be war. But I do not propose that we should go into it alone. The King of Spain, as you have just heard, intends to strike at Ireland. That, he considers, is the weakest spot of our armour. But he has a weaker. The Netherlands. Oh no,' she said quickly as a murmur of " '82 and '85 all over again" rose from the table. 'I do not propose to shed any more English blood about Zutphen. I suggest that it is time the Netherlanders helped me. They have had our men and our money repeatedly. They owe us money now. Our shores have ever been a sanctuary to their refugees. In Lavenham they weave their wool, in Norwich dye their silk.' There was no need for her to point out that all this hospitality had been offered tongue in cheek. The Flemish silk and woollen weavers were an asset to England, spreading the knowledge of their crafts, but she preferred to think of them as a burden, poor homeless refugees, living upon English charity. 'We will approach the Netherlands, reminding them of past favours and present friendship, and promise that in return for men and ships we will overlook, for the time being, only for the time being—that must be quite clear—the money that they owe us which otherwise must be paid at once that we may fit out ships for ourselves. They have the ships; about the money I am not too sure. I think there is no doubt about their decision. Then we can attack the Spaniards on their own ground, through Cadiz, probably.'

The councillors murmured their agreement and the Queen went on: 'We may as well appoint the commands now, then the fleet can be set in order that there may be no delay when we have word from the Netherlands.'

Burghley took up his pen and the orderly air of the Council

chamber dissolved into a babel of voices as suggestion, counter-suggestion and disagreement met and clashed through the cold air. In this debate the Queen took no part. She sat straight and silent at her end of the table with her cold hands thrust into the shelter of her wide sleeves. Finally, Burghley laid down his pen and handed her a fair copy of the sheet that lay before him covered with names and scratches where other names had been written and then obliterated.

Elizabeth picked up the paper and walked with it to the window. Her eyesight was failing slightly and the afternoon was darkening; and though, in ordinary circumstances, she would have avoided the unflattering light of the north window against which she now stood in revealing profile, she was always sufficiently master of her vanity to leave it outside the door of the Council chamber. She ran her eye over the list. Essex and Howard of Effingham in a joint command; she nodded, that was good. The appointment would appease Essex's uneasy ambition and the joint command would be a check on his impetuosity. Vere and Clifford to command the land forces if the landing were made. Sir George Carew as Master of Ordnance. She frowned at that, as she was not fond of Carew; still, she knew his work. Lord Thomas Howard in charge, under his kinsman of Effingham, of the navy.

Elizabeth looked out of the window and drew her chin through her hand, frowned, pursed her lips and tapped the toe of her shoe on the floor, all signs to those who knew her and were watching that she was on the brink of some decision. She turned over the paper and studied its reverse, blank side; flicked it impatiently and then came back, quickly, to the table. Seizing her gilded peacock pen she drew it once across her lips, dipped it in the ink, wrote a name below Howard's, linked the two with a bracket and pushed the paper across to Burghley. The old man looked at the name, elegantly written, still gleaming wet, and his eyebrows rose. He glanced at the Queen, his breath indrawn, his lips just ready to part in protest; but Elizabeth was watching him and in that twinkling, half-amused, half-pugnacious eye, in that curved close mouth he read a determination that would

break into anger in the first breath of opposition. The breath
that he had drawn for protest served him to say:

'Sir Walter Raleigh is appointed to share Sir Thomas
Howard's command.'

A rustle, like the sound of wind through standing corn,
ran through the room but it took no voice. The Queen's eye
travelled slowly from face to face around the table. Not an eye
of them all took up the challenge.

And so, in due time, as Effingham led down the Channel in
the old Armada veteran the *Ark Royal* with the crimson flag
proudly afloat, following with Essex's once-disputed tawny
colours and Lord Thomas's brilliant blue, came Raleigh in the
Warspite with the white banner riding the wind. Raleigh was
putting to sea in splendour. Below in the cabin the gold tooling
shone on the books that went with him always and the jade
Buddha stared at a bed-cover as near his own colour as Lisbeth
could find at the silk-mercer's. And Raleigh's heart beat high
and hard. He would wring honour from this expedition, wring
it, in Will's phrase, 'from the pale-faced moon.

II

The white-walled Convent of Our Lady of Sorrows stood on
a little eminence in the centre of the city and from the upper
windows the streets between the convent and the harbour
and the harbour itself were clearly visible. All the day before
the Sisters had, in stolen moments, watched the fighting and
reported upon it in surreptitious whispers. But today there
was no time for staring from windows, or wondering upon the
fortunes of war, for the convent had been turned into a hospital
and the little Sisters, who had renounced the sight of men and
the touch of their bodies, were called upon to administer such
comfort as they could to the shattered flesh of the soldiers
who, the Mother assured some who shrank from the sight and
smell of the blood, had 'suffered in the same cause as Christ
Himself'. All the narrow straw pallets were dragged from the
bare, virginal cells and laid out in rows in the sunny south
cloister and all day the Sisters pattered in and out, plastering

gaping wounds with herbal ointments, bandaging broken limbs with strips of sheeting and forestalling fever with infusions of lime and red clover.

From such of their charges as were able and willing to talk they learned details of the battle and by the evening they knew all about the two mad Englishmen who had brought all the Spanish plans of defence to nought. There was a tall one on the ship with the tawny flag who had thrown his hat over the side of the vessel in his excitement and who had ordered down boatload after boatload of men in an attempt to rush a landing. But in that God had defeated him, causing the boats to sink in the piling surf of the harbour. The other was the commander of the ship with the white flag; he was possessed; he was the one who had started the grappling and the others had followed him, sinking their octopus claws into the great new galleons, so piously named after the twelve apostles, so there was nothing to do but to fire the precious vessels in the hope that the flames would destroy the enemy as well. The Sisters paused in their work sometimes to listen to the sound of the firing; and to the new arrivals who were often now suffering from burns as well as wounds, they began to put the tremulous question, 'Will they land, think you?' And at last when the darkness fell, revealing the extent of the glare in the harbour, one soldier, newly admitted, answered the question, not with the familiar 'Assuredly not,' but by the terrifying words, 'They have landed.'

There was little sleep in the convent that night, or indeed in any part of the fallen city. Fighting went on, even in the darkness, around the barricades hastily erected in the street. English and Flemish sailors, afire for loot and blood and rapine, poured tumultuously through the streets; they sacked the wine shops and added the madness of the grape to the madness of victory. Women and children ran screaming towards the untaken parts of the city or, intent upon preserving their property, leaned from the grilles of the tall white houses to drop heavy, copper cooking-pots, stones, stools, boiling water and flaming tow upon the heads of the invaders.

'They will be here in the morning,' whispered one nun to another, as they hurried about their errands; and according to the temperament of the wearer, varied feelings leaped to mastery in the minds beneath the demure coifs. Sometimes many feelings strove for the mastery of a mind, terror, resignation, courage, vaguely sensual wonder. The English had thrown their own nuns out into the world, what might they not do to the nuns of a conquered enemy?

Even in the face of such danger duty must be given pride of place and morning found the Sisters pale and haggard, for they had spent all night without beds, busy in the south cloister with bowls of soup and boxes of ointment and rolls of linen. The Mother Superior had ordered the gate to remain closed and bolted and she herself took up the position at the grille, that she might judge when it should be opened. For urgent as it might be that no Englishman should enter, it was equally important that no one seeking succour should be turned away. But no more wounded found their way there that morning, defeat had broken down all organisation and those who were wounded now must depend upon their own efforts or lie where they had fallen. And presently, realising this, the Mother Superior left the gateway and returned to the temporary hospital. So, it was not until the small doorway in the gate gave way before a party of drunken sailors that the nuns and the wounded knew the enemy had arrived.

It looked, for a moment, like an invasion of devils; they were blackened with smoke and many of them caked with blood as well. The thick English heads, accustomed to mild ale, were aflame from the unaccustomed wine. They carried bundles that had been part of last night's booty, incongruous things like copper lamps, lengths of silk, Spanish boots and bits of tableware. One man wore a woman's comb driven into his bushy beard and most of them had several rings upon their little fingers, sometimes only pushed on as far as the knuckle. They had not spared women then, thought the Superior as she rose from her knees beside a pallet and tried to bring some order into the situation by inquiring what they wanted. She might as well have addressed the wind. The man with the comb in his beard wound his left hand in her rosary, snapping the links at a touch, and holding her firmly between the shoulders with his right, drew her lips into his bearded mouth. For a long moment she was utterly helpless, mentally and physically chained, then the horror and revulsion in her mind found voice in a prayer no longer than a thought, 'God deliver me, strike him dead!' And for an instant she thought that God had answered, added another of His long list of miracles. The hot, terrible mouth fell away from hers and the man dropped, full length at her feet. But deliverance had come from her from the hand of the man she had been tending the moment before; reaching out he had pulled the sailor's feet from under him and brought him down so that his head cracked on the cloister pavement. ('All the same, it was God's answer, through human agency,' she told herself for ever afterwards, thinking of that dreadful day.) A glance at the pandemonium around her prompted her almost to wish, but that would have been a sin of course, that she had worded her prayer, 'Strike me dead,' instead.

Some of the Spaniards whose wounds permitted them to rise were endeavouring to protect the Sisters but scream after scream testified to the failure of their efforts and aided the spread of the panic, while one hysterical giggle proved that Agatha was as unbalanced as the Superior had always feared. Mechanically and quite hopelessly she went to Agatha's aid, for while a screaming woman may be in danger, a giggling one may be on the brink of sin. But she never reached the side of the frail one, for a volley of shot passing overhead turned the whole Inferno into a mass of statuary. The Superior turned her eyes towards the entrance to the cloister. Four men stood there, three with smoking muskets in their hands, the fourth leaning upon a stick, an improvised stick, a rough grey branch of an olive tree. All the nuns and all the sailors had turned that way, too, and the sailors were coming, unsteadily and reluctantly, to attention. To them the man with the stick spoke vigorously and sharply in a language that she could not understand. But she saw the sailors stumble hastily into couples and begin to march in some semblance of order to the gateway. The man with the stick stood aside to let them pass and two of the musket-bearers turned and followed the fellows who were suddenly only drunken men and not inspired devils after all. The man who remained with the musket stood at the gate, the other came forward a painful step or two and she saw that he had been wounded in the leg. The rough bandage twisted around his calf was soaked with blood and it had dripped down his pale silken hose. As he came towards her the man took off his hat and at a respectful distance stopped and bowed to her.

'I apologise, madam, for the behaviour of certain of my countrymen. The wine of yours is to blame. I trust that you have suffered no more than a temporary fright.'

His Spanish was beautiful, she thought, and so was his face, for all it was so pale and drawn with pain.

'It was a great shock,' she said simply; 'I dread to think what might have befallen us had you not appeared. To say that we are grateful expresses nothing of what we feel.'

She became aware of the nuns pressing close, looking at the stranger, looking at him doubtless, her heart smote her, as she had looked, with admiration. She turned and said sharply, 'Be about your duties, redeeming lost time.' Meek as lambs the nuns obeyed her, took up bowls and boxes and bandages from where they had dropped them and went on working as if nothing had happened. She turned back, intending to add something to her thanks; instead, she darted forward and thrust a stool beneath the stranger, who was swaying upon his stick and whose one attendant was running towards him with an expression of alarm.

'It is but faintness, occasioned by loss of blood. Do not concern yourself, madam,' he said faintly.

'But I must concern myself over the suffering of so good a friend,' said the little woman firmly. 'Would you like to lie down?—any one of these'—she pointed to the recumbent figures—'would be proud to give you his mattress.'

'Indeed, no. I am in no need of a bed. I am better already; such faintness soon passes.'

He smiled up into her bothered little face, so earnest and childlike under its grubby white bands.

147

'Some cordial then,' she suggested and, rather to humour her than from any faith in her innocuous potion, he said:

'That would be welcome, indeed.'

He was pleasantly surprised when, after darting away and returning at incredible speed considering her garments, she put into his hand a little silver beaker of choice Benedictine. Encouraged by the pleasure with which he sipped his cordial she suggested that a new bandage upon his wound would be more comfortable, but the stranger shook his head.

'It is very good of you but I must waste no more time. God knows what mischief some of those fellows will be in.

'You will see a doctor, soon?' she persisted.

'Faith, no. He would but bleed me. And sooth, that has been done already. Yon fellow with the cutlass was both wounder and healer at once.'

Once more he smiled at her and she could hardly hear his answer that they would have no more to fear from wandering bands of sailors. He had been rounding them up since daybreak and judged that her visitors were the last of them. She wished that he could have stayed amongst the patients in the sunny cloisters. How pleasant to have ministered to him, to have brought out the honey and killed one of the hens in the pen for his use! Foolish and wicked thought. There would be penance to do for this. He was bowing again, on the verge of departure, when a thought struck her.

'If you would tell me your name. You are a stranger and were an enemy but you have been our friend this day and as such we would pray for you.'

He smiled at her and immediately she knew that he was not of the many benighted ones who despised the prayers of the faithful.

'Raleigh is my name. Walter Raleigh. And I am proud and happy to have served you.'

He replaced his hat and turned, leaning heavily upon the olive-branch, and walked slowly but doggedly towards the doorway and through it.

The little Mother Superior stood for a moment, repeating

the harsh and awkward syllables that made up his name. Then she went slowly and closed the door behind him. The door in the gateway closed easily but one in her mind that she would have given much to close remained open. She thought of him often and often did penance for the thought. And it was part of her punishment, she considered, that the face of Christ as she had always imagined it, clear and shining, should every now and then become obscured by another face, pale and narrow, racked with pain but smiling. Sometimes there was a hat above the face, a jaunty hat with a feather. And then her mind would recoil with horror. Who ever heard of the Blessed Lord in a hat? A very confused and distressing state of mind for an earnest and simple woman. But gradually, with the years and the presence, her memory of the strange English face faded and it was only rarely that the imagined face of Christ called to mind, through some mysterious and unholy channel, the name of Walter Raleigh.

III

Twenty-four hours later Lord Howard of Effingham sat in his cabin facing the distasteful task of writing a report of the action. He was falling gradually into the old man's habit of talking to himself when he was alone and troubled and he was now muttering, 'Spoilt Puppy', 'Jackanapes', 'Head-long fool', at intervals. The difficulty was to keep such phrases out of his official letter, for he was an honest old man and wont, in most circumstances, to speak his mind. Still, he was sufficiently clear-sighted to see that now, in the middle of a rather delicate report of an only half-successful action, was no time for attacking Essex who was, when all was said, dearer to the Queen than any other member of the expedition. Yet it was, thought the old man, laying down his pen and muttering again, entirely that young fool's fault that so many lives had been thrown away. He thought again, hot with anger, of Essex's behaviour over the launching of those ill-fated boats. No fewer than four had he ordered down and every one had been swamped and every man in them drowned. It was not the loss of the men or the

boats, though, that had most annoyed Howard, boats were built
to sink at one time or another and men were born to die; but
the abortive attempts at landing had informed the citizens of
Cadiz that the English were not out for a cut-and-run naval
engagement but bent upon landing. Consequently everything
of value had been smuggled out of the city long before Raleigh
with his grappling tactics had actually effected a landing. And
after sacking Cadiz the successful leader must now sit down
and write to his Queen to inform her that the loot taken was
far, far from paying the cost of the expedition. From Peru, from
the Indies, from the East the treasure galleons had borne down
upon that city to lay their wealth upon the limestone quay and
yet the English had only found there a few hundred pounds'
worth of hides, a quantity of church silver and similar things of
little value. 'We could have taken as much from Copenhagen,'
Howard muttered. It would have been such a relief to have
been able to write, 'My Lord Essex ruined the expedition
financially and was only restrained by Sir Walter Raleigh and
myself from ruining it in every other way.' How gladly he
would have sealed a letter containing that sentence. But he put
away the temptation. He would have quite enough to explain
as it was; he and Essex, as joint commanders, must tell the
same story, that by some chance the Spaniards had received
warning of the impending attack and had cleared the city. He
must forget the long mule trains that had been seen leaving the
city within an hour of Essex's first premature boat launching.
But, he thought, taking up his pen again, his letter, which dared
not blame, should not praise the Queen's favourite. No, all the
praise was going to the man that had rowed so rapidly from the
Warspite to the *Ark Royal* and had shouted, 'Can you see what
the young fool is at? Unless you, as Admiral, command this to
cease, he'll have drowned all his men without striking a blow.
We must aim at the ships first, then at the city.'

Walter Raleigh was going to be the hero of the Admiral's letter.
And perhaps, in some obscure way, that might even please her
Majesty. After all, she had been fond of him once and had herself
appointed him to this expedition. He might prove, even yet, an

effective foil to Essex. 'Though he, too is a conceited fellow but not, like the other, a rash fool. I like him little better. But the world is run for such nowadays,' The old man twitched his nostrils and sniffed contemptuously. Next time he spoke aloud he was trying over the sound of what he hoped was a stately phrase.

And while Howard wrote, and paused, and crossed out, and tried over his phrases, Sir George Carew was writing his private impression of the affray for Cecil's uneven eyes. Carew was a fluent writer and, although no lover of Raleigh, a sensitive judge of the way that the winds of favour were likely to blow. 'I do assure your honour that Sir Walter's service was so praiseworthy that many of his former enemies do hold him in great estimation.' Did Carew speak of himself or of another? 'That which he did at sea could not be bettered.' From cousin Carew that was high praise and Cecil, always on the look-out for a spoke to put into Essex's giddy wheel, read the letter with pleasure and with pleasure made his plans.

Raleigh came back to Durham House, nursing his leg and his disappointment about the paucity of the plunder, and amongst the first of his visitors there was the nervous, crafty, far-sighted man who had been so pleased to apologise for a disloyal word when it was a question of sharing a responsibility.

IV

Lisbeth came too. She came unwillingly, for she hated London as much as she loved Sherborne. One was the abode of enmity and unrest and danger: the other the place of peace. She had never forgotten that a casual word had once thrown them both into the Tower and every moment of her visit was clouded by the fear that the Queen might hear of it, might suffer a revival of that old jealousy, might say another of those fatal, casual words. Still she came; she was eager to see Walter, to assess the damage he had sustained and to show him their son. Those were the reasons that she gave herself as she made the difficult journey and faced the dreaded city. The deep inner reason for her coming was hidden, as yet, even from her.

Walter had grown from a dimpled baby into a sturdy little boy with his hair curled up into a tuft of his crown. He was still tanned with the sun of the past summer and looked, with his fair hair and lashes, rather like a little golden image of a boy. He was shy with his father at first but soon, with smiles and gurgles of pleasure, recognised his old play-fellow.

Raleigh, crawling about the floor with the child astride his back, forgot both his years and his stiffness. Lisbeth watched them and wondered—would the boy succeed where she had apparently failed in luring the father back to Sherborne's peaceful acres? She had talked much of the estate, telling of the harvest, just gathered, and the stock and the timber; but though Raleigh had listened with courteous interest it was plain to her that his mind was elsewhere and that her words were waking in him no desire to return. He began to mention things that he wanted her to tell to Meere, the steward. Ask him this, remind him of that. And every message to that inoffensive and efficient man was an arrow aimed at her hope, until at last it died like Edmund under the Danish barbs. And when hope was dead, she could speak.

'Has the Queen sent for you yet, Walter?'

'Not yet.'

'You think that she will,'

'I know it. Cecil is busy in my cause.'

'In *your* cause! Since when has he been any one's friend but his own?'

'Don't be bitter, love. If you knew what it does to your mouth, to your eyes. You become a stranger.'

'I *am* a stranger. But whose is the fault? My mouth, you say. If you knew what this absence does to my heart...'

'There is no cause for absence. This will be your home as long as it is mine. Stay here.'

'I hate it here. The boy thrives at Sherborne. Besides, the place needs a master. Every day there is something that only you, or in your absence I, could do. The whole countryside sickens because those who own it prefer to be toadying it at Court when they should be ruling at home.'

152

'You enjoy that, don't you Lisbeth?'

'What?'

'Being a little Queen at Sherborne?'

'Why judge all women by her?'

'By whom?'

'Her. The Queen. Or if you must apply her measure to us all, think of me. Do you think that if someone younger and fairer than I, for I am that to her, took you from me I'd ever forgive her? And she will never forgive me. As long as I remained here, she would be watching... and one day... do you remember Amy Robsart and the stairs? Whose hand was it that sped her? I can't stay here, Walter.'

'Your fear preys on your nerves and eats away your reason, my love. Leicester was the Queen's lover or the world lies.'

'Any you?'

'Lisbeth!'

'Forgive me. I let my tongue run away with me. And yet what else can I think? Why should she have taken your marriage so ill that for four years she could not bear to look on you while Essex she forgave almost the next day? Why should you linger here now like a patient suitor waiting her word? Why do I feel that she has only to look on me to blast me?'

'You imagine it all. The loneliness of Sherborne has bred all these fears in you,' said Raleigh patiently. Lisbeth saw that she was as far from understanding as ever. She left her chair and fell on her knees at his feet.

'Listen to me, Walter. Let me speak once and I will be silent for ever. You threw Guiana at her like a challenge. She ignored it. Everyone's tongue is loud in praise for your conduct at Cadiz. She alone is silent. And so you sit here waiting. The years are passing. You are a young man no more. The ague comes on you unawares. Now you are lame, too. Come back and live at peace. What does it matter? The great and the obscure, they sleep at last in the dust and none can tell one from the other. What is fame or honour? A little passing glory in the eyes of men as human and frail as yourself. Will one of the men whom you call your friends love you as Walter would if you spent

153

an hour teaching him to ride or read? Will the Queen herself ever love you as I do? You'll eat your heart out, my darling, searching and waiting and striving for the wrong things and in the end, you will be naked...'

Raleigh jumped to his feet and pushed past her, striking his hands together with a gesture curiously like the Queen's when she was angered.

'No more, I beseech you.' His voice was urgent and Lisbeth knew that some of her words had found a mark; but when she looked up at him, something in his face brought her to her feet. 'There may be truth in what you say. In any hundred words there must be some truth. But I have chosen my path. I married you because I loved you; I love you still but control me you shall not. I shall stay here until the Queen sends for me. If you care to stay, stay and be welcome. Everything that is your due shall be yours, *malgré* Queen, man or devil. Or if you choose Sherborne, go there and rule as my wife, as I shall always esteem you. But in God's mercy spare more of this.'

Lisbeth tilted her chin. She was defeated. Her reason for coming had been revealed to her. She had hoped to take him back with her. The obsession was too strong. She was defeated; but she was not beaten. There was still Sherborne and the boy.

'I shall leave tomorrow,' she said in her usual quiet voice, strangely quiet after her impassioned pleading. 'Someone will certainly tell the Queen. How pleased she will be!'

Raleigh struggled for speech. There must be something that could be said that would make all well; but he could not think of it. Lisbeth went out of the room while he was still struggling.

Next day she left for Sherborne. They parted like friends whom custom had staled: and probably Elizabeth knew all about it, for her spies were everywhere, and very soon after she sent for Raleigh.

Chapter 18

Hampton Court
1597

Elizabeth was seated amongst her ladies. One of them was plucking at the strings of a lute and a boy was singing:

> *'Though roses were opened*
> *The winter returned.*
> *The snowflakes fell down,*
> *Where the young roses burned.*
>
> *Like you were those roses*
> *So icy at heart.*
> *Your lips are the petals,*
> *Soft pink, just apart.*
>
> *And where the sweet warmth*
> *Of the summer should be,*
> *There is only the frozen*
> *Hard heart turned to me.'*

'A very foolish song,' said the Queen, without choler. 'If that is the best you can do, be silent.'

There was silence for a moment, then Elizabeth turned her head sharply and said, 'Go on, sing. Am I to sit here, hobbled by my foot and blinded with headache, and have nothing to distract me? Find a better song and sing.'

The silks she wore rustled as she turned back in her chair and lifted her hand to her aching head. The lady with the lute and the singing boy conferred together in a frightened whisper. Then, with wary eyes on their mistress, they began again.

> *'Love comes tripping down the way,*
> *Hey ho, sing hey ho.*
> *Will he go or will he stay?*
> *Not the wisest one can say.*
> *Hey ho, sing hey ho.'*

Elizabeth pressed her lips together as if she were nearing the end of patience but the next verse, in its first word, promised better.

> *'Honour comes and Honour goes,*
> *Hey ho, sing hey ho.*
> *Where it comes from no one knows,*
> *None can tell how honour goes.*
> *Hey ho, sing hey ho.'*

The Queen put her other hand to her head, driving her knuckles into her temples as though she were crushing the enemy. The clear boy's voice went on:

> *'Wealth's a goodly thing to gain,*
> *Hey ho, sing hey ho.*
> *Will it buy our youth again?*
> *Spare us just an hour of pain?*
> *Hey ho...*

The Queen leaped from her chair and the sudden movement sent such a pang through her throbbing head that for a moment she felt as murderous as she looked. In a single stride she was beside the singer, had seized the lute and broken it across his head and flung the pieces full in the face of the player.

'Is there no song but that? You do it a-purpose. God's blood! The very Bedlamites would know better than to sing of pain to a woman who was crazed with it. Out of my sight all of you.

156

Out of my sight, I say. Go and sing of roses and youth and honour to such as to have a good leg to stand on while they kick your behinds with the other. Would I had...'

She stumbled back to her chair as the attendants scuttled through the door. She folded her arms on the back of the chair and laid her forehead on them. Bedlamites, forsooth. She would be one herself soon if this aching in her temples did not abate. How many mad people, she wondered, had been driven into that state by their aching heads? Tomorrow she would inquire and if there were any such they should not be whipped to drive out the devil but should be laid in cool, darkened rooms with vinegar clouts on their heads... They were not the Queen of England, they had no need to keep upright. A few tears of self-pity ran down over her painted cheeks and lost themselves in the crumpled folds of flesh between her chin and her ruff.

She realised that she was crying and stopped abruptly. Of late she had found self-control easy to lose and perilously nigh impossible to regain; and tonight she had arranged an interview that was going to demand more of her than she cared to admit. She began to regret the fit of temper that had made her drive out her attendants. She would have liked Raleigh to come upon her when she was in high spirits and surrounded with chatter and merriment, defying her years and the frailty of her flesh. And then tonight this headache had assailed her. She determined suddenly that she would not see him, nor Cecil who was supposed to be bringing him. With an impetuous movement she leaped to her feet and went to the door. It was heavy and stiff on its hinges and resisted her for a second. Only a second but long enough for her heart to think, 'This is what it means to be old, the very doors defy me.' She threw all her strength into the second effort and the door swung open, to reveal John Best on the point of knocking upon it; he had his hand raised and behind him Cecil and Raleigh.

The sight of the Queen, unattended and in an obvious hurry, surprised them all. John Best opened his mouth but before a sound could come from it Raleigh had pushed him aside and had thrown himself on his knees at Elizabeth's feet.

Almost automatically the Queen stretched out her hand to him. He seized it and lifted it up to his lips. Still without speaking Elizabeth put out her other hand behind her and took hold of the half of the door that had remained closed.

'Thank you, Sir Robert, I won't keep you,' she said graciously; and laying her hand upon Raleigh's shoulder as he still knelt before her, she seemed to pull him in one movement to his feet and into the room behind her. The door swung in the faces of the two astonished men and Cecil, with raised eyebrows and shoulders, took himself out of the palace.

Behind the closed door the Queen stopped beneath the chandelier that held twenty candles and taking Raleigh's chin in her hand raised his face to the light. Not a line that time and hardship and thwarted hope had graved there escaped her eyes. The white hairs that had begun to show at the temples drew from her a curious smile, half tenderness, half pleasure.

'Four years have dealt harshly with you, Walter,' she said, and the voice that had been a raucous screech ten minutes before was now the voice of a crooning dove.

'They were spent in your service, your Majesty,' said Raleigh and, in his turn, he looked at her. He looked long and deliberately and then said, 'With you they passed as trackless as the twenty before them.'

'They have not robbed of your silver tongue, at least,' said the Queen; and then the pain, forgotten in the moment of excitement, assailed her in double force. She put her hand to her head again, pleased at that moment that the hand, still, would bear the closest inspection, and staggered to her chair. 'It is my head,' she muttered dolefully, 'it has been very troublesome all evening.' She closed her eyes but opened them again, wary as a cat, as Raleigh made a movement to fumble in his pocket of his doublet. With great care he drew out a packet which, unfolded, disclosed a pinch of brownish powder. He held it towards her. 'If you would but this upon your tongue and swallow it I guarantee that in five minutes or less the pain would be gone.'

Elizabeth looked at the powder cautiously and then at Raleigh's face. All her life she had been in danger of dagger or poison and caution was now deep-rooted in her. Besides, her conscience warned her that she had dealt hardly with this man... and nothing was too unlikely... 'What is it?' she asked.

'An Indian drug more effective than any we know. I have never been without it since I tried it first.'

'I have been warned against strange nostrums,' Elizabeth began but just then her head gave a sickening thud and she put out her hand. 'Give it here. As well as dead as suffer such agonies.'

''Tis perfectly safe. I would not offer it else,' said Raleigh.

Elizabeth opened her mouth so that, watching, he could see the line where the paint ended upon her lips. The powder covered her tongue, she swallowed hard and closed her eyes. Raleigh stood silent. For four years he had waited for this moment and fortune had arranged that in it he should be able to serve her. He sent a grateful thought winging to poor old Topiawari who had introduced him to this and other remedies. The silence continued for about three minutes and then the Queen opened her eyes.

''Tis a miracle,' she exclaimed, and now there was a look of genuine wonder as well as relief in her eyes. 'Its all gone. Have you known of this long, Walter?'

'Some months. Had I but known that you were in such need of it I would have brought it unbidden. Even if you had cut off my presumptuous head the next day.'

'You needed never to fear that. It is much too handsome a head and much too full of wisdom. Where did it gain this fragment?' She touched the empty packet with a pointed finger.

'In Guiana...'

'From Topiawari, King of Arromaia?'

'Your Majesty read the book?'

'I read it. There was one part of it ill done, slurred over.'

'And that?' asked the author, strangely humble.

'There was no mention of this miraculous powder which has cured not only my maddening head but eased also the pain in my leg.'

'And had there been?' asked Raleigh, with one of his old mocking smiles.

'It would have spared me much ill ease,' said the Queen demurely.

Raleigh laughed and after a moment's rather puzzled hesitation Elizabeth joined him. Did the man think so lightly of her favour that the thought of all those wasted months could move him to mirth? Something of interest, which she had lacked sorely of late, moved in the royal breast. This was so subtle a man. Set midway between the droning sobriety of her old councillors and the boyish gaucheries of her young favourites his personality shone for a moment, rich and mellow like well-matured wine. She promised herself much of his company in the immediate future.

'And how is your wife?' was her next question.

'She is well. She is at Sherborne.'

'At Sherborne, eh?' said Elizabeth, raising her darkened eyebrows, 'and the children, are they at Sherborne, too?'

'The child is. There is but one, a boy.'

'Only one? Has the marriage bed lost its charm so soon?'

Raleigh flushed darkly. This had been bound to come, but...

'Lisbeth detests London,' he said shortly.

The Queen drew her hand across her mouth as if to wipe away a smile that had come unbidden.

'And you detest Sherborne?'

'I could hardly say so if it were true, Sherborne was your gift. But you are not at Sherborne.'

And that, although flatteringly said, was true enough as a reason for his preference for London: and the Queen was pleased by the picture that it called up of herself as a bright light around which men hovered like moths while their wives sat neglected in the outer darkness at places like Sherborne.

She reverted to business with a sudden twist of her attention that seemed to bring about one of those astonishing changes in her actual physical appearance. With eyes shrewd and hard and hands folded in her lap she settled herself to talk and to listen.

'And what news of Guiana since your return, Sir Walter?'

'Bad,' he said bluntly. 'We missed the tide there. Had you struck at once, as I suggested, with a couple of thousand men the land would have been ours now. As it is I sent Keymis back with two ships, all I could afford, but they couldn't get up the river farther than where the Caroni joins it, Berrio had fortified the junction.'

'That would never have happened if you hadn't allowed Berrio to escape,' said Elizabeth, swift to throw the blame onto any shoulders but her own.

'That may be true,' Raleigh admitted, 'but I could hardly have taken him on the expedition with me; and he escaped during my absence. Besides, it was a question whether I had the right to bring him home. It was not an open war.'

'Then why destroy St. Joseph?'

'It was necessary. You know the saying about half a loaf?'

'And the specimen ores, have they been tested?'

'About half have been proved to contain gold. I marked the localities on the maps. Next journey I shall waste no time nosing around the red soil district.'

'And the land is as rich as you believe?'

'I believe that it has stores of gold that have never been tapped.'

'And the natives, they seemed friendly?'

'I was careful for that. The row was well hoed before me by their hatred of the Spaniards and I watered it well. I never but once took what I didn't pay for, and the one time was when we were starving and the Indians fed us of their charity. I never abused one, however stupid he might be. Above all I never allowed one of my men to touch one of their women. The Spaniards have made a great mistake there. The land is full of half-breeds; and although the morals of the people seem strange to us, actually their own codes are very rigid and the forcible infringement of them has caused more ill feeling than the robberies, I believe.'

'But their feeling for the English is friendly?'

'That was the only cheering thing about the report that Keymis brought back. That the natives asked after me and sent me messages of good will and affection.'

'Well, I hope sincerely that their loyalty lasts. There will be need of it. The war with Spain is far from ended... Tomorrow, since my leg is better, we will go riding and talk more of these matters. Meantime your deputy would be glad to be relieved of his duties as Captain of the Guard.'

So, the dream that he would one day stand again at her door and wear his silver armour in her sight came true. Lisbeth was wrong: one strove and dreamed and suffered but the coming true of but one dream was more than payment for all that one had done and borne.

Raleigh and the Queen rode side by side through the green meadows starred with buttercups and daisies, along lanes where the scent of the wild roses mingled with the fragrance of new hay.

Raleigh and the Queen danced under the chandeliers until the warmth of the candles and their own exercise drove them out into the cool gardens where the roses shone under the moon. Raleigh and the Queen played cards until the candles wilted and had to be renewed. All the time they talked and schemed and laughed; two subtle, rare minds that had been very lonely apart.

And down at Sherborne Lisbeth kilted up her gown and ran nimbly beside young Walter as he learned to ride on the small pony whose fat sides his own sturdy legs were still too short and stout to grip. She dared not trust the task to any one else for, as the weeks and months drew out, she realised more and more that Walter was all that remained to her of the strange, dark, hag-ridden man she had married. Yet she must bring up her son as his father would have wished, had his desires ever turned to homely things. So, she taught the boy his letters with a stick upon the ground, or the coiling peel of an apple or with sugar sticks which the dutiful scholar would devour as soon as the lesson was ended. And in all she did she had little reason to think that she was preparing perhaps the finest offering that was ever laid at any man's feet. Raleigh, busy amongst the great, Effingham's friend, Essex's boon companion, the Queen's 'dear Walter', seemed little in need of devotion from two flushed and tousled beings capering about the Sherborne meadows speechless with mirth and the effort of catching a small frisky pony who refused to come at lesson-time.

162

Chapter 19

Hampton Court
November 1599

Summer sped away, Raleigh accompanied Essex upon his unlucky expedition to Flores and managed to wrest for himself what honour there was to be had in the ill-fated trip. Late autumn found Elizabeth lingering at Hampton Court. Generally, she left it by the time that the great vine had ripened its burden, but this year she lingered, apparently unable to make up her mind to face the journey. She was annoyed with Essex and though anger could spur her into action beyond her strength, annoyance wasted her force. She complained bitterly of the cold. Old Topiawari's drugs could deaden the pains that racked her head and shrunken limbs but they could not keep her warm. She avoided the great chambers where the hangings were ever aswing in the draught and had two small rooms fitted for her use with great fires always blazing on the open hearths. Over her rustling silks and heavy whispering velvets she wore a cloak of ermine with a high stiff collar upturned around her neck. In repose she looked like a snow woman finished with a carnival mask.

Raleigh found her so one November morning and was struck for the first time by the thought that she was, after all, only a mortal woman and that the time was approaching when Death would 'call for her every day' as he had done for the old dirty Indian king in his dripping adobe hut. Raleigh himself was feeling fit and ageless. It was a frosty morning and the white cloud of his horse's breath had come up and mingled with the thin stream of his own as he rode. The sun had risen redly and glittered on the rime frost of the fields as he came along the river

163

road and he had sung the verse about honour coming none knew how and going knew whither without realising its sting. Who cared whence it came or how it went if it were but here today? And for him it was, in his hand. He had landed at Fayal, against all orders, before Essex had arrived and when his men refused to go forward into the teeth of the Spanish fire, he had waved his white scarf and shouted and run ahead himself. Two, ten, twenty men had joined him and the rest had followed them like sheep. That had been a moment to live for, and to live again in memory, with the shots rattling out and the bullets striking the rocks all above them. Essex's anger had been a sight to see, too, when he had arrived too late and had threatened court martial and had been defied. The mutual apologies and the dinner together afterwards had also been sweet. And now, because he had been busy for some days and left the Queen to her own devices, she had sent for him in haste, saying that she needed his advice. And here he was, aglow with the hard riding, standing before her as she stretched one hand towards the fire while with the other she waved away her women and signed for him to be seated.

'I have been waiting for you,' she said peevishly.

'Your Majesty, I received your message last night at midnight and set out as soon as it was light.'

'I mean for the past week. You haven't been in your house for a week. Where have you been?'

If she had said, 'Have you been at Sherborne?' her meaning would have been no clearer.

'I've been to St. Ives.'

'In God's name, what for?'

'There was a talk of a Spanish scare. The Sheriff sent for me to hearten the folk, which I did easily.'

The Queen looked at him, her outthrust jaw and sulky eyes belying her thoughts. He was a man to hearten a flock of sheep. Lame he might be, a prey to the ague, greying at the temples but that flashing eye, showing a little more white than ordinary, like the eye of a spirited colt, and that ringing voice: no wonder the men followed him at Fayal. Were she a woman to be led, this would be her leader.

'I'm in a nasty coil again, Walter,' she said. 'And that's God's truth.'

'What is it?'

'Three days before Robert landed, I made Howard of Effingham Earl of Nottingham. 'Twas his due. He is an old man and has served me well. Now he will precede Robert in Parliament and Robert is sulking like a baby. I cannot withdraw Howard's honour... but I must have peace about me. Think of a way for me, Walter.'

Raleigh brushed his hand over his face and then propped up his chin. He thought; but not immediately about a solution to the pretty little problem. What a fool Essex was! His constant petulance was such as a capricious young girl might show towards an elderly and infatuated lover. Reverse the sexes, thought Raleigh, and that was the exact position. But caprice could overreach itself and the Queen was Henry Tudor's daughter. There was a point beyond which she must not be tried. Give Essex but rope enough; let him imagine that his wildest demands would be humoured, then, like an unbroken dog, he might work his own ruin. And while the surface of Raleigh's mind was occupied by thoughts like these, deep down, far and under the layers of craft and annoyance at Essex's power over the Queen, beneath his hope that by good advice he might cement his own favour, there moved unbidden a thought that would have annoyed Elizabeth beyond all bearing, had he revealed it. It was a thought of pity for her, so old, so frail to be bothered by questions of precedent by a cub young enough to be her grandchild. It was the most real, the most manly thought in all that master mind but it gained no attention. It passed through and was gone, a pale ghost of the sensitive onlooker at life that Raleigh, in a less robust age, might have been. And as it passed unnoticed the solution to the problem leapt into the upper storey of that populous house, his mind.

'I have it,' he said. 'The office of earl marshal has been vacant since Shrewsbury died. Give Essex that. A marshal takes precedence of an admiral, so there you are.'

Elizabeth smiled. 'You are a genius, Walter. I'll do that. Then perhaps I shall have a little peace. Now if you could but think of something that would warm me.'

'I could think of something; the question is, would you do it?'

The Queen shivered, 'Anything,'

'A tot of rum, then. And a walk in the sun.'

'The wind would kill me.'

'Not it. Will you try it?'

He stood by her while she gulped down the burning spirit and called for stouter shoes. Then, with her leaning heavily on his arm with her own that felt like a well-swaddled stick, he led her out to where an old red wall kept away the wind and attracted the warmth of the pale sun. There he kept her moving about until with her own hands she unhooked the collar of the fur cloak.

'Warmer?' he asked smiling.

'I must admit it, yes.'

After that they moved more slowly and Raleigh looked above him and saw clinging to the wall one belated rose, its pink petals browned at the edge and its green leaves purpled with the frost. He jumped up at it and brought it away in his hand. He sniffed it and offered it to the Queen.

'There is no rose that smells so sweetly as one that the frost has fingered,' he said.

The glance with which he said it encouraged the vain old woman to seek and find the metaphor in the speech. Much restored by the walk, the rum or his company she was suddenly strong enough to order the Court's return to Whitehall on the morrow. Raleigh returned to Durham House assured that it was only a question of time before he was made a Privy Councillor. Essex had but to take one slight advantage of the extra rope that Elizabeth had, on Raleigh's advice, paid out to him and a seat in that Council would be empty.

Chapter 20

Essex House, The Strand
1601

The woman who had been Lettice Knollys and Lady Sydney and who was now Lady Essex was walking about in Essex House. She had ordered candles to be lighted in every room and corridor and now she was walking through them with the set, abstracted gaze of a sleep-walker. Her servants had obeyed her orders about the candles and were now huddled together around the fire in the kitchen and had she rung every bell in the house not one of them would have ventured into her presence again that night. For ten days, ever since Essex had been dragged away on a Sunday morning to answer a charge of treason she had not been to bed or eaten more than a crust of bread standing at the table. The servants regarded her as bewitched or, rather, as deep in some spell of witchcraft herself. The ghastly pallor of her face, her shrunken figure and glaring eyes terrified them and now, as the wind rushed through the house banging the doors that she left open on her journey, they drew nearer the fire and feared to go to bed.

Presently there came a hammering upon the street door. Not one of the servants stirred. The mistress had been praying the devil to save the master and they had no reason to doubt that here he was in person to seal the bargain. The knocking continued for Sir Robert Cecil, standing in the street, could see that every window was lighted and could not understand why his summons should go unanswered. And presently Lettice herself heard it and came to the door. At the sight of Cecil she put her hand to her breast and reeled against the door-post.

'I must speak with you a moment,' he said. And she replied

167

with menace in her voice, 'And I with you.' She led him into a little room near the door where Essex had been wont to transact his business and see his many suitors for favours. There was no fire there and the February evening was raw and cold; but Lettice stood in her short-sleeved gown impervious to cold and fatigue alike.

'It's over?' she asked.

Cecil nodded.

'And the sentence?'

'The worst. To be hung, drawn and quartered...' Lettice screamed, and the sound made the servants clutch one another and shudder. Cecil continued smoothly, 'But the Queen will remit that and he will be beheaded in an honourable manner. I will see to it.'

'There is no chance of a reprieve?'

'None whatever,' said Cecil, and he might have added as before, 'I will see to it.' For now that Essex was down, it was not going to be Cecil's upturned thumb that would save him. Far from it.

Whether Lettice guessed that or not, she had decided that time had come to show her hand. She laid one hand on the bosom of her gown and Cecil heard the crackle of paper.

'I have here a paper left by my husband that contains the details of a plot that you and Raleigh are concerned in to make the Infanta of Spain Queen of England. Tonight, unless you and I come to terms, I take it to the Queen.'

She eyed Cecil narrowly but saw no blenching in that narrow olive face.

'That would do your husband small service. You would be silencing the one tongue that can save him from disembowelment. Besides, I doubt whether the Queen would care. Who succeeds her interests her little. It is the date of succession that is her concern.'

Lettice narrowed her eyes.

'Then we must look to the future, you and I. The Queen might not care about the plot as such but it would ruin you with her. You admit that?'

Cecil nodded.

'You admit also, it would be foolish to deny to me, that you are in communication with the Scots King who will claim the throne, whether he gets it or not?'

Again, Cecil inclined his head.

'Then this is my bargain. I shall keep the paper and say nothing about it until the Queen is dead. In return you will use every grain of influence you possess to save Robert. And then, the moment that the Scot makes his claim good you will use all your power to break Raleigh.'

Cecil pondered.

'What is your grudge against the man? He asked at last.

'He was ever Robert's enemy and mine,' said Lettice shortly.

'I see. You hold the paper until we can use it against Raleigh alone. And I go to the Queen now to plead for the Earl. Is that it?'

This time Lettice nodded. Then after a moment's thought she added; 'If that sentence is carried out as it stands, I shall go mad and may expose all in my frenzy.'

'Be assured that I shall do all in my power to persuade the Queen to mercy.'

Lettice relapsed into her sleep-walking state and Cecil let himself out into the street. He had walked a good way before he remembered that he had not even asked to see the paper. He hesitated and half-turned. But it was of no matter. He had only promised to do what was in his mind already. Lettice had threatened him into no action that he was not prepared to take before he had knocked on that door. He would beg a seemly execution for Essex because so shameful a death for a Privy Councillor and an Earl would be an evil precedent and a thing that Elizabeth would repent the moment it was done; and he had promised to work against Raleigh and that he had already planned to do at the new King's accession, for Raleigh was no comfortable rival though he was a useful tool.

So Cecil went to call upon the Queen and missed meeting the man he had just promised to ruin by the fraction of a moment. Raleigh had been present at the trial with forty of his guardsmen. He had heard the accusation brought against the young Earl; had listened to Essex's muddled and contradictory defence; had seen the Lord Steward snap his staff in two as he pronounced the awful sentence.

All through the day his mind had been busy, working backwards and forwards. He remembered the morning, so long ago, so far off down the misty path of years when Essex and he, thirsting for one another's blood, had faced one another across a space of dewy grass. He thought of Essex's marriage and how it had brought him hotfoot from Ireland and opened the second period of his favour. He recollected that morning at Hampton when he had advised the Queen to make Essex the earl marshal. What effect had that upon the young hothead's subsequent behaviour? None could tell. Essex had been sent to Ireland, had failed there and returned unbidden. He had thrust himself upon Elizabeth before she was dressed and had been forbidden ever to come to Court again. Then, instead of acting as Raleigh in identical circumstances had done, with cunning and patience, he had made some hair-brained plot against her and this was the end. Essex was being led off to the Tower with the headsman behind him, carrying his axe with its edge turned towards its promised victim. There was much food for thought in that story and Raleigh's manner was absent as he dismissed his guardsmen and left a place of justice. As a poet he was touched by the sudden ending of a bright and meteoric career, as a man he was sorry for the horrible fate that was the price of foolishness; but as Raleigh he was most concerned with the fact that there was now an empty chair in the Privy Council.

Chapter 21

The Tower Yard
Ash Wednesday 1601

Ash Wednesday and a frosty morning. Every blade of grass,
every thin twig bleached with frost. The sun, silvery pale,
shining for a moment and then obscured by the lowering,
purplish clouds.

Raleigh stood by the block in the Tower courtyard with
the order of Essex's execution in his hand. Huddled in their
cloaks and deathly silent, the people awaited the last act in the
tempestuous drama that had been the Earl's brief life.

Standing there, so near the spot where life was, in a little
while, to be so violently taken, there was no jubilation in his
heart. He felt as he had felt on that long-ago morning when
he and Essex faced one another across the dewy grass of the
Ring Meadow. Rivalry did not necessarily imply enmity. True
there would be that seat at the Council Table but he would have
preferred it to have been emptied in some other fashion. Essex
had been so vividly alive in his impetuosity, his rages and his
good-fellowship. The friendly meal that had followed so hard
on the quarrel at Fayal stuck in his memory. The Earl would
never drink wine, never laugh, never flout authority again.

Blount and other of Essex's friends failed to read his mind.
To them his stately, sombre presence in that place was an
affront and just before Essex arrived upon the scene Blount
came near and said in a low, venomous voice, 'Could you not
gloat equally well elsewhere? Friends, not enemies, should
surround a death-bed.'

Raleigh looked at him and beyond at the men whose angry
faces and low murmurs showed them of Blount's opinion.

171

Without a word he turned on his heel and walked to the White Tower where, from the window of the Armoury, he could see, unseen, and carry out his duty of being present without affronting Essex's friends.

The silence was unbroken, yet a stir ran through the crowd as the young Earl, all in black and attended by three clergymen, appeared upon the scaffold. All the sanguine colour had drained from his face and his haunted eyes looked out without a vestige of their old proud disdain. With his hat in his hand, he walked to the front of the platform and bowed to the spectators. Then in a low, unsteady voice he began a public confession of his sins. He admitted his lust, his vanity, his worldliness, his pride and especially his last sin, '... this great, this bloody, this crying, this infectious sin, whereby so many for love of me have been drawn to offend God, to offend their sovereign, to offend the world...'

The watcher in the Tower stirred uneasily. What good did this self-abasement do? The man was doomed, the order of his death was sealed. Death waited. He could neither escape nor postpone it. Better, surely better a thousand times to have called upon the ingrained arrogance of his thirty-four years and gone to the block disdainful. Why shroud the bright memory of his fiery years with this shabby cloak of confession?

The recital ended, Essex fell upon his knees and engaged in passionate prayer. The assembly knelt uncomfortably on the cobbles and prayed with him. A sound like that of bees in clover blossoms announced that all were joining in the Lord's Prayer. In the succeeding silence Essex rose and laid aside his white ruff and the black doublet. The executioner knelt and, as was the custom, begged his forgiveness for what he about to do. Then Essex knelt at the block and stretched out his arms in the long red waistcoat sleeves. Crying 'Lord be merciful to thy prostrate servant' he turned his yellow head sideways on the block. A gleam of the wintry sun caught the upraised blade of the axe. Three times it fell before the strong young neck was severed and the executioner could lift the head by its bright hair and hold it, dripping blood, before the eyes of all the people.

'God save the Queen!' he cried, and the voices that had been silent since the ending of the Lord's Prayer repeated, 'God save the Queen.' But the customary 'So perish all traitors' was no louder than a sigh.

No premonitory pang struck Raleigh as he turned from the sight and gathered his cloak about him. No shadow of an event some seventeen years ahead fell upon his path as he left the Tower, warning him that but for some slight varying detail he had this day looked upon his own death. But he did think, as he turned homewards, that had he been in Essex's place his prayer would have been not for mercy but courage. Then, dismissing the affair, he began to muse upon the future and the Privy Councillorship.

But Cecil had not been idle. Essex had been defeated and never again, the Secretary had determined, was a favourite to gain any power except what came from favour. Raleigh, looking for a seat at the council, received instead the Governorship of Jersey.

173

Lisbeth fixed the last wreath of holly and stood looking at her work with a pricked finger in her mouth. 'Gather up the pieces and the nails, Walter, and take them out to the kitchen, your father will be here at any minute now.'

She threw several logs on the fire and their sudden breaking into blaze lit up the pleasant room. The twelve peacocks glowed on the seats of the chairs, the holly berries gleamed scarlet and the mistletoe pearl from the dark panelled walls. The table was laid with silver and coloured glass that Raleigh bought from a Venetian caravel that had put in at Plymouth during one of his visits there.

Lisbeth went round with a taper and lit the candles in their heavy silver sconces. Another inspection assured her that the room was ready. She lifted the curtain of stamped Spanish leather that hung over the door and went through to the kitchen where a turkey and a haunch of venison were turning sizzling on the spits. She peeped into the saucepans that contained the spiced puddings, the simmering gravies and the sauces. All in order there. She visited in turn Raleigh's room, the guest room and their own bedroom to see that the fires were burning brightly. In the last room she paused and gazed into a little dim mirror. Yes, her hair was smooth and shining; two days of hurried preparations had left her looking neither tired nor ruffled. She had not seen her husband for ten months. He had come to Sherborne in February and stayed one night. Now it was Christmas he was coming with guests to stay for a week.

Suddenly, as she stood smoothing her dress of yellow silk,

her ear caught the clatter of hoofs on the frozen drive under the beeches. Gathering up her skirts she ran down the slippery oak stairs and flung open the door. Raleigh and two other men were dismounting. One was unknown to her and the other's face was hidden as he dismounted. As he turned, however, she saw with dismay that it was Lord Cobham. Her heart sank. It was not going to be a peaceful week of domestic bliss, then, after all. Politics and intrigue had come to Sherborne with Cobham, for they were inseparable. She offered her welcome, warm to Raleigh, gracious but reserved to the stranger who was presented as Lord Compton, cool to Cobham; then she led the way to their rooms where they might change out of their heavy riding-clothes and wash after their journey. She sat with Raleigh and as he bent over the basin asked, 'How did you leave the Queen?'

'Poorly,' he answered, blowing through the water as he splashed it on his face. 'She has never recovered from her attack in October when she collapsed at the opening of Parliament. She has bursts of vitality but they grow shorter and more rare.'

'Seventy is a great age,' said Lisbeth with the indifference of one-and-thirty. 'Has she named her successor?'

'There, now that you have asked it I think that that has been asked by everyone in England,' exclaimed Raleigh, towelling vigorously. 'No, she hasn't. Not a word of this but that is what Cobham and I have to talk over. Popular feeling is Scotch James. But Cecil is his man, I know, and I have more than a suspicion that he worked against me over the Councillorship, though why I have no notion, we were always friends. I've more than a mind to back the Infanta.'

'A Spanish Queen sounds a strange choice for England.'

'I don't know. You can fight a nation until you have a queer affection for them. And it would mean an alliance of power such as the world has seldom seen.'

'I thought balance of power was the idea amongst statesmen.'

'You're getting extremely clever, darling.'

'I've had plenty of time for thought and study. Have you any other reason to favour the Infanta, besides Cecil's partiality for James?

175

'Yes, two. She is younger and more easily influenced. He will be set in his ways and bring his Scots friends with him. Also, men have more power under a Queen. Under a King, women often rule. In fact, if he wins, I shall have to consider a bid for power through you, my pretty one.'

He stooped and kissed her, smiling at the idea of blunt and forthright Lisbeth as a power behind the throne.

'If I ever wheedled a king for anything it would be to banish you to Sherborne, on pain of death if you crossed the boundary, my dear,' said Lisbeth dryly. It was a light enough reference to a sore subject but it made Raleigh say, as he shook out the frills of his cuff:

'Come, we must go down. By the way, I've not seen Walter yet.'

'No, he was hanging around in the passage. He was shy of coming forward before strangers.'

'He's too old for such vagaries. He sees too few people. He should be in London with me more.'

'Yes, I've been thinking that he needed his father. We may come up in the New Year.'

Raleigh gaped at her. Was it the Queen's illness or her own thought that he had brought her to that startling decision? He could not know but the announcement pleased him. With a light-hearted gesture he put his hand on her waist and ran her down the stairs.

Young Walter, tall and grave for his years, was shyly haunting the passage at the stairfoot, ready at the sound of a strange voice to dart back into cover. Seeing only his father and mother he came forward and clasped Raleigh round the waist. 'I have been wanting to see you for so long,' he said. 'I want to know whether you ever went back for that gold.'

'What gold, son?'

'He's been reading your book about Guiana,' put in Lisbeth.

'Oh that. No, I haven't been back yet.'

'Oh good. Well, when you go, do take me with you, please, father.'

The child spoke earnestly, as if it were a matter of life and death to him. Raleigh looked down with interest. It was his own face, long and narrow, but with Lisbeth's clear eyes, fair hair and black lashes.

'Why do you want me to take you?'

'Oh, I'd love to see all those strange things and the brown people. I'll never ask you for anything else if you'll only take me. Do you think that old man with the funny name will still be there?'

'Topiawari? I shouldn't think so. He was a very old man and that was a long time ago.' Turning to Lisbeth he added, 'He's just like I was at that age. There was an old sailor called Harkess who used to tell me stories about the places he'd seen and drive me almost crazy with longing to see them.'

'He's your son all right,' said Lisbeth and turned away to the kitchen. Remembering the alphabets of sugar sticks and apple peel she thought, bitterly, he might never have learned to read for all Walter cared, now I suppose he will fill his head with crazy tales and I shall lose him. As she rated the wench who had allowed the pudding to boil dry, she was thinking of the growing interest that young Walter had been showing in his father since that last visit. She was shocked to realise that she was jealous of it. Yet behind it all she was willing as ever to admit that her husband had a indescribable fascination. This very afternoon the sight of him, looking a little older, a trifle less lusty than of yore had moved her so that she had, on the spur of the moment, determined to face London in order to be near him and surround him with those wifely attentions that she was sure he needed, though he had never mentioned their lack.

When she left the kitchen she found that her guests had descended and were seated before the fire. The boy was perched upon the arms of his father's chair, answering Lord Cobham's questions with every sign of self-possession. True, Cobham had chosen a favourable subject, ponies, but it did not please Lisbeth to see Walter shed his shyness with such ease, in such company.

'Run into the kitchen, Walter,' she ordered, 'I forgot to tell Martha to mull the ale for the wassail cups. They'll be here very soon.'

NORAH LOFTS

Walter rose, obedient though reluctant, and almost as soon as he had gone the sound of singing rose clearly on the frosty air outside the windows of the cosy room.

> *We sing of a maiden*
> *That is matchless.*
> *King of all kings*
> *To her son she chose.*

> *He came all so still*
> *Where his mother was,*
> *As dew in April*
> *That falleth on grass.*

> *He came all so still*
> *To his mother's bower,*
> *As dew in April*
> *That falleth on flower.*

> *He came all so still*
> *Where his mother lay,*
> *As dew in April*
> *That falleth on spray.*

> *Mother and maiden*
> *Was none such as she,*
> *Well may such a lady*
> *God's mother be.*

There was some shuffling of heavily shod feet on the hard ground, coughing and clearing of throats, then they began again.

> *As Joseph was a-walking, he heard an angel sing,*
> *This day shall be the birthday of Christ your*
> *Heav'nly King.*

178

He neither shall be washed in white wine or in red,
But in the pure water that on him shall be shed.

He neither shall be lappèd in purple nor in pall,
But in the fair white linen that babies usen all.

He neither shall be cradled in silver nor in gold,
But in the oxen's manger that lyeth on the mould.

As Joseph was a-walking thus did an angel sing
And Mary's son at midnight was born to be our
King.

'Shall I bid them in now?' asked Lisbeth, 'the meat spoils in waiting.'

'Let them sing one more,' said Raleigh; 'I love these old songs. And the meat can wait, it is but once a year.'

The virgin sat a-nursing the babe upon her knee,
Three wise men entered kneeling, and gave her
presents three.

The two lines were hardly completed when Lisbeth sprang to her feet. 'I can't bear this one,' she cried, 'I knew that would be the next.'

'It is new to me, what's wrong with it?' asked Raleigh.

But Lisbeth was already at the door.

'Good people, I wish you a Merry Christmas. Come in and welcome.'

They came in, six men and six boys, all wearing over their heads and shoulders leathern hoods, roughly shaped to represent some animal. Under the long ears of donkeys, the sharp ears of cats and the drooping ears of mastiffs the rosy yokel faces peered out. They drank their ale and presented their Christmas wishes in a quaint chant, 'God bless the master of this house, likewise the mistress too, and all the little children that round the table go.' Then they departed to repeat the performance elsewhere.

'Those hoods interest me,' said Raleigh, as they sat at the table. 'They seem to have no real connection with Christmas, yet it's one of the oldest customs.'

'It may have some reference to the animals in the stable,' said Lisbeth, looking along the table to see that both the guests had all they needed.

'Martha said that on Christmas Eve at midnight all the animals knelt down. But it isn't true, father, I stayed up last Christmas to see for myself,' said Walter

'I shouldn't think that animals have any idea of the time,' said Raleigh, 'still it's a pretty notion.'

'It's like the story about five thousand people having their dinner off two little herrings and some bread,' said Walter very seriously, 'I never could quite believe that.'

Raleigh laughed and Lisbeth shot a reproachful glance at him.

'Such dreadful talk for Christmas Eve, Walter,' she said, 'You must believe that God can do anything.'

'Then He could have made the animals kneel down.'

'Why should He? He probably knew how naughty and headstrong you had been about staying up so late and didn't let them on purpose. Now get on with your supper and don't speak again.'

Lord Compton said, 'I heard a droll story just before we left. Not a word of this, but I was solemnly assured that Harington, the Queen's godson, has sent James a Christmas gift, a lamp bearing the words, "Lord, remember me when thou comest into thy kingdom." Apt enough but amusing when you remember whose words they were.'

'A thief's,' said Cobham, smiling.

'It's horrible,' said Raleigh, 'She's not taken to her bed yet. What would she do if she heard?'

'Nothing, she's past it. Besides, it is no good waiting till the throne is vacant. That's what we want to talk to you about.'

'It'll be the end of an era, and I for one will be sorry. We shall not look upon her like again.'

Chapter 23

Hampton Court
March 1603

Sceptre and Crown,
Must tumble down,
And in the dust be equal made
With the poor crooked scythe and spade.

Despite the winter weather and her own increasing weakness, the Queen had moved the Court to Hampton and installed herself in the two small, well-warmed rooms from which Raleigh had once lured her to walk in the garden. Looking back on that day it seemed now as if she had been still a young and lusty woman. She could move still, but with difficulty. The Indian drugs were losing their potency as she became more and more addicted to their use. She could not take her food and would sit at the table clasping a beaker of wine in both hands, sometimes for an hour on end, and then set it down untasted.

Her illness had stirred an interest in her people and old foul tales were circulating freely. She had borne Leicester a daughter who was now married to a French prince and would claim the throne. Her son by Raleigh had been strangled at birth at Hampton. Burghley and Walsingham had had their pleasure of her and asked no other reward.

And if the subject of these stories heard anything of them, she gave no sign; no one hanged, no one's ears were nailed to the pillory, no hands were cut off. Sunk in a melancholy from which nothing could rouse her the Queen of England prepared for death. They had thought she would never stir from her rooms again but one windy day in March, when the smoke

181

billowed out from the hearth and the tapestries billowed from the walls, one of the waiting women whispered to another who had just come in, 'How is she?'

'Dying,' was a reply.

Elizabeth roused herself. 'I am not dying, malapert. How dare you say that!'

'Oh no, your Majesty, not you. It is the Countess of Nottingham.'

'The Countess? Oh, Lady Howard. Why was I not told? Because I am not too cold to go abroad in this Devil's weather, why must I be treated like a Bedlamite? Fetch me another shawl. And you, fetch me a man. Get Raleigh if he can be found. I suppose he's languishing round with that whey-faced wife of his but you can see. And make haste.'

Raleigh, speedily summoned, thrust away the little book of melancholy poems that he had been reading and hastened to the Queen. All through the passages the words of one he read for the first time that day, haunted him.

> *O mortal folk, you may behold and see*
> *How I lie here, sometime a goodly knight.*
> *The end of joy and all prosperity*
> *Is death at last, thorough his course and might.*
> *After the day there cometh the dark night.*
> *And though the day he never so long*
> *At last, the bells ringeth to evensong.*

The Queen, he thought, as the icy draught in the corridors struck him, had had a long day but there was no comfort in that. She greeted him with, 'I've come low enough to ask for an arm before it is offered, Walter. I want you to lead me to Lady Howard. They tell me she is dying.'

'I'm afraid that is true, your Majesty.'

Swathed in her shawls she was no more substantial than a child and the hand that she thrust through his arm was thin to the point of transparency and blue at the tips of the fingers. She stepped out bravely, however, and walked far better than

182

Raleigh had thought possible when she first announced her intention.

All the way she grumbled continually about the way she was treated. 'Lady Howard was ever my friend and they would have let her die and not have told me. Let the spring once come and warm my blood so that my bones thaw and I will make my women skip.'

The Countess's room was full of people and there were two doctors by the bed. Raleigh opened the door and, seeing the aperture blocked by someone's back, Elizabeth threw all her weight on to his arm in order to give the back a sharp poke with her stick. The victim turned round sharply and immediately a stir ran through the room. The Queen was here. Still leaning heavily upon Raleigh, Elizabeth made her way to the bedside.

The dying woman raised herself on one elbow and said, 'Send everybody away. I have something to confess to you. They said you couldn't stir and I dreaded to die unforgiven.'

The Queen turned. 'Get out,' she said briefly. 'Walter, wait outside the door, within call.'

As he closed the door, he saw Elizabeth seat herself stiffly on the bed and heard her say in her most soothing voice: 'Now old friend, what silly trivial thing had been troubling you?'

The idea of the women behind the closed door, one easing the other along a path she was so soon to tread herself, brought a lump to Raleigh's throat and moisture to his eyes. Lisbeth might say what she would; she misjudged the Queen. There was in her a rich streak of tender unselfishness. At some cost to herself she had come on this visit and her 'Now, old friend,' had been deeply sympathetic.

He could hear no sound from the room. The Countess was grappling with her last weakness and Elizabeth had a gathered throat which made speech painful.

He had been waiting for some time before the silence was suddenly shattered. 'God may forgive you, I never shall,' the Queen screeched. The door was flung open violently and Elizabeth strode into the corridor. She was a horrible sight, her eyes were starting and blood and mucus were pouring from her

183

lips. She wiped her mouth on her sleeve and as Raleigh offered his arm, said in a loud voice, 'It is nothing, this thing in my throat has burst. I am better. But follow you me, I have much to say to you.'

Straight as a stick and almost as narrow she marched back to her rooms, Raleigh following as he was bidden. To the women who were crouching over the fire there she shouted, 'So you let the fire out in my absence, do you? I suppose you thought I shouldn't come back. Well, here I am and I'm better, so mend your paces. Mend first the fire and then take yourselves away.'

Hurriedly the women threw logs on the fire and withdrew.

'Now,' said Elizabeth, throwing herself into a chair and fighting for breath, 'I'll tell you what that wicked woman has told me. My throat burst with rage, I wonder my heart didn't break. If she hadn't been dying already, I would have killed her.' She stopped and struggled for air. Raleigh saw her shoulders heave and her nostrils contract as she breathed fiercely inwards.

'Long ago I gave Essex a ring.' Her voice faltered on the word, it was a name that she hardly ever mentioned or permitted in her hearing. 'All through those last days I waited for him to send it me, for I had promised that when I received it back from him, no matter what he had done, I would forgive it. It never came and I regarded it as the last insolence, that he would die rather than use that symbol. Do you know why it never came?' She leaned forward, staring at Raleigh and breathing noisily through her nose. 'He flung it from a window and told a man to take it to Lady Scrope. The fool took it to Lady Howard, the sister of Lady Scrope and she, for spite, kept it and told me of it but now. Now, when the worms are at him. Now, and he died thinking me unforgiving in the face of a promise.' She finished on a high note of hysteria. But before Raleigh could think of something soothing to say she cried, with a dramatic dropping of the voice and a pointing finger, 'And whose doing was it that Lady Howard was his enemy?'

'Howard and Essex were ever...' Raleigh began, and then suddenly the answer burst upon him. He did not need to listen to the Queen's shaking voice.

'It was yours. You in this very room showed me the way to set Robert over Howard when I had made Howard Earl of Nottingham. With that stroke, Walter, you cut off Robert's head. I once stopped you from killing one another, I always tried to hold a fair balance between you. I loved you both. Differently, he was such a boy, more like a son. But I loved you both. I shan't see you again, Walter. That is the least I can do. I may live a long time, until I am eighty maybe, but I won't see you again. It wouldn't be fair after you did that to him.'

'But' said Raleigh, falling into his old error of trying to reason with her. 'I only advised you to make him earl marshal and so put him over the Admiral. I didn't do it. You did it.'

Elizabeth put her hands to her face, and began to cry.

'I did it, yes, I did it. I killed one of those I loved and now I will not look again upon the other. Get you gone, Walter Raleigh, and if you know how, pray for me.'

Raleigh flung himself on his knees beside her.

'Don't banish me now,' he pleaded, 'we're neither of us young any more. There isn't time for partings. We both made a mistake there but we meant no ill. I swear I never meant Robert any ill in my life. I regretted his end as much as you did. We're all that are left of the old days. Banish me not.'

Elizabeth pushed him away and said, straight ahead at him, 'I always listened to you when I had better not have done and refused to when I should. Now you must go. I punish myself more than you. Understand that, and go quickly.'

Turning her head, she kissed him abruptly and fiercely on the mouth.

'Now go,' she said.

Raleigh rose slowly, her kiss still bitter on his lips, and for the last time went out of her presence.

Forbidden her presence he still haunted the Palace, gleaning what news he could. On the Saturday word ran round that the Queen was genuinely demented. She had risen from her cushions at eight o'clock in the morning and standing upright with a terrible effort, had cried, 'Death, I defy you!' And there on that same spot she had stood all through the day. Fearing that the strain would hasten her end her people had begged to lie or at least sit down. To that she replied, 'If I quit standing, I am done.' They had placed cushions around her to soften the fall when her strength finally collapsed, they had offered her wine and succory potage; she would have none of them. Rigid and staring she had remained upon her feet. The afternoon darkened towards evening. 'She is still standing,' came word from the scene of the strange conflict. Night fell; Robert Carey, who was to set out for Scotland at the moment of her death, looked to his horse, standing ready saddled at the stable. Not a soul in all Richmond doubted that death would strike her as she stood.

An hour before midnight, when she had been standing for fifteen hours, she said, 'You may put me to bed. I have conquered. Have the Great Chapel made ready for service at ten tomorrow.'

Superstition, never far away in that age, flared through the Court. Raleigh, in the ante-room where he had spent the day, was conscious of its thrill even through his sceptical soul. Perhaps there were souls too strong for death and if there were he was ready to believe that Elizabeth Tudor's was one of them. Suppose Death had been facing her through all those long hours and had at last turned away defeated.

Fresh cloths were spread on the altar in the Chapel. Early in the morning some of the women went out to gather the pale wind-blown daffodils that grew under the wall from which Raleigh had once gathered a frosted rose. They arranged them in the silver vases which Elizabeth, despite the Puritan tendencies of the day, insisted upon retaining on the altars of her private chapels. At ten o'clock everything was ready, the candles were lighted, the Archbishop of Canterbury, little swarthy Whitgift, was waiting. Raleigh and some of the guard were ready to escort the Queen. There was no sign from the Royal apartments until close to eleven when Agnes Lawley opened the door softly and approached Raleigh.

'She can't get to the Chapel. Will you ask the Archbishop to hold the service in her room?'

As many of the congregation as could squeezed into the Queen's room on the Archbishop's heels: the rest stood without with the guard and listened to the responses.

Within the room the dying woman lay stretched, fully dressed in all the panoply of majesty upon the cushions in the middle of the floor.

A cloud of terror and dread hung heavy over the whole Court. The prayer for the Queen's majesty sounded like a prayer for the dead. Whitgift's strong voice was unsteady, the women wept aloud.

The service ended and the room was cleared. Raleigh remained in the ante-room. He tried to pray for her, as she had bidden him, but instead of prayers old half-forgotten verses thronged in his mind. Peele's

> *Goddess allow this aged man his right*
> *To be your beadsman now that was your knight.*

Dead Gasgoigne's

> *Lullaby my youthful years,*
> *It is now time to go to bed*
> *For crooked age and hoary hairs,*
> *Have won the haven within my head.*

And Nashe's lines that had once so disturbed the Queen –

> *Dust hath filled Helen's eyes.*

As the afternoon lengthened the past came near him, Holland, Ireland, Guiana. What had been the comrades' talk? The Queen. Whither had all their hopes winged? Queen-wards. And now that bright Deity was brought low, an old sick woman moaning on the floor. 'Man, that is born of woman hath but a short time to stay, he flourisheth like the flower and is cut down like the grass.'

The sky clouded and a fine blinding rain began to fall,

obscuring what was left of the dying daylight. Cecil arrived, dripping wet, and was admitted. When he came out again, he stopped by Raleigh and spoke.

'I told her that to content the people she must go to bed; and in her old manner she said to me, "Little man, must is not a word to princes". I asked her about the succession and she has appointed James.'

'Appointed?'

'Well, she said, "No base man but a King." That means but one that I know of.'

'She cannot have known what she was saying. She always hated him.'

'I think you impute your own feelings to her.'

'I should hate anyone who took her place.'

Cecil gave a half-smile and left him.

At eight o'clock, having eaten nothing all day, Raleigh went towards the buttery for some wine and a manchet of bread. Coming back through the cold and dimly lighted passages he met Agnes Lawley flying on feet of terror. She flung herself upon him.

'I now saw her walking in the long Gallery, fully dressed and moving with ease. I went back to look and she was lying on the cushions as I had left her with her finger in her mouth. It was her ghost I saw. It is a sign of death.' She whimpered and clung to his arm.

'Your overwrought senses deceived you,' said Raleigh soothingly; 'stay here with me a little.'

Presently old Howard, Earl of Nottingham, arrived. He had been absent for his wife's funeral. Garbed in black and with a face stricken with grief he looked frail and pitiable, very different from the bluff old sailor who had once controlled young Essex. But his spirit was unimpaired.

'They tell she refuses to go to bed,'

'Cecil tried to persuade her this afternoon,' said Raleigh, 'but she wouldn't listen to him.'

'I'm not going to persuade her,' said the old Earl, 'I am going to lift her upon the bed.'

'Would I might aid you,' said Raleigh.

'I don't want your aid,' said the old man curtly. He went through the door and shortly returned, bidding Agnes go and help disrobe her mistress.

Night thickened over Richmond and the Queen slept. Bald head covered with a shawl, sunken eyes closed under the arched brows, railing, cajoling tongue still at last, restless hands at peace, the Queen slept.

Just before dawn, bending over the bed they saw that the coverlet moved no more to her breathing, the pulse in the shrunken neck was still.

Robert Carey flung himself upon his horse and set out for Edinburgh to tell James of Scotland that England was his footstool.

The Queen's Guard went on duty for the last time. In sable doublets and hoods, with points reversed, they stood along the route of the procession. The hearse passed them, bearing the laden coffin covered with a pall and over it the waxen image of the Queen as she had been upon her Coronation, proud pale face, lovely in its intelligence, golden red hair, royal robes. Behind walked old Howard, loyally making this last effort for his Queen; Cecil, whose allegiance was already transferred; courtiers; ladies, their faces marred with weeping. Slowly they passed the tall grave man whose mind was busy with another April day; another day when the clouds had sailed before the sun and the Queen had asked, 'Heaven. But shall I be Queen of England there?'

All that wit and grandeur, those rages, that kindliness, all that courage, that learning, that life, that whole being, reduced to something that must be lifted upon men's shoulders and put away and forgotten.

At a word of command, the Guard fell in behind the mourners and followed to the Abbey. The scent of ancient incense clung to the air, mingling with the smoke of the wavering candles. The grand, solemn words of the service rang out over the sobs

189

and snuffles of the assembly. In due time the Queen was laid with her fathers, cautious clever Henry the Seventh, bluff and lustful Henry the Eighth. They had their part in her but she had been greater than either.

The choir ended its last sad chant, the candles guttered towards their end. Raleigh brought his Guard outside into the April sunlight and dismissed them there. There was no need for a guard now. There was nothing left to guard.

PART THREE

Chapter 24

Windsor Castle
1603

JAMES, by the Grace of God King of England and Scotland, Defender of the Faith, looked at Raleigh and Raleigh looked at James.

So, thought James, this is the redoubtable Raleigh. He saw a tall, thin, dark man, slightly lame and very white at the temples, sombrely but richly dressed and holding himself proudly.

Raleigh thought, this is a king! A man with a flat sallow face, a thin straggling beard and nervous, rolling eyes; dressed in a paddled doublet and stuffed breeches that went ill with his thin weak legs. His linen was dirty and the frequent sweats of terror that soaked him gave all his clothes an acrid, repulsive scent. His soiled hands with their bitten nails lay on the arms of the chair where Elizabeth's had often rested.

He spoke in a thick Lowland Scots voice, his utterance a little impeded by the largeness of his tongue.

'We are glad to see you, Sir Walter Raleigh, though so late. Most public men have presented themselves ere this.'

'There was a proclamation, your Majesty, bidding public servants refrain from resorting to you,' said Raleigh, with a glance at Cecil who had issued it.

'And are you always so scrupulously obedient?'

'I endeavour to be.'

'I had heard otherwise. The late Queen's men were represented to me as a very headstrong sort.'

Raleigh was silent: if the King wished to be disagreeable, well, he must, nothing could stop him. But his eyes flashed. That had been Cecil's line, had it? To play upon the cowardice of the new King.

James saw the flash.

'Still, let that pass,' he said, 'and arrange to ride with me tomorrow. I would have your opinion upon various matters.'

Raleigh retired and James turned to Cecil.

'You were right in your judgment of that man; he is proud and dangerous.'

'And an atheist,' added Cecil, who had gauged the depths of James's half-Puritanical religiosity.

Next morning's riding was a sore test of Raleigh's gravity. A splendid horseman himself, accustomed to riding with Lisbeth and Elizabeth, James's performance struck him as comic in the extreme. He rode so clumsily that only his stuffed breeches saved him from doing himself some serious injury; he sawed his horse's mouth, he struck out his knees and his elbows and the conversation that was the ostensible reason for the ride was continually broken into by his admonitions to his steed.

Raleigh was guilty of a little exhibitionism, not thinking how it was annoying James who lumbered along hating this popinjay's long legs, straight back and easy seat.

'You're a man who has fought the Spaniards more than once; tell me, is there still any danger to be feared from them? Steady now, you brute, steady!'

'Both their fleet and their army are bigger than they were in 'eighty-eight, your Majesty.'

'Is there enmity?'

'Every established nation hates a growing one. Look how we are beginning to hate the Dutch.'

'I wonder, curse you, keep your head up, I wonder that there was no attempt made upon the throne. That has always been their pigeon,' said James craftily.

'There wasn't a chance,' said Raleigh honestly. 'The whole country was solid in your favour.'

'Solid?'

'With individual exceptions, of course. But that shouldn't disturb you. The late Queen, God rest her, was the most popular monarch ever known in England and her accession was not unanimously applauded.'

'Indeed. Now to revert to Spain, gently, gently! To revert to the question of Spain. What policy would you advise?'

'What I always have, action. Unless we hasten, we shall have the whole of the New World under Spanish rule, its minerals, its rich virgin soil, its enormous possibilities of wealth and employment for people who have in England no prospect of either.'

'Go on, what do you propose?'

'I'd attack the Orinoco basin. You'd have a great weapon in the Indians. In 'ninety-five I destroyed a whole Spanish town in Trinidad with a couple of hundred men. The Spaniards had called up the native levies and with the first shot they turned round and fought for us. And they would again, especially if I were there.'

'Why?' James looked distastefully at this swashbuckler.

'I know them, they know me and trust me. I took enormous pains to leave a fair name behind. I continually get messages from any English captain that touches on that coast. They haven't forgotten me even yet.'

'Indeed,' said James, 'shall we turn now?'

'I'll raise two thousand men at my own expense,' Raleigh offered, as they wheeled and cantered back. 'And with your permission, I'll lead them. It would be a glorious opening to your reign.'

'The question requires much thought.'

'One shouldn't delay. They wouldn't expect action so soon and that would be to your advantage.'

James was silent. He rode back, quite satisfied. This Raleigh was all that he had been reported, a hothead who would plunge the whole country into war to please his own vanity: a braggart: an insolent fellow who would dictate to the King and who had only once addressed him as 'Your Majesty' in the course of the whole conversation. James thought of Cecil, suave, obsequious, ill-favoured and crooked. There was the man for him.

The King of England dismounted stiffly from his horse and went to confer with Cecil. And the Secretary, now Raleigh's most bitter enemy, paid him perhaps the greatest compliment of his lifetime.

'Arrest Cobham first,' he said, 'he will betray Raleigh. From Raleigh we shall get nothing.'

Chapter 25

The Tower
1604

Sir John Peyton, the Lieutenant of the Tower, was a man with a great gross body and a very kindly soul. He had noted Raleigh's gloom during the first days after his arrest and decided to ask him to dinner. There could be no harm in that, he thought; the man was only awaiting trial, he was not yet condemned for any crime. And, judging from his own experience, a good dinner was a great heartener. So he ordered a rich broth of eels, turbot stewed in white wine, young ducklings and apple sauce and a monstrous pie of mixed fruits covered with ornamental pastry. He panted down to his cellar and returned with four dusty bottles, two under each arm, purple Malmsey, sweet Canary and the rich red wine from Oporto. There, he thought, when all was ready, such a meal would hearten me were I on the brink of the grave and he is yet far from that. He eased his belt and unbuttoned his doublet as he sat down to the groaning table and was pleased to see Sir Walter do likewise.

'I shall be but a poor guest, I fear,' said Raleigh, 'a heavy heart is bad company.'

'You mustn't despair too easily,' said the good man as he dipped his ladle into the broth. 'From all I hear there is only Lord Cobham's word against yours and he hasn't every one's ear.'

'The King and Cecil will listen to what they want to hear, as we all do. And they have condemned me already in their hearts. Why else take away all my monopolies and the Governorship of Jersey?'

'They've given that to me,' said Peyton, laughing. 'I suppose

195

you didn't know that. It was none of my seeking, though, mark you,' he added, grave again immediately.

'I bear you no malice if it were. It's every man for himself in this world, Peyton. I wish you joy of it. Tis a sweet pretty place.'

'So, I'm told. But I doubt the office will be too grand for me.'

'Not it. Aim to impress the people at the first: wear your finest clothes for every public occasion. They're half French you know, fond of outward show. For the rest the place runs itself; they're half-feudal system of government that there's no need to understand. I didn't but I wasn't there long. Apart from sudden, violent feuds amongst themselves they're very peaceful, pleasant folk.'

A thought struck him, reminding him so poignantly of past hopes and present impotence that he had to drink deeply of his wine before he spoke.

'I wish you'd have an eye to my potatoes. I planted a number there in the spring. It seems to have the right climate. The crops mature earlier there and potatoes travel well. I see no reason why they shouldn't build up a flourishing export trade in time.'

'I'll see to them, never fear. I'll just harvest the first crop for you and after that you'll be free to see to them yourself.'

The shiny streak of grease that ran over his fat chin did nothing to diminish the kindness of the glance that he gave his guest.

His certainty of a favourable outcome to the trial disturbed Raleigh. He had abandoned all hope upon his entrance to the Tower. He had plotted with Cobham, there was no denying that. And though the plot had been made and abandoned in the Queen's reign, malice could easily twist into treason against James. Cecil would pack with enemies the court that tried him: it would all be very easy. He put Peyton's assurance upon one side, as the outcome of ignorance, optimism and good nature, and strengthened the resolve he had made early in the day when the invitation had been given.

With several complaints of his guest's small appetite, Peyton worked his way steadily through his gargantuan meal and finally, after consuming a pound of fine strawberries, heaped his plate with young stem ginger preserved in syrup, an Eastern sweet that was then attaining great popularity in England. He filled both the silver cups with the red Spanish wine and raised his spoon.

Raleigh watched him. Would what he was going to do spoil Peyton's appetite? Probably not, but the possibility deterred him. He watched the spoon rise and fall: he listened to the vigorous crunch of Peyton's teeth; the scrape of the spoon on the plate as the syrup ebbed. He had faced death in many forms, in many places, in the company of many good fellows. Now he was to die, not to the sound of spattering bullets but to the sound of a gourmand munching ginger. He smiled and picked up his table knife as Peyton, with a sigh of pleasure, laid down his spoon. One movement of the left hand opened the loosened doublet while the right drove the knife hard into his breast. He saw the red blood spurt out onto the table, heard Peyton cry out, felt the knife jar on the bone and knew that he had failed.

The Lieutenant seized his arm in a paralysing grip with one hand, thrust a handful of the tablecloth into the wound with the other and began to roar lustily for the servants.

'Don't call anyone,' said Raleigh, ''tis nothing, a mere scratch, God curse it. I struck a rib.'

'Are you mad?' gasped the fat man.

'Not I. I'm sorry to have done it at your table, Peyton, but as you know, prisoners are not served with knives.'

'But why try to do it at all?'

'I wanted to save Sherborne for my wife and son. They couldn't try a dead man for treason and unless I'm condemned for that my lease on Sherborne must go to my son. There'll be nothing now.

He smote his bloody breast with his hand and Peyton stood silent, dumb and helpless before a grief that made fleshly pleasures suddenly seem small and foolish.

Chapter 26

Whitehall
1606

'I want it and I must have it,' said James.

'Then my son is to be beggared?'

'That is the lot of traitors' sons.'

'My son is not—'Lisbeth began hotly. Then she saw that that was not the line to take. Gracefully she bowed her proud neck and sank with a rustling of petticoats to the ground at the King's feet.

'Your Majesty, be merciful. Out of all England spare us just the home where my son was born.'

'I have been merciful,' said James smugly. 'Your husband was condemned to the block as a traitor. I reprieved him.'

Fierce words crowded to Lisbeth's lips. She burned to spring to her feet and hiss into that ugly face. 'Yes, you did, and why? To save your face. To buy yourself a little popularity.'

She crushed the rash words back and said meekly:

'His life you spared and for that I thank you upon my knees. Spare now a few acres of Sherborne for my son and render your clemency royal.'

The last cunning word touched him. Above all things James aspired to be royal. And every day in this strange new country he was reminded of a predecessor so naturally royal that even his most ambitious attempts seemed poor and studied beside her careless legended gestures. For a moment he was minded to bid the kneeling woman rise and enter upon her right. But as he was steeling himself to renounce his claim a shadow went past the window. No more. But the passing glimpse of that blunt young profile recalled the King from his dangerous dalliance with abstract royalty. Young Carr wanted Sherborne: he should have it. The traitor's brat and the traitor's wife must beg or starve. How fine to be a king and have places like Sherborne in one's gift! How sweet to be able to give dear Rob so lordly a token of love!

He turned once more to Lisbeth who fixed her fine eyes on him, melting, beseeching. She was thinking of Raleigh's laughing words, far back in the old happy days, 'I must bid for favour through your charms, my pretty one.' She was pretty still and what harm to use her charms to soften the King on Walter's behalf? But with James her sex played against her. If she had been a pretty boy, with fair smooth hair and blue eyes, black-lashed, then James might have given her Sherborne and anything else she desired. But a woman, no!

'The estate is forfeit. I have already disposed of it,' he said.

Lisbeth rose from her knees.

'Then, your Majesty, may I change my plea? Give me your leave to take my son and live in the Tower with my husband.'

The shadow fell across the window again. Rob was pacing outside, waiting for this weary audience to be over.

'I see no objection to that. You would be willing to abide by the rules, I suppose?'

'Certainly, your Majesty.'

Raleigh was fortunate, thought James. He wondered whether anyone would be willing to share his imprisonment were he in such a case. Not Anne certainly. Rob might.

With a belated and rather difficult effort at graciousness he dismissed Lisbeth by saying, 'I am sorry, Lady Raleigh, that the other favour was less possible to grant.'

'All things are not possible, even to kings,' said Lisbeth unkindly and went out of the presence.

The door was hardly closed behind her when Carr, who had been waiting, as James had guessed, for Lady Raleigh to end her suit, slipped round the corner and entered. At the same time a woman, hastening down the corridor, stopped within arm's length of Lisbeth, stamped her foot and exclaimed, 'God rot him!'

Lisbeth stopped and stared. She looked at the short, spare squarish woman with the plain intelligent face and reddish-brown hair without knowing her. Their eyes met. The little woman moved on a step and then stopped again.

'Isn't it Lady Raleigh?' she asked in a voice rendered attractive by a faint foreign accent.

'Yes,' said Lisbeth.

'I thought so. I've been longing to see you. I am the Queen.' Lisbeth gave her lowest curtsy.

'Forgive me, your Majesty. I did not recognise you. I am but lately come from Sherborne.'

'Are you in haste? Could you spare a little time to talk to me?'

'Of course, your Majesty.'

'Come this way then.'

She led the way into the garden and sat on a seat in full view of Lisbeth's old window.

'I'm so glad your husband was pardoned,' she began. 'I did all I could to bring it about.'

'My deepest gratitude is yours then,' said Lisbeth.

'I've quarrelled with my husband about the Sherborne business,' the Queen went on, 'but since that rat of a Carr set his great greedy eyes on it, remonstrance and pleadings have alike been vain. He was loitering there just now, all aquiver lest your prayers should have prevailed. How I hate him! Where are you living?'

'We, that is my son and I, have been staying with my brother but I have just obtained leave to go into the Tower. Not as a prisoner,' she added as Anne gave an astonished gasp; 'it is possible to live there, if you can bear the restrictions. It will be best for the boy to be with his father. No woman can really bring up a son.'

'I do my best with mine,' said Anne sharply. 'And I'll see to it that he grows up to be a proper king.'

'Ah, but he sees his father, he has other men around him. He is not alone with you as Walter has been with me.'

An expression of extreme scorn appeared on the plain brown face.

'Henry is better with me than he would be with the fellows that hang around the King now.' Her voice changed a little. 'You probably regard me as strange, talking to you like this, but I always speak my mind. Since the day that Carr fell from his horse at the Tournament and landed at the King's feet nothing has been the same. I try to be tolerant. I remember my husband was blighted before his birth, strangely born and ill-used in his childhood. He loved me once, too. But if you and I are to be friends, as I hope we are, you must not suggest that a father is a better mentor than a mother. In fact, you must help me to fulfill my task alone.'

'Help you?'

'Yes. Your husband, by all that I have gathered, is a man after my own heart. I shall visit you. I shall bring Henry. I want him to know a man. To talk to him. To hear about the grand days that seem to be gone forever but which may return with him if we do our work well. Promise to say no word of this; promise to aid me and in return I vow that whatever my voice and hand can do to release him shall be done. After all I am Queen of England.'

'Nothing that I could do would ever repay you for those words. The future has seemed very dark of late.'

'It will lighten,' said Anne, 'I have had dark times too. When I saw Carr go through that door this afternoon I felt like murder. Then you see, I met you; now I'm strong again and full of hope for Henry. I shall come to the Tower very soon.'

Chapter 27

The Tower
1606—16

WHEN Lisbeth came to him, Raleigh was standing by the window, looking down-river. It might, he reflected, be the last glimpse of that busy artery that he would see: for the new Lieutenant of the Tower had ordered a wall to be erected across the window and tomorrow, or the next day, when the topmost bricks were laid, that view would be sealed for ever. He thanked God that the laying had been deferred just long enough. For today, upon the ebbing tide he had seen the *Sarah Constant*, the *Godspeed* and the *Discovery* set off for Virginia. Three little ships to found an empire: but there was a man aboard them. Captain John Smith turned his eye to the Tower as the river bore them past it and a thought of respect and sympathy winged towards the prisoner in that grey pile, meeting upon its way a fellow thought of respect and well-wishing directed to the soldier who was bearing the prisoner's banner. Smith did not see the pale face at the window, Raleigh did not see the brown face on the deck but they were, for a moment, conscious of one another and the bond that held them. In his mind Raleigh saw the grey wash of the seas, the sand and the pines under the blue Virginian skies. He felt the remembered stir of the spacious hopes that once that land had held for him. Sighing, he turned back to the pallid present and the two grey rooms that held him. Two small rooms and a pacing space on the terrace when Sir William Waad was in a generous mind. Without, the spring might scatter the banks with snowdrops, the summer twine the hedges with wreaths of honeysuckle. No spring would ever fire his blood again nor any summer warm it. The two grey rooms had closed around him, inviolate as the tomb.

202

He turned his head at the sound of the opening door and set his face into the insensitive mask that he always showed to Waad. But it was not the Lieutenant. It was Lisbeth in a gay gown of grey silk sprayed with roses and tied with wide pink ribbons. The mask fell as he went towards her, crying with mingled pleasure and anxiety:

'Lisbeth, what are you doing here at this hour?'

'I can come in at any hour now.'

'You're not imprisoned too?' he asked in sudden fear.

Lisbeth nodded, laughing.

'I've put myself in, darling. I wanted to be with you.'

She had said, 'I love the air and the open spaces.' She had said, 'Banishment I could bear but imprisonment, never.' And he had turned from the sight of the ships going down-river and deemed himself the most wretched man on earth! Even then Lisbeth's hands were pulling at the bell. It was an omen. He was almost prepared for her next words.

'And I bring news. Good and bad. I'll tell you the bad first. Sherborne is gone. Carr wanted it and James has given it to him.'

'He had no right.'

'I think he had no choice, Walter. He's in love with the man.'

Raleigh stared at her incredulously for a moment. Then:

'Well,' he said, with a great shout of laughter, 'that is almost worth losing Sherborne for. Did ever man hear the like since the time of Piers Gaveston who wore the crown jewels for Edward the Second? Are you sure you didn't dream it?'

'The Queen herself told me as much.'

'The Queen?'

'Yes,' said Lisbeth, seating herself and drawing him beside her with her fingers linked in his. 'I went to the King today, to beg Sherborne for Walter. I begged hard. I went down on my knees and, as you see, I looked my best. But it was quite useless. All I could gain was permission to come here myself. As I came out a man hurried in and there was a woman coming down the corridor: when she saw him, she said, "God rot him", and I suppose I stared at her rather hard. She looked at me and

203

called me by name. And Walter, it was the Queen. We went into the garden and had some talk. She wants to visit you and bring her son, Prince Henry. She wants him to meet a man. That's you, my love. Moreover, she said that she would spare neither her voice nor her hand to get you out of here.'

'That is news indeed. What is she like? Has she any power?'

'You'll see when she comes. She's short and thin but sturdy. Her face is rather plain, square too and hard but lovely when she smiles. Her voice is delightful, deep, and her speech is broken. But she knows what she wants and is full of plans for her son. Walter, a woman after my own heart.'

'I'm glad one of the Queens of England has managed to please you,' said Raleigh, amused at Lisbeth's enthusiasm.

'She'll please you too,' said Lisbeth confidently.

'Maybe. But meantime, Lisbeth, much as I love you for thinking of it, I don't want you to stay here.'

'Why not, pray?'

'You'll hate it. It wouldn't suit you. You'll wither and wilt. Every room is damp, the sun never shines. And the rules will drive you distracted.'

'Oh no. Oh no. What you can bear with your ague we can bear.'

'We?'

'Walter and I. He is without now.'

'This is no place for him.'

'No? What will be good for the Prince of Wales will surely be good for Raleigh's son. And that is his father's company. I want my son to meet a man, too.'

She gave his fingers a final squeeze and then went to the door.

There she paused and said seriously:

'You can't dissuade me; I have always lived where I liked. That is the right of a free woman.'

A free woman, she thought, as the door yielded to her hand. She thought of the deep woods and the green fields of Sherborne, the gracious rooms, the garden that had been her delight. The thought of the Tower struck her coldly, she had

204

already dreaded it. But she had chosen it now because, for all her boasted freedom, she was nothing more than the slave of the proud man whom misfortune could not break. And nothing less. She called young Walter in.

II

'Go on, go on,' urged the Prince.

'But that is the end of the story. There was nothing left to do but to go home,' said Raleigh, leaning back in his chair and filling his pipe.

'And you never went again?'

'No, various matters arose to make it impossible for a little time and when I sent Whiddon out scouting again he found the river junction fortified by Berrio. If I'd had enough money to have gone back directly the rains stopped... I might not be here, spinning idle yarns.'

'Who but my father would keep such a bird in a cage?' said Henry. 'Don't lose heart, Sir Walter, or let your spirit fail you, easy as that would be in the circumstances. One day I shall be king and then I promise you you shall have all the ships and men and money that you can use.'

Raleigh smiled. 'Come with me, I'll show you something.'

He led the young Prince to a converted hen-house which Waad, impressed by his prisoner's popularity with the Queen and her son, had placed at his service. He had fitted it as a laboratory with distilling plant and a furnace for trying ores. Here he prepared his unguents and cordials according to Topiawari's recipes. And here he made his experiments. He reached up to a shelf and took down a flask. Drawing out the stopper he offered it to Henry. 'Taste it.'

The Prince drank, lowered the flask with a puzzled expression and sniffed at it.

'This is only water,' he said, thinking that Raleigh had made some mistake.

'Good water?'

'Yes, good plain water. What of it?'

'I made it. Have you ever considered the battles that have

205

been lost, the explorers who have had to turn back, the glorious ventures foiled and the men who have died of thirst because the water casks were dry? And around them for miles there was the sea. No sailor need have died of thirst, no explorer turned back for lack of water. That you have just tasted was distilled from sea water. Whiddon brought me that cask. I boiled some, caught the vapour, poured it from vessel to vessel to restore the air (it was flat tasting before that) and you didn't know it from well-water. Is that a discovery?'

'One worth these years of imprisonment to make.' Henry spoke solemnly.

'Maybe. I sometimes wonder whether anything in this world can happen without fulfilling some secret purpose. I should never have thought of that outside.'

'And I might not have known you.'

'Not so well, perhaps. In the whirl of Court life, the story of Guiana would sound like the droning of a dotard.'

'Oh no. The world has ever a use and an ear for a brave story. And you have the bravest and the best told that I ever listened to. The time remaining to you should be short now. Carr is disgraced and Villiers, my father's new man, hates the Howards and is friend to my mother and to me. I shall have power now, I have my own establishment already and I shall never rest until you are free, my friend. But in that little time... but it is audacity in me to suggest aught to you...'

'Go on,' said Raleigh.

'In that little time, you might achieve an immortality by your pen.'

'My story is already told.'

'There is a bigger. You who alone of those I know can look backwards and forwards should write a history of the world.'

A history of the world. A fine phrase. Man had fallen; Jerusalem had been sacked; Rome had gone down before the barbarian hordes. And the long years in the Tower had taught him patience alongside despair. He did not believe so readily as the Prince did in his imminence of his release. There was plenty of time.

'I'll do it,' he exclaimed. 'I'll write a history of the world for you.'

Afire with the idea, he closed the hen-house door. The great experiment had been made, successfully. There was a good store of unguents. His attention would be undivided. Doctor Burrel would lend him books and advice. Ben Jonson would see the completed work through the press. And for himself the book would mean escape. From the two rooms and the terrace and the tiny laboratory he would escape. He would fight at Salamis.

> *Peloponneus, your four thousand sons*
> *Sleep, after battle, with three millions.*

Through Thermopylae he too would fight his way to freedom. The voice of the young Prince broke upon the dream that it had begotten.

'Give me a pipe, Sir Walter. My father has just uttered a blast against the pernicious habit, so it must be needs to be a manly one, I think.'

III

Propped up upon many pillows and with a hot brick at his feet Prince Henry fought back his weakness long enough to finish the book.

'O eloquent, just, and mighty Death,' he read with failing eyes. 'Whom none could advise, thou hast persuaded; what none have dared, thou hast done; and whom all the world have flattered, thou only hast cast out of the world and despised; thou hast drawn together all the far-stretched greatness, all the pride, cruelty, and ambition of man, and covered it over these two narrow words, "Hic Jacet".'

'The last words I shall read, and worthy ones,' he said so faintly that Villiers had to stoop to catch them.

'Work for him, George. You alone must plan what we planned to do together. Fail me not. There was never a man with brain so able, soul so lofty or courage so high. He must not die a prisoner. That golden tongue!'

207

'You hand over your task too soon,' said Villiers brokenly. 'You will live to get him out yourself, never fear.'

'Not I. When I used to stand by Raleigh while he made that cordial, I heard him say repeatedly that all ills not caused by poison gave way before it. A quart of it has not served me. Poisoned I am and I shall die. My hopes, my future kingship, all that I might have done are stillborn and will scarce need even the narrow words "Hic Jacet".'

'You talk too much. It increases the fever,' said Villiers.

He walked to the window and stood watching the rooks winging through the red afternoon to their nests in the black elms whose leafless tops netted the sky. It was sad, he thought, to die in the spring of one's day and when the spring was swelling the buds on every tree in England. He knew that the world regarded harshly his allegiance to the Prince, putting it down to his desire to be as much in favour with the future King as he was with James. The world did not know, and he was not the man to bother to inform it, that the young Prince, now dying upon that bed, had a real and powerful claim upon his worldly and superficial heart.

He turned from the window and said gently, 'Let me lay you down. Your mother will be in with the doctor in ten minutes. I heard them bidden to wake her at four.'

'Countermand the order, George, as you love me. It is her first rest in six days and she can do me no good. It tears her heart to see me and mine to listen to her crying. Do that, George, and then come back to me and shut the door against the leeches.'

Unwilling but obedient, Villiers did as he was told. He hoped that this show of spirit augured well. Henry might be feeling stronger.

When he returned, he found the Prince sunk deeper into the pillows, one hand still clasping *The History of the World*.

'One last favour, George. Light me a pipe. I doubt if I can smoke it. But if I must die, how better could I do than with his book in one hand and his pipe in the other?'

In death, thought the worldling, the eyes saw clearly. The dying thief could look at his battered fellow felon on the Cross

208

and call him 'Lord'. And the Prince in death, for there was no doubt now in Villiers' mind, saw something so attractive in that old prisoner in the Tower that he must imitate his pipe-smoking, as in life he had imitated his walk.

Handing him the pipe he pulled the bell that would bring in the Queen and the doctors and then returning to the bed said solemnly, 'I promise you that I will spare no effort on your Raleigh's behalf.'

It took him two years exactly to fulfill that promise.

Chapter 28

London
1617

He set out to walk from the Tower to the house that Lisbeth had taken and left the Tower a week earlier to prepare. Passers-by took no note of the tall, stooped man with the white hair, the stiffly held, useless left arm and dragging walk. They did not know him. The days when Sir Walter Raleigh was stared at and pointed out in the streets were gone. Nor did they guess that to him they were all as fair as angels in the gay March morning sun. The watermen with their pails, the housewives with their baskets, the vegetable vendors with their strings of onions and bunches of carrots, he stared at them all, enthralled. After twelve years he was walking the streets again, the dust was blowing in his face, the cobbles irking his unaccustomed feet, the voices of his fellows sharp in his ears after a long quiet.

A lady, passing in a sedan chair, saw him staring and drew the curtains, half in coquetry and half in annoyance. How could she guess that she was the first passenger of the kind that he had ever seen?

Staring and pausing, slightly dizzy in the bustle, he came to the modest little house that Lisbeth had thought suitable to their straitened means. She and Walter had been at the window and hastened to the door to welcome him. She was wearing the same rose-sprinkled dress that she had worn when she had waited upon the King. It had been laid away in lavender since that day, it smelt strongly of the herb, and in the gathers at the waist the folds of the silk had cut themselves through.

'Poor Lisbeth,' he said, when the moments of emotion upon his arrival had gone, 'we must get you a new dress.'

'I do well enough,' said Lisbeth. 'The man who sold me this was a rogue. Twelve years in a press have worn it out worse than if I had worn it every day.'

'It fits you still. Are you never going to be matronly, Lisbeth?'

'I have enough grey hair and shall have more. Walter, go into the kitchen and fetch the wine and the sweetmeats.'

Obedient to his mother at twenty as he had been at ten, Walter went. As soon as the door had closed behind him Lisbeth dropped her gay manner and spoke urgently.

'Walter, I've had a terrible week with him. As soon as he heard of the reason for your freedom, he began recalling that promise that you made him when he was eight. He swears that you vowed he should go with you next time you went to Guiana. You must deny it, swear that he imagined...'

The door opened and Walter appeared with a salver in his hands.

'Thank you,' said Lisbeth. 'Did you look at the fire, Walter?'

'No.'

'Then just go and see that it is mended. I must get the dinner going in a moment.'

Walter looked at her and laughed. 'Oh no, mother. You won't get me out of this room again until I have asked father my question. You'll be persuading him into denying what is true if I give you time. Father, didn't you promise me at Sherborne that I should go with you next time you went to Guiana?'

'I don't remember. My memory was never as good as I could have wished.'

'I asked you at the foot of the stairs on the Christmas Eve when you came with Lord Cobham and another man for Christmas. You didn't say yes or no then, you just laughed at me and asked me why I wanted to go. Then after that, one day, that day when you came riding with me, I asked you again and you did solemnly say that you'd take me. I can remember your very words. Shall I repeat them?

'It's all invention, Walter,' said Lisbeth sharply. 'Your father would know better than to promise such a thing to a child.

211

Why, he might have gone back the next year. How could he have taken you then?'

'You said,' Walter went on, addressing his father and ignoring his mother. '"My son", so you see it was a solemn occasion, he began, "my son", mother. "My son, I promise you that I will take you. To have one to follow me by the call of blood would be the greatest comfort I could know." There.'

'He would never have said that to a child and you couldn't have remembered it if he had,' Lisbeth spoke with finality.

'As a matter of fact, those were my very words, Lisbeth.'

He thought back to that bright January morning when he had ridden beside Walter under the avenue of beeches at Sherborne. Now the plump little boy was twenty, almost a man, and holding him to his promise with a stare as steely as his own.

'It will need some consideration,' he said in answer to the stare. 'Circumstances have changed since those days.'

Sick fear seized Lisbeth. She, too, remembered that Christmas and the carol which she interrupted because she words hurt her.

'Stand by your word, father. I'd be more useful to you than anyone else would be. I'd forget that you were my father except that my obedience would be more prompt and faithful than any other's. Please, father. I've longed for it all my life.'

'A week ago it was all unplanned, your father was still soliciting Villiers for the King's permission. All your life! Are you but a week old? Faith, one would think so to hear you talk.'

'Let the boy be,' said Raleigh, observing the young face take on a mutinous, sullen look. 'I made the promise, not thinking how things would be when I was faced with it again. We'll talk it over, Walter, later. But I'll say now that I rather you didn't come. After dinner we'll go down and see about putting the ship in hand. I shall call her *Destiny*, for mine she is.'

On the way back from the docks they met George Percy, one of the few who had visited Raleigh in the Tower. He fell into step beside them and began to talk of the expedition.

'So he's let you out on condition that you bring him back a gold-mine. I hope you may do it. But a word in your ear—the

Spaniards know all about it already. Don Diego, the Spanish Ambassador, has offered to secure you a safe passage. You know what that means. He'll know all your plans. And you'll get just as far as they intend you to and not an inch further.'

'I know. All this hob-nobbing with Spain is enough to make an Englishman sick. Still, I'm out on those conditions and must take things as they come. I wasn't in a position to dictate my terms. And a word in *your* ear—I've given the Spaniards the slip before and with God's help may again. Any other news?'

'There's a native Virginian staying at the *Bell Inn*. They say she's a princess in her own country, I'm on the way there now. Would you care to come?'

'Care to? Come on, man, mend your pace.'

A Virginian! One who could tell him how Smith's colony was faring.

'It wouldn't be Pocahontas herself, I suppose?' he asked, breathless at the pace which he himself had set.

'That's the name,' said Percy, 'she was at the races at Newmarket with the King and Queen the other day.'

Raleigh entered the *Bell* almost reverently. Pocahontas, tall and slim and the colour of dead oak leaves, rose to greet Percy whom she already knew. He presented Raleigh, half jeeringly, to the 'Princess', for to Percy's limited insular mind royalty was the prerogative of white skin and he was surprised to see Raleigh go down upon his knees and kiss the brown hand with every sign of deep respect. Young Walter in his turn did likewise. Powhatan's daughter, who had met with kindness and curiosity in England but little reverence, beamed with pleasure on this tall and stately man with the beautiful manners and the handsome son.

'You know Captain John Smith?' she asked, in her broken English.

'Well. He is my man. I sent him to Virginia.'

'You sent him? And you are proud of him?'

'Very. His energy and his courage have got the colony going at last. How are they faring?'

'Well, now that they look for gold no more but grow tobacco

213

and the potatoes and the Indian corn for bread. It was not so always. And but for me there would be no Captain Smith.'

'No?'

'No,' said Pocahontas, shaking her head. 'You have not heard the story of how I buy his life?'

Her eyes shone with the spurious brightness of phthisis, its easy vivid colour flooded her dark cheeks.

'No, tell me. I have heard very few stories of late.'

'My father captured him one day when he hunt in the big forest. My father not love the white men, he ordered his head off. They bring the stone and the axe. Looking out I see him. That lovely white neck, the beard like the sun. I run from the hut and put my head upon his so they strike me first. But I am the King's daughter. They do not dare to strike. He is save. I talk with my father and the next day we take corn and buffalo meat to the white man and I show them how to plant the seed.'

'A grand story,' said Raleigh, 'let me add my gratitude to his. We could ill have spared such a man.'

Pocahontas looked wistful.

'He is not grateful to me now. Once maybe, not now. He sent me here, far away.'

'You'll go back, Pocahontas. Back to Virginia.'

'Some time perhaps. But Captain John Smith, he loves me not. It matters little where I am.'

Tragedy stirred in the little room. White man, brown woman. How many more would there be, Raleigh wondered, before the white men's flags waved over all the earth.

They took their leave of the tragic Princess, destined to give her love to the Englishman, her health to the English winter and to lay her bones in an English graveyard, and went back to the little house where Lisbeth, weary of eye and hot-cheeked with cooking, awaited them with their supper.

The *Destiny* grew upon the stocks: the Spanish Ambassador and the King whispered together until every plan, every plank, every barrel were known in Madrid: and Lisbeth made her last stand. Life, that had taken her love, her comfort, her wealth and freedom and pride, was now bidding for her son and with every breath and nerve she fought that last battle. And it was the harder because, as well as the fates, the two beings on earth that she loved were ranged against her.

'You are too young to know what you want,' she said desperately to Walter.

'I am nigh on twenty-one. Older than father was when he went to war in the Netherlands,' was Walter's stubborn answer.

'It's all so wrong. You shouldn't go under the conditions that the King and the Spaniards have enforced,' she said, turning to Raleigh, 'but I've given up trying to reason with you. But you shouldn't encourage the boy. Say no, and mean it, and spare me my son.'

'He is my son too, Lisbeth.'

'Your son! Did you ever think of that you were waiting for the Queen's word and I was bringing him up? Never. Then he was a troublesome child who pined in the London air. Now, when thanks to me he has grown to man's estate you only see in him one more sacrifice to make to your God of adventure. Why don't you offer me a place as cook or sail-maker aboard your ship and make a family affair of it?'

'You are unfair, Lisbeth. You were never fair where my ventures were concerned.'

'How could it be? It was the last Guiana voyage that brought us to ruin, I see that plainly now. It wasn't because you were supposed to have plotted against him that James is your enemy but because you were known as an enemy to Spain, whom he was anxious to placate. That is why we lost Sherborne and spent twelve years in the Tower. Now you are fool enough to go looking for gold on the Spaniards doorstep and promise not to strike a blow. And they know where and when you go. And you expect to take Walter with you. How can you be so, so damnably blind?' She drew a deep breath and said more quietly, 'You go, if you have a mind to. Your life is your own. You never did belong to me for more than a few fleeting hours. But Walter is mine, flesh of my flesh: I bore him and trained him, nursed him when he was sick, taught him when he was well. I will not let him go.'

She pressed her hands together in her lap and stared at them both with hard defiant eyes.

'But, mother, other men leave their mothers. Hundreds of boys would gladly sail with father and their mothers would be proud for them to go. George Raleigh is going. I couldn't stay behind. I won't. If you talk father into forbidding me to go with him, I'll do something else. I'll go to the Muscovy Company, they'll have me and be glad of the chance. I know that you've done all for me, looked after me and brought me up,'—he moved uneasily, thinking with embarrassment of the not-so-distant dependence of childhood,—'but so did your mother for you. Yet you went out into the world and had your own way. I should think perhaps your mother would have advised you against marrying the Queen's favourite and going to the Tower as you did. But you wouldn't have heeded her.'

'I should have been wiser to have done,' said Lisbeth bitterly.

And so saying she turned her defiant eyes to Raleigh. Immediately she wished the words unspoken. There had always been a hard streak in her. Misfortune moved her not to tears but to anger; and she could look at life uncompromisingly and without self-deceit. The last years had strengthened that hard streak with layers of cynicism and fortitude but she was still not hard enough. For twelve years she had lived with Raleigh in close quarters and so the changes that the years had brought had established themselves unnoticed before her eyes. But now, as she saw him start and gaze at her, hurt by her bitterness, she saw too that he was an ageing man, frail and vulnerable in his body as he had never been before. The sorry realisation of the brevity of life struck her. Youth had flown, they had wished away the days, counting on this chance and that to do this or that for them. And now in the end life had cheated. He was bent on a perilous venture for which he was ill-fitted and he was the man whom she loved. For the last time she experienced the old familiar weakness, knew that in a moment she would, in her own heart, capitulate. She struggled against herself for a moment and then said in a queer new voice, 'Walter, leave us for a moment… no, I won't try to persuade him, I promise.'

Reluctantly the boy went out, not quite closing the door behind him and lingering in the passage ready to dash into the fray at the first sign of battle. Lisbeth went over to Raleigh and laid her hand on his thin bowed shoulder. He looked at her dumbly. The whole scene, and those similar ones that had preceded it, were inexpressibly painful to him, seeing as he did so plainly both Walter's point of view and Lisbeth's. But now she was speaking softly.

'Years ago, I gave you everything I had, Walter. There is nothing left now but the boy. You need more than I do. Take him.'

'But, you said... a moment ago...' stammered Raleigh, disconcerted by this change of front.

'I know. Forget it. I didn't mean it. His place is with you.'

Relief and pleasure at the anticipation of Walter's delight, and joy in this end to an unpleasant situation, took twenty years from Raleigh's age. He rose and seized her hands.

'You shan't regret it, Lisbeth. He'll be safe with me, I promise you. Let's call him in and tell him.' The old excitement danced for a moment in his tired eyes.

Lisbeth shook her head, 'You can do that,' she said, and loosing her hands she hurried through the door, stumbled over Walter and ran upstairs where she flung herself upon the bed in a flood of tears. The early days of their passionate loving, the secret wooing, their estrangements, reconciliations, the trials borne together swirled through her brain as she lay sobbing. Where did it all lead and to what purpose? That one might go naked and weary to the grave. Perhaps that was life's sole object, to so reduce one's strength and pride and high hope that in the end of the grave was a desirable and pleasant place.

Chapter 29

The Canaries
October 1617

Time drives flocks from fold to fold

The Governor's house at Gomera in the Lesser Canaries was a
low white building surrounded by a deep veranda paved with
bright Spanish tiles. Climbing plants swarmed up the pillars
and nodded freely at the top; a tame monkey amused himself
by running along the veranda roof pelting any passer-by with
flowers.

The Governor's wife was casting a last critical glance at
a table laid for supper in a room separated from the veranda
by a flimsy door of threaded canes. Usually, a task of such a
domestic nature would have bored her and she would have left
it to the black servant who at that moment was following her
round, terrified that unwonted interest boded ill. She found no
cause for complaint in the table spread with a cloth of lace and
bright with silver and flowers; and the servants breathed a sigh
of relief as she nodded and, pouring some wine into a beaker,
strolled out on to the veranda and threw herself upon a couch
that stood there, heaped with cushions.

This would be the first time in her life that she had entertained
a man alone, she thought as she sipped her wine. Carlos would
probably be furious if he knew. She shrugged her shoulders
at the thought. He was always in a rage about something
whether she gave him cause or not, so what did it matter? He
was busy with a court on the other side of the island and when
the messenger had arrived with a letter from the captain of an
English ship that had just put in at the harbour, she had been

seized with a half-mischievous, wholly irresistible impulse to turn his timely arrival into a mild adventure. She would not have done so but for the gloves. They had arrived with the letter which she had sent by the runner to her husband, a pair of soft white English gloves with embroidered gauntlets. They proved their sender was a man of state as well as imagination and she had forthwith bidden him to supper. Now, with every curl and jewel in place she awaited his arrival. He might be old, she warned herself, or impossibly ugly but even so she would have the pleasure of hearing the English speech once more and gathering news of the civilised world. That, to an exile, would be worth a meal and the risk of a jealous man's displeasure.

With a quickening heart she heard the ringing of the great bell at the gate and sharply bade the chattering monkey to be quiet. He retorted by throwing down a spray of pink rose that lodged amongst her dark curls and she was carefully though furiously detaching it when the black servant ushered the Englishman through the main door of the house. Holding it in her left hand she went forward with her right outstretched and a smile of welcome and a gracious speech upon her lips. Then suddenly the smile froze, she dropped the rose and with a little gasp put her hand to her breast.

Raleigh stopped, arrested by her change of face, wondering why the sight of an invited guest should startle her so. She looked at him unsteadily, her bright green eyes blinking and darting as if at every glance they expected the vision to vanish.

'You do not remember me?' she asked at the end of a half-minute that seemed ten times its length.

'I crave your pardon. My memory is defective. And yet... the voice, the face... are certainly familiar.'

She pulled herself together with a visible effort and took a step or two towards him with her hand outstretched again. He bowed over it and lifted it to his lips, aware of its trembling and icy cold. Then he looked at her again. Who the devil was she and why was she so horribly discomposed? He saw a tall slender woman in the last flush of a beauty that must have once been considerable. Green eyes, black hair, creamy skin. Where

219

had he seen her before? Wrinkling his brow he stared at her dress, as if by that he might gain some clue. Lilac silk, a rather outdated stomacher of amethyst, amethysts in her ears and on her fingers. He lifted his eyes to her face again. His obvious bewilderment restored her poise and gave her time to make a successful bid for control.

'Never has been a long time, hasn't it, Captain Raleigh?'

Never. A long time! He had it. The castle at Bally-in-Harsh: his heart all atwitter lest his ruse had failed: Lady Roche saying farewell to her husband and himself bending above just such a quivering cold hand.

'Janis,' he said.

'And you, after all these years. Oh, I am so glad to see you.'

'And I you. I was expecting some very stiff Spanish lady who would ask me all the awkward questions that her husband boggled at. Of course, you knew whom to expect from my letter.'

She shook her head. 'No, I sent that on to my husband, who is from home. I was bold enough to ask you to supper with me, just myself.'

She laid one hand on the cane curtain but at its first rattle a black hand on the inside pulled it away and they stepped into the room, lighted now with candles.

Two dark eunuchs, silent on their bare feet, served the food and wines and Raleigh, newly recovered from a vile bout of sea-sickness, was glad that the conversation took on the casual nature that permitted him to give his attention to the meal.

'I hope your father forgave me,' he said in one of the easy pauses.

'Forgave! He admired you above all men. He was never tired of telling the story of how you arrested the whole town. He used to vow that if a few more of the English were like you he'd be a rebel no more.'

It was like hearing some stranger praised, some boy whom one had known a little and who was dead. How brightly it had opened, the little saga of his life... He banished the wistful thought and straightened his shoulders with a determination that the end should at least be worthy of the beginning.

'How do you come to be here?' he asked to divert his own attention from himself.

'That is a long story,' said Janis, 'and,' with a glance at the attendants, 'one that I will tell you later. Tell me about London and the new King.'

'I know so little of either. I have been in the Tower for more than twelve years.'

'So long? I heard something of the affair at the time. The Spaniards were glad. They felt that Guiana was safe while you were imprisoned. You are married, of course?' There was a shade too casual a tone in that question.

'Twenty-one years ago.'

'You have children?'

'A son. And you?'

Janis shook her head.

Fearing lest that admission had been painful to her he betrayed Walter's adoration to say:

'They are a mixed blessing. They grow from children into people for whom one feels responsibility without having authority.'

'Your son has disappointed you?'

'Oh no. He thinks too highly of me. He insisted upon accompanying me upon this venture. That means that I sail vulnerable as I have never been.'

'The ancients speak of children as hostages to fortune.'

'In that, as in many things, they spoke the truth.'

In conversation such as this the meal drew to an end. Janis addressed a terse sentence in Spanish to the servant and rose. With her hand on the cane curtain that covered the veranda doorway she paused and turned.

'It will be more comfortable within,' she said, and led the way to an inner room, hung with tapestry, furnished with low cushioned couches and containing many books.

'We can talk here,' she said.

Before she seated herself, she took from one of the shelves what looked like a thin book covered with leather and she tucked it behind a cushion as she sat down.

221

'You were going to tell me how you came here,' prompted Raleigh, anxious to trace the road that had led her from the cold bare Irish castle to this luxurious, half tropical island.

'It is little of a story, really, unless I you the reason; and I am not certain that I should do that. But I will...'

She pulled up a cushion behind her head and leaned back.

'It was the Armada that brought me here. I had stayed at Bally for six years after your visit and I intended to stay there all my life. Then, one morning a wreck was stranded on the rocks. The men went out with boats and got off some of the people, they were Spaniards. One of them was the man I married.'

Her voice trailed off into silence as she sat in this strange company, remembering that far-away morning when the stumbling, exhausted men had crept into the hospitality of the Bally Castle. She drew out the slim leather-covered case that looked like a book and opened it. It was a portrait in a folding frame. She stared at it a moment and then handed it to Raleigh who took it and looked down, with astonishment, upon what seemed for a moment his own pictured face.

'That is my husband,' said Janis.

'He is like... I mean, have you noticed the resemblance?'

'To you? But of course. For a moment, that morning, I thought that some strange chance had brought you back.'

Simple words, simply spoken. Yet they betrayed her. The waiting, the hope, the prayers to the saints and to the Virgin for a return that was never made: all the dreams of her girlhood were laid bare by that one sentence. She had waited for six years and at the end of them had greeted a stranger who had worn a familiar face.

'Not many galleons were cast up upon our coast, more went to the west. Some of the common sailors stayed and are there now, or their children are, but the important ones waited their chance and then slipped home. When Carlos left, I went with him. That's how I came here... Do you ever think when you look back over your life, how different it would have been but for some quite accidental thing? We don't make our lives, really, do we?'

Suppose, she was thinking, it had really been Raleigh on that bright morning; suppose he had loved her as Carlos had done, what different paths she would have trodden. And suppose she had never seen Raleigh, what charm would the silent, alien castaway have held for her then?

And Raleigh thought, suppose I had seen the charm of her that evening and married her before ever I saw the Queen. I should never then have suffered that fatal set-back over Lisbeth. I might have been in Cecil's place by the time the Queen died and not now staking my all on this perilous venture.

'We make them, in a sense, but we can only use the material that comes to hand and some of it too unwieldy and swamps our efforts to deal with it. And to look back on life is like reading a story from the end backwards.'

'Your story should look well from either end.'

'Mine? Why?'

'You've been important and had power. Even I, in this backwater, had heard of you.'

'I haven't attained much of what I wanted. There have been the good times and may again. If this venture succeeds. But who can tell? And the time is too short for failure now.'

'Would you really like to know what the future holds?' She looked at him queerly, hanging upon his answer.

'I should, but who knows save God?'

For an answer she rose and went across the room and opened a drawer. She rummaged in it for some moments, then slammed it shut impatiently and opened another. Diving into it she drew out a parcel wrapped in black velvet and with it in her hand came and seated herself close to him. Without unfolding the parcel she said:

'I can tell you. I haven't done this for some years. My last confessor regarded it as a deadly sin, so I put away and forgot it. But the one I have now is very lenient and will absolve me, especially if I do it for you, not for myself.'

Raleigh watched her unfold the velvet and expose a ball of crystal, faintly green and with a wreath like smoke coiling in its depths. She curved her hands about it, warming it in her palm.'

'Look in it,' she said at last, 'you may have the gift too. An old Spanish woman gave it to me, long ago in Seville. I discovered that I could use it quite by accident.'

It dropped into his cupped hand, heavy and cold. A chill struck the back of his neck and crept up his scalp.

Superstition and scepticism combined to silence the protest that rose to his lips. He believed in the thing sufficiently to long to know what might be learned of it; and he disbelieved it sufficiently to discount the warning tremor that struck through him as he looked down at the harmless glass.

Nothing stirred in the pale green depths, the smoke wreath was invisible now, all was clear and empty. He handed it back to her. She spread the velvet over a cushion and placed the globe upon it, touching it with the tips of her fingers on either side.

The silence was thickened as she bent her head above the crystal: and it grew deeper until it seemed that the whole world had stopped to listen to Raleigh's fate.

When Janis spoke at last her voice was strange, low and impersonal and awed.

'You have so many enemies,' she said, 'and so few friends. There is a boy... of course, your son, and a woman with fair hair. Your wife? They are faithful. There is a sailor, too, who will die for you and some brown men who are your friends.'

Silence again and nothing in the crystal, for the seer's eyes had strayed to the hand which lay on the arm of the chair near by. She remembered dressing herself in the early evening; she had anticipated then, at the best an evening of discreet flirtation, at the worst one of gossipy interest. And then the hours had brought her this memory of an old and powerful infatuation and here she was gaping into a glass globe to see what the fates might hold for him, when all the time she longed to take that splendid, shattered body into her arms and smooth away the lines that the unkind years had traced upon his face with kisses that had been kept from him these five and thirty years.

With an effort she dragged her eyes and her thoughts back to the matter in hand.

There was another long silence and then the strange voice said, 'Your men will reach the mine. You'll never see it, you are going to very ill, very ill indeed. Then...'

Raleigh leaned forward, conscious of sudden tension in her body. He saw her mouth drop open, her eyes start in horror. With one hand she covered the ball with the corner of the velvet, the other flew to her throat as she leaped to her feet, deathly pale, breathing hard and struggling for words.

'Dear God,' she stammered, 'it was a sin in me but did it merit such punishment?'

'What is it? What have you seen?'

She dropped her hand at the question and dropped her lids over the horror- stricken eyes.

'It was nothing,' she babbled, 'nothing to do with you. It was myself. I saw myself... it was nothing to do with you.'

Her effort to reassure him was too obvious. The sceptic in him gave way before a full flood of ghostly fear.

'What is it? You must tell me!'

But Janis had recovered herself and the next lie came more convincingly from her blanched lips.

'It was nothing to do with you. That is God's truth. My mind slipped. I tried to see it for you and I saw myself instead. I'll never touch the thing again.'

She picked up the silver bell that stood on a nearby table and rang it violently. To the servant who appeared as if by magic in answer she said sharply, 'Bring wine, and quickly.' Waiting for the man's return she picked up the crystal and opening the window threw it far, out into the darkness. 'I'm so sorry,' she said as the curtain fell back into place, 'it was an unfortunate chance. But we will not let it mar our meeting, will we?'

She mustered a smile and when the wine arrived, poured it out with a steady hand and said, 'A toast to your mine. May it be all that you hope it.'

'And one to our meeting, that has been more than I had hoped,' Raleigh responded.

She seated herself again in the same chair and dragged it a little closer to him. There was a subtle change in her manner.

'Have you ever thought of me?'

'Often.' And that in a way was true, for whenever he had remembered that midnight march from Bally to Cork, he had pictured the meal at the Castle and both Lady Roche and her daughter had been recalled as puppets in the background of the little drama.

'I'm glad of that,' said Janis, 'I had thought of you so often and wondered if I would ever see you again. I never dreamed that it would be like this.'

She had never realised that the years would touch him; whiten that black hair; hamper him with that dragging leg and unsteady hand. She had led so sheltered and undisturbed a life that the years had dealt gently with her. There were a few faint lines around her eyes that deepened as she smiled; one or two white hairs that could be tweaked away from the shining curls. Yet there were only thirteen or fourteen years between their ages and although in youth such a gap loomed large, in the later years it narrowed. And yet it seemed as if she were looking at a very old man. And a doomed man. For there had been no mistaking the significance of the scene that had formed in the smoky depths of the crystal. Something more than a memory of her youthful adoration stirred in her heart. A desire to console, to protect, to save him, shook her. It found no more adequate outlet than the stretching forward of her hand towards his, she curled her warm white fingers around the cold, nerveless ones that lay on the arm of his chair.

'I suppose you must go on this errand?'

He laid his other hand over hers.

'It is my only hope. Why? Did you see disaster in that globe?'

'Oh no. Only, if you are to be ill... You'll be so far away. And only men with you...'

'They are excellent nurses, you know. Besides, your vision may all be wrong.'

'I'm sure I hope so.'

But there was no doubt in her mind. And at the thought she drew away that inadequate hand. In the face of what she had seen advancing relentlessly towards him, any gesture seemed

226

silly and futile. He must go; and, for her own peace of mind, she must forget. The bright charm and fire of his youth, the pathos and shock of his age, must be alike forgotten.

Almost as though he had felt the retreat of her mind, Raleigh rose to take his leave.

'I will send down some fresh fruit and sugar in the morning,' said Janis. She spoke with an effort that made her voice sound flat and forced. She knew this time that she would never see him again. He had reappeared in her life as the last line of a song reappears sometimes at the end, rounding it off rather sadly.

And Raleigh, with her hand against his lips again, cast up at her a glance that seemed to imply that he understood it all, past dreams and present sorrow. Even his formal words of gratitude spoke thanks for more than mere hospitality or the promised gifts of the morrow.

Janis left him at the main door and then walked as if in a dream back to her seat on the veranda. The moon was high and brilliant and by its light she could see the monkey playing with something. Idly she called him and he came sheepishly and laid the crystal in her lap. She jumped up screaming. With no pretence to arm her now the full horror of what she had seen in that harmless globe smote her. As the first black eunuch dashed breathlessly from the house she fell in a faint at his large bare feet.

Raleigh walked back to his ship. Even by its evidence of the distance of youth the meeting had failed to disturb him. He recalled it already as mistily as one recalls a dream. It meant something, had enormous significance; but the numbing touch of the years, the press of present care were merciful anaesthetics to his once so lively mind. Moving slowly through the warm bright night he wondered whether he would ever feel anything again.

Chapter 30

Trinidad
December 1617 — March 1618

Red sails in the sunset

He rolled his aching head upon the hard pillow and moaned. For the fourth time that morning, he had attempted to leave his bunk and had fallen back defeated by weakness that no determination could overcome. And now, though impatience was shaking him to the heart, making it flutter and miss its beat, he must lie here and let another day pass. Another day, twenty-four hours in which he might have done so much. Apparently that devilish globe had shown the truth. He had been warned of this.

Keymis came quietly and stood in the doorway, peering in to see if his leader were asleep.

'Come in, man,' cried Walter impatiently, 'I want to talk with you.'

'How do you find yourself this morning?' Keymis asked gently.

'Damnably ill still. How are the other sick?'

'Four are recovering. Two more...' He bit back the words, fearing their effect upon the suffering man.

'Dead? That makes forty-two on the *Destiny* alone, Keymis. This is unbearable. Here we lie, waiting upon this devilish ailment of mine and the men are dying every day and every day the Spaniards are better prepared against us. I must go today. I *must* get up. I tried just now and failed. But perhaps with your help...'

228

'I daren't help you,' said Keymis gravely. To help you to leave your bed would be to help you to the grave.'

'Keymis, you must. There's no other way. With a friendly arm to cling to when I first set foot to the floor I can manage. You know what this delay means to me. I appeal to you. You must help me.'

'Very well,' said the sailor, moved against his better judgement by the words, 'You know what this delay means to me.'

He came close to the bed and thrust his strong arm behind the thin shoulders, aware of the prominent bones, the heat and the sweat. Raleigh moved his legs feebly over the side and rose to his feet, clinging to Keymis as a drowning man might. Keymis saw the bearded underlip disappear as the teeth bit over it and the cold sweat appear on the lined brow. Raleigh moved his arm from the supporting shoulder and said, breathing hard, 'All right. Loose me. I shall do now.'

Very cautiously Keymis withdrew his arm.

'My breeches, if you please.'

The sailor reached out for the serviceable dark garments that had replaced the courtier's finery. And Raleigh, with his hand outstretched to take them, dropped like a stone.

Keymis picked him up easily and laid him on the bed again. The eyes were closed and the teeth still clenched the lower lip. It was a dead face.

A bottle of brandy stood on a locker beside the bunk and Keymis reached for it, uncorked it and with no gentle hand prised open Raleigh's mouth. The strong spirituous smell filled the cabin as the first tilt of the bottle sent the liquid showering over the sick man's chin and chest. The second attempt was more successful, Keymis could see the throat muscles move as Raleigh swallowed the draught and in a minute or two the eyelids fluttered and Raleigh said faintly, 'I see, it is useless. Sit down a minute, my friend. I must make other plans.'

There was silence in the cabin for some five minutes. Keymis stared round at the paintings and the books and the jade Buddha, as if he were seeing them for the first time. He

229

knew in what penury his leader had made ready for the sea and was puzzled, not for the first time, at the mentality of a man who, desperately poor and bound on a reckless and desperate errand, should yet surround himself with such state. Spartan and rather Puritanic as he was himself, he saw nothing to blame and something to admire in such a man. And that puzzled him too. He looked at me thin face, lying with closed eyes on the pillow, and wondered what new plan was afoot behind that shuttered façade. He was soon to be enlightened.

'There's nought else for it, Keymis. You must go without me.'

Keymis was well aware what that statement had cost Raleigh. And he was flattered, too, that in this last hopeless position he was the man whom Raleigh chose to take his place. There was pleasure in his consciousness that he was as well fitted for the job as any man could be.

'Very well, Sir Walter. I shall do my best, you know that. When shall I start?'

'Today, if that is possible. You'll take the five small ships. They'll manage the river. And two hundred and fifty of the fit men, if there are so many to be found. I'll give you sole charge, Keymis, and I'll trust your judgment. But avoid war, if that is possible. All the same,' and here the faint voice gathered strength, 'get to that mine, Keymis, and if you are attacked, hit back hard. Not to reach the gold would be a personal disaster; to flee before the Spaniards would be a national disgrace.'

'Never fear for that. I'll leave you now and get things afoot. I'll come back as soon as I'm ready.'

Raleigh nodded and Keymis made for the door.

'And Keymis...'

'Yes, Sir Walter.'

'My son will go with you. I've never sent a deputy where I wouldn't have gone myself and now, brought thus low, I'll send my son instead.'

'There is no need...' Keymis began, but Raleigh cut him short.

'I wish it. He will too. Watch his face when you tell him. Tell him, and then send him and Herbert here to me.'

*

He lay for a little after Keymis's footsteps had died away, savouring the most bitter moment that life had yet brought him. To be condemned to lie here, useless, when the last, the greatest advance of all went forward. To have to rely on Keymis at a moment when a change of plan, a flash of effrontery, a daring decision, might mean all the difference. Keymis was a good fellow, trustworthy, loyal, brave, but it wasn't his venture. Why must this fever come now? And God, why to him?

Walter came in, breathless with excitement. 'Thank you for sending me, father. We'll succeed, somehow. You won't fret, will you? Stay here and recover. When you see me again, I shall have glorious news for you.'

'I hope so, son. Help Keymis all you can. And remember, he's in charge. He knows the country.'

Walter nodded.

'The pikemen are mine though.'

'The pikemen are yours but I hope to God they'll not be needed.'

'Of course,' said Walter, rather flatly.

'We've got to regard the Spanish as our friends now, until they're proved otherwise.'

Walter pulled his underlip... he had known that, of course. It had been amongst the fleet's sailing orders... but the repetition of it now made the venture sound rather tame.

'The old days were the best,' he said regretfully.

'Yes. They were. You were born a little late, Walter. And I, I have lived too long.'

'Don't say that. Don't even think it. Your great day is still to come... when you sail back with the gold. What a day that will be!'

'What a day indeed! Oh, is that you, Herbert? Come in. I want you two to lift me into that chair and carry me on deck. I must at least see the ships set off.'

'Will that be wise?' asked Walter.

'Wise or not, I want you to do it. I'm too old to begin acting wisely.'

They wrapped a blanket around the lower part of his body and spread his cloak, with the collar bravely upturned, around him. And so, carried by their strong young hands, he went on deck again. From his chair he overlooked the hasty fitting out of the five vessels and the sorting of the picked men. The heat of the midday hours suspended the operations but Raleigh refused to go below, choosing rather to doze in the chair upon the deck. Exertion had heightened his fever and when Walter and Keymis came at last to take their leave it seemed to him that between these living, vigorous men and himself a curtain had already fallen. He could see and hear them, could talk sensibly still about the expedition, but an air of unreality hung over all.

Slowly the five small ships drew away. Slowly the colours of the individual vessels faded until they were only dark blurs against the brightening western sky. And then the tall topmast sails caught the glow and blazed for a moment in the sunset. There was the old tawny red colour which he had always loved. The colour of hope, about which he and dead Essex had once quarrelled. Was it an omen, that sudden, ruddy glow as the small fleet lessened and disappeared in the distance? The West. Scene of all his hopes, magnet of his soul. Or was it an omen of something else? Topiawari's words, spoken so long ago, sounded again in the ears of the sick man drooping and dreaming in his Dolphin chair. 'The young nations rise in the East, the old nations die, like the sun, in the West,' something like that he remembered, and something more, something about knowing defeat in the body of your son's son. 'Farewell, Walter,' he said once again, softly this time with a sigh.

The horizon was unbroken now and the air was cooler. Turning his head, he called for someone to carry him below. The long years in the Tower had at least taught him the value of patience. Raleigh thought often of that other waiting during the month that followed. This was bound to end with some news, good or bad, shortly. The other had been indefinite. He wrote in his journal; kept everything seaworthy about the waiting ships so that part, at least, of the fleet could set off when the good tidings that he still hoped for arrived; and on days when his fever left him for a little time he landed and hunted for herbs and gained further information about the island.

There were yet moments when he could forget that he was Raleigh, unlucky and almost broken, dependent for his very life upon the fate of this expedition; moments when the discovery of some new thing in this strange, tropical island could thrill him anew with the wonder of the world and of being, for a brief lifetime, the witness and partaker of its age-long drama. From moments like that he would wake again to be the impatient, hobbled leader of a fleet that had sailed without him and which no news had come.

On February the fourteenth the blank sea was broken. A ship was coming back. From the moment when it was sighted until the first man boarded the *Destiny* with a letter in his hand was longer than all the time in the Tower, longer than all his lifetime before. What had happened? Was this vessel the sole survivor of some unimagined disaster? Was Keymis aboard her, or Walter? And the gold. What of the gold? At last, he had a letter in his hand.

He spread it out with his shaking fingers and ran his eyes over the writing, absorbing the contents in one rapid glance. No, that was impossible. His eyes were deceiving him. He had read it too quickly. Like a stunned man he went back to the beginning and read every word again, slowly, like a child with its first lesson.

'The Spaniards attacked us at San Thome.' He had expected that. 'We rallied...' Yes, that too was news that might be believed and understood. But the next... 'Walter Raleigh and Captain Cosmor were killed.' There it was, written. No hallucination then. Walter was dead. That strong young man who had wrung his hand and kissed him and left with promises to do his work for him. That little curly-haired boy who had implored him at the foot of the Sherborne stairs to bring him to this very end. Walter, who had spent all his vigorous boyhood days in the gloomy precincts of the Tower, bursting out only now and then into some innocent piece of horseplay. His son, whom he had so long neglected, who had repaid that indifference with adoration and devotion. He was dead. In some alien soil that golden head was already laid. Guiana had sealed those bright eyes for ever.

Raleigh pressed his hands to his face and groaned. Bitterly he blamed himself for letting Walter go. And yet, it had been the boy's own wish. Sadly, he realised the tie of fatherhood; it was as if a part of himself had died.

For a long time, he sat there with the letter between his nerveless fingers. First the long illness and then the blow. That was the order of events that had killed Drake and Hawkins. There came a time when there was no more resistance in a man. When to lie down and die seemed more natural and far, far more easy, than to face life devoid of hope and courage. He could die now. It was only, as the Bible said, a matter of turning one's face to the wall, to the blankness and peace of the grave and then death was easy. But there was Lisbeth still. He owed her what comfort his return could give her. And he must go to her with words of comfort, too. What aspect, then, of this disastrous affair could be constructed into comfort? Walter had been young, cut down in his flower. No disease had battened upon him; he had never known the sickness of hope deferred. Love had not had time to betray him; the ills and frustrations of age would never touch him. He had died suddenly and cleanly in the heat of action, in a place that he himself had chosen—at the head of his pikemen, at the hand of the enemy. He thought of himself at Walter's age. He had been in the Netherlands, risking death in the same way. Suppose he had died so. Would he have missed so much? Hadn't everything that had come later been dearly bought? Lisbeth's love, those nights when he had stolen in at her window. He was paying for those now; facing the fact that he must break to her the news of what had befallen the fruit of their love. A little glory, sweet at the time but gone, leaving him that most dismal thing, a fallen power. Perhaps one should envy, not pity, Walter. Perhaps...

234

*

At last he picked up the letter that had fallen unnoticed to the floor and read the part that dealt with the mine. Keymis had located it and was now in ambush within reach. He had hopes, at the time of writing, of making a lightning dash, opening the mine and returning with enough treasure to justify the expedition.

So again, there was nothing to do but wait.

Sixteen burning, airless, fever-stricken days and at the end of them Keymis, empty-handed.

They faced one another across the narrow cabin. Faithful Keymis, big and brown, who for three months had faced death daily in a cause not entirely his own. Shamefaced with failure, tongue-tied in his efforts to justify himself, he faced the broken man whom, he understood that now, he had finally failed.

Desperately Raleigh clung to his last shred of patience.

'You found it, you say. I still don't understand you, Keymis.'

'Oh, we found it. What you can't understand is out not opening it. I tell you the Spaniards were all round us, waiting only for us to move, show them the place, then they would have fallen on us. What could our handful do, cut off from the ships where the food was, against half the Spaniards in the New World?'

'Since when have we altered our plans for the sake of food, or the thought of what the Spaniards would or would not do?'

'You won't see,' said Keymis, stung to anger against his will, 'that we were hopelessly outnumbered. The whole thing has been a plot from the start. The King betrayed us. The Spaniards were thick as bees in a hive, they knew everything. How many men, how many ships, how much food and ammunition. The only thing they didn't know was where the mine was situated. Was I to show them that?'

'You seemed to think of everything, Keymis, except the fact that owing to your unusual caution we go back defeated and empty-handed. God, if I could only have gone myself. They

235

meant to defeat us, did they? I'd have gone on if I'd been the last man, crawling on my belly.'

He sank down on the Dolphin chair and stared, sick-eyed, at Keymis who said, uncomfortably fumbling for words:

'There was another thing, too. When I left you, you were ill, so ill that you didn't look... as if you were going... to live long. And the King hasn't forgiven you yet. I wasn't going to open any mine for him. I mean, if it wasn't going to do you any good...' He faltered into silence before Raleigh's stare. Raleigh said slowly, ignoring the heart of loyalty revealed in those last words:

'You mean that you counted upon my death so far as to kill me. For that what you have done, Keymis.'

The sailor took one last look at his Admiral: realised that he would never make the crazed, disappointed mind understand, turned on his heel and left the cabin.

Three minutes later a shot shattered the quiet. Through heat and hunger, through pestilence and the plague of flies, through danger and bitter disappointment Keymis had been faithful. What was death?

But Keymis with that shot had stilled more than his blundering loyal heart. The demon that had gnawed at Raleigh's vitals was no more. Suddenly the world was quiet and the way was clear before him. The old notion which had been reborn early in the expedition, when the wide sea opened once more before him — the notion that if the venture failed there were still the wild ways of piracy to try, troubled him no more. He would keep his parole and in quiet resignation preserve his dignity. He did not even think, in that new mind of his, that by his return he would preserve his legend, too. That the picture of the lonely, beaten man, returning willingly from an unlawful freedom to certain shame and death would seal, in the minds of men yet unborn, his claim to a place amongst the immortals.

Janis might see in her crystal that a sailor would die for him. He saw more clearly still. Worldling he had been and a worldling would condemn him. Schemer he had been and now to further another's schemes he must be sacrificed. James, with his eyes upon the Spanish marriage for the Prince of Wales, could not condone the battle of San Thome. And so clear of sight and without bitterness Raleigh, turning his fleet and his eyes towards England, could write:

> *Blood must be my body's balmer,*
> *No other balm will there be given;*
> *Whilst my soul like quiet palmer,*
> *Travelleth towards the land of heaven.*

The sails filled, the good ships ploughed the water's unstable furrows and the voices of the sailor men rang out as they had done when he and all the world had been young and gay. But the good old days had gone and evening had clouded. The Queen, Gasgoigne, Sydney, Marlowe and Will, they were all returned to their clay. Only Lisbeth was left to shake his heart at the thought of another meeting and parting. But in his new clear sight the little time that would divide them now was negligible. After all, it was not so long since he was a small boy listening to old Harkess's stories far out on some summer sea.

The Conclusion

Old Palace Yard
Friday 29 October, 1618

Golden lads and girls all must,
As chimney sweepers, come to dust.

It was morning when he opened his eyes. The thin October
light was filtering in, showing the candles that had been left
burning dead in their pools of tallow. He had not meant to
sleep, had grudged the time; sleep's brief unconsciousness was
for those who had busy hours to face. But now, stretching out
his hand, he was glad for during those few hours the miracle
had happened, the ague had left him. He had so hated the idea
of going to the block all atremble before those who would see
his shaking limbs evidence of fear, not of disease. Now, if this
respite could endure but for a little, he would be able to go
steadily as a man should. He was grateful to Lisbeth who,
leaving him for the last time at midnight had, after a spell of
weakness and weeping, suddenly become strong again and had
said in her firm voice, hoarsened with tears, 'Sleep now, that
you may be strong to face the morrow.' And as one always did
in the last issue, shuffle as one might, he had obeyed her.

It was light enough to write now. Rising, still proudly and
gratefully aware of his steadiness, he went to the table, drew up
the stool, tried the point of his pen on his thumb and began to

set word on word in his old easy way. For a time his attention was not thoroughly fixed, pictures came between him and the writing. He saw the sails shaking out under the October sky as the ships made for the Indies. Here was Cadiz, shining white above the sea, and there in Youghal the sun was creeping over his myrtle trees. For everyone else the day was just beginning while for him... But he put the weakening thought away. All these people, on sea or land, were doomed to die soon or late; many that he might envy now would never attain his age; would die suddenly with their sins on them or lingeringly of some disease that would turn their loved ones from them in disgust. Lisbeth's kiss had been as warm and fervent last night as on any night of their loving. Comforted by the thought, for he was a proud man, he gave his whole mind to his writing.

Presently with a shriek of iron on iron, the door was opened and Heron the gaoler stepped in, a big man trying to move softly. He stood for a moment, fearful of interrupting, but Raleigh did not lift his head so he said quietly:

'There's less than an hour, Sir Walter, and the Dean is waiting in the chapel.'

Raleigh ended the line and looked up.

'Is that so, Heron? Well, I'm nigh finished.'

He referred to the writing but in that place and in that hour the words had an ominous and sinister meaning; he became aware of it and repeated, 'Nigh finished' as if the previous words had been spoken by some other person.

Heron waited. Raleigh added a line or two and laid down his pen. They walked together to the chapel where the Dean waited with bread and wine of his office all ready. Raleigh knelt in the place where young Elizabeth Tudor had knelt long ago, striving to keep her soaring thoughts upon the matter in hand. Her thoughts had been of the future, Raleigh's were of the past. He thought of George Gasgoigne who had lived as an atheist and then died in mortal terror, aghast at the thought of meeting the God he had denied. Good bread, sweet wine, transformed by some divine alchemy into the body and blood of Christ. Christ who had faced unflinchingly a death more terrible than that which awaited him and so must surely love brave men above aught else.

'Enable me to die fearless. Receive me into Thy Kingdom. Comfort Lisbeth... and any else who may grieve for me.'

He rose steady upon his feet.

Breakfast awaited him and, stupid as it seemed to nourish a body that would be dead ere the hour was run, he ate it, flicking the crumbs from his black silk breeches with the old fastidious gesture. And so to the last pipe of tobacco against which the King had once launched his virulent tirade. 'He misses much,' reflected Raleigh, as the sweet smoke rose blue and curled with a faint bitterness around his tongue. Before the pipe was finished Heron appeared again at the door. With the pipe still between his teeth Raleigh rose and fumbled in his pockets. He brought out a miniature cased in gold and studded with diamonds. He laid it beside the sealed papers on the table and then put the pipe, warm from that last smoking, on the table too.

'These are for you, Heron. ''Tis all of value that they left me. The miniature you can sell but if you are wise, you will keep the pipe. 'Twill be as good as a friend to you as it has been to me. And dispatch the letters for me.'

Heron choked.

'Of course, I will. It won't be long, Sir Barker's a good man and the axe, I saw to it... is sharp.'

'You've been a true friend to me, Heron. I've never found many. But maybe I've looked in the wrong places.'

He stared ahead of him for a moment, thinking of the places in which he had looked but not, he admitted, for friends.

''Tis cold in here,' said Heron thickly, 'and there's a fire without. Would you care to warm yourself before...?'

'I'd sooner dispatch the business,' Raleigh said.

And they began to walk through the long corridors to the Old Palace Yard. He thought as he walked of those who had gone this way before him. Anne Boleyn, with her 'I have but a very little neck'. And old Sir Thomas More, precisian to the end, moving his beard aside and saying, 'Twere pity it should be cut, it has not committed treason.' He wondered whether

240

he would find some last word by which men would remember him.

There they were all waiting, the men who had come to see him die: the common people who had resisted the Lord Mayor's pageant. And there, with his last defence spoken, he knelt at the block and there the last inspiration came. He kissed the axe, sharp as Heron had promised, and said clearly: "'Tis a sharp medicine but a sure cure for all diseases.' A moment more and the cure was his. No more devouring ambition, no more chafing at restraint or bitter passing of youth and vigour, no more laying word on word in a poet's agony at the unattainability of loveliness. One stroke, and it was all over.

Back in his prison the letters lay at the table and the sun, creeping forward, dried and loosened one insecurely fastened seal. The sheet opened so that Heron might have read, coming in to fulfill his last duty, Raleigh's own Requiem, the verse that was to go with the English language wherever the Empire of which he had dreamed should spread.

> *Even such is Time, that takes in trust*
> *Our youth, our joys, our all we have,*
> *And pays us but with earth and dust;*
> *Who, in the dark and silent grave,*
> *When we have wandered all our ways,*
> *Shuts up the story of our days;*
> *But from this earth, this grave, this dust,*
> *My God shall raise me up, I trust.*

But Heron couldn't read; and had no idea of what a story had ended that day before his eyes or what ways had been wandered to reach that sorry conclusion.

Lightning Source UK Ltd.
Milton Keynes UK
UKHW041806171122
412353UK00001B/18